CW01498101

THE
HEATH

An Inspector Love Story
by AJ Munro

Dear Craig,

Thanks for your letter
and support note. Hugely
appreciated.

Enjoy The Heath!

AJ (AJ Munro - he)

Copyright © 2017 by AJ Munro

All rights reserved. No part of this publication may be reproduced, distributed, or transmitted in any form or by any means, including photocopying, recording, or other electronic or mechanical methods, without the prior written permission of the author, except in the case of brief quotations embodied in critical reviews and certain other noncommercial uses permitted by copyright law.

Published by WriterMotive
www.writermotive.com

1

The bullet ripped into the back of the Labrador's head exiting between the dog's snout and right eye as it tore into the water. A group of ducks immediately took to the air in a flurry of flapping wings and splashes. The dog's head lolled to the side briefly before he sank beneath the surface. His owner bent over and reached into the water for him, and despite the weight of the sodden animal, he cradled him like a baby. He had no idea how long he stood there cradling him. He simply sobbed, gently murmuring 'my Prince, oh my Prince, my lovely boy,' as he stood forlorn in the pond holding his dog.

A runner stopped, took in the scene then quickly went to the man's aid. He looked around as if expecting to see the reason for this pathetic sight, then shouted something at the man and ran for help. Neither the runner nor the owner noticed a man jump down from a tree and leave the scene.

Albert Johns had left his cottage in Highgate Village at 7 o'clock sharp with his white Labrador, Prince, for their early morning constitutional up to Parliament Hill and wherever took their fancy after that. After all, there was no reason to rush back. Albert had been retired twenty years after forty years' service on the buses with London Transport. His wife Marion before her death four years ago often ribbed him about his early rising especially when he'd retired, but he had reasoned that old habits die hard and as an old soldier they died harder. In any event, he was wide awake by 06.30 without fail and always felt the need to be up and about.

The slight chill in the air that morning was a relief as early August had been hot and humid. This particular morning Albert and Prince made their way along Southwood Lane, and Albert was struck by the brilliant orange sky lighting up East London. It invigorated the old man, and he lengthened his stride feeling nowhere near his 89 years of age. Prince constantly looked up at him and bounced along in expectation. They quickly made their way across the already traffic-laden High Street and were striding past The Flask pub and down Highgate West Hill towards Merton Lane, a warm breeze teasing the giant trees and swaying the branches flush with summer green.

Albert and Prince had reached the Heath, and Prince had been finally released from his lead. He bounded off gleefully with a couple of sharp barks for good measure and revelled in his freedom. As usual, and for no apparent reason, he promptly plunged into the first pond that they came to. He swam a bit and looked around as if wondering why the hell he had jumped into this murky expanse of water. It was a scene Albert would never stop playing in his head as the horror of that morning engulfed him.

DI Jack Love rose early after a very good night's sleep. Ravenously hungry, he set about preparing a hearty breakfast for himself and a strong coffee for his still-sleeping wife. He flicked on Radio Five Live, picked up his Guardian from the door and put two slices of maple-cured bacon under the grill. Soon the inimitable aroma was filling the kitchen, and all seemed well with the world. A cursory glance at the front page of the paper soon gave way to a thorough digestion of the sports pages (or more particularly, the football pages). The season was but a couple of weeks old, and the tables showed unfamiliar names making the early running.

The smell of the spitting bacon drifted upstairs, and Jack knew that heady smell would rouse his adored wife from her slumber. Sure enough, Annie Love entered the kitchen uttering a barely audible 'got enough for two there, love?' Jack looked at his wife taking a seat, smiled and threw another couple of rashers on the grill. She looked so fragile in the morning, slow movements exaggerated by her short stature and slim figure. If Jack was full of beans in the morning, Annie was the complete opposite. She turned the radio down and sat staring forlornly at the grill while Jack brought her juice and made some toast. Jack never ceased to be amazed by her transformation once her breakfast had been digested and a shower taken. It was the school holidays, however, so without a doubt, Annie would be heading back to bed exhausted as the summer term hangover was still in full blaze. Jack gave his wife a quick peck and walked the short distance from East Finchley to Muswell Hill Police Station.

Jack thought of the pile of paperwork that awaited him and sighed as he made his way along Fortis Green, the relentless rush-hour traffic crawling by. He did smile as he remembered how it came about. A nice little run of successful cases meant spirits were high in the station, and Jack's step hastened as he passed The Clissold, scene of a good few celebrations just lately.

No sooner had he sat down, the threat of paperwork quickly receded when his phone rang.

'A dog? On Hampstead Heath?' said Jack. A 'shot dog' was a new one. Jack looked out of his window onto Fortis Green as a woman passed with an Italian greyhound and shook his head, muttering 'bloody hell' to no one in particular. He swung round in his chair, shouted over to Sergeant Ray Merton to forget his cup of tea and instead join him in paying a visit to the poor dog's owner. Merton, with as much reluctance as he could muster, grabbed his jacket and followed his boss down the stairs.

'So, sir, how do we approach this one?' enquired Merton as they got into the station Mondeo. 'Did your dog have any enemies Mr Johns? Can you think why anyone would want to shoot Fido, Mr Johns?'

'I was hoping you'd have some ideas, Merton.'

'Brilliant.'

They drove in silence to Albert's house in Highgate Village. Albert made tea for the detectives and sat hunched over his steaming cuppa, his eyes red, and his thick white hair slicked back. Love looked around the room and noted how immaculate the place was. The furniture and fittings were old, but the place had an evocative aroma of polish. It reminded Love of the smell of church and his failed attempts to miss Sunday school as a kid. Albert Johns was clearly a proud man, popular too judging by the photographs that were neatly framed around the place. Old football team photos, big group holiday snaps and many with his wife and children. One photo particularly caught Jack's eye, a baby boy perched on his proud father's lap in the cab of a *Routemaster* bus, the expressions bursting with love and pride. The house dripped with memories.

'Prince was all I had left.' Albert's voice was barely audible.

'I know this is difficult, Mr Johns, but can you just run through exactly what happened to you and Prince this morning.' Love asked, briefly wondering how many times he had said 'I know this is difficult' in all his time in the force.

Albert insisted they used his first name and quietly but eloquently relayed the events of that morning. He stared into the middle distance, a determined look discernible upon his grief-stricken face. He wanted the detectives to get the clearest account of what happened to his beloved Prince. He wept gently when he finished talking, apologised for his tears and wiped his eyes, clasped his hands together and stared right at Detective Inspector Jack Love.

'I have to ask you this Albert', the detectives shared the briefest of glances 'do you know anyone who has anything against you, a long-held grudge, have you fallen out with anyone lately?' Jack already knew the answer. Albert merely shook his head slowly and let out a big sigh. Of course, he had no enemies he could think of. The whole notion was ridiculous.

Merton clarified some of the finer points of the story and the two men left Albert in peace, promising they would do all they could. They strolled the short distance to the village, the heat of the late morning already intense, and made their way down to the pond on Hampstead Heath where Prince was shot. There was a sole uniform talking to people out walking, and that was it. The PC told Jack and Merton that Albert seemed to be a well-known face around the Heath and truly loved his dog. People were genuinely shocked and shook their heads with a 'what's the world coming to' weariness all too familiar to the police. The locals had also told the PC that Albert was a regular in the Prince of Wales pub up in the village. Jack and Merton needed no persuading that should be the next port of call.

The cool dark interior of the pub was a welcome contrast to the heat and glare of the street, and two pints of ice cold lemonades were swiftly ordered and dispatched.

They talked to the landlord and the few early drinkers reading their papers and a picture began to emerge of the sort of man Albert Johns was. As Jack suspected, no one had a bad word to say about him. He would come in during the odd lunchtime with Prince for a couple of pints and was a regular on a Friday night and Sunday lunchtime without fail. He was a quiet man but liked to talk to the other drinkers and was generally considered nice and amiable. When Jack told them what happened, they took some convincing it wasn't a wind-up.

Jack and Merton adjourned to a table at the back of the pub overlooking Pond Square, the bangs and clatters of the kitchen hinting at the lunchtime rush to come, not to mention some hunger-inducing aromas.

'What do you reckon sir?' asked Merton as he took a sip of his drink.

'Looks totally random at this stage, I can't believe anyone would have anything against Johns, do you?' replied Jack.

'And Johns was a good distance from the dog, so the gunman wasn't aiming at him,' said Merton looking out of the window.

'So we have a dog-hating maniac on the loose. God almighty. Get uniform to talk to neighbours, friends and family, and we'll dig as deep as possible and see what we can turn up. There may be a dark secret somewhere, you never know. It may only be a dog, but someone out there has fired a live round in a public park, so we have to take this seriously, spread the word will you Ray?'

The two men nodded to the landlord and headed back to the station, their heads buzzing with questions.

Mark hated Clarence and Clarence hated Mark. It was a hate-hate relationship. Every morning when his 'mummy' had gone to work, he would stand in the bedroom doorway glowering at Mark. It was a look Mark knew to take seriously given he was a fully grown Rottweiler. His calves still held the scars, looking like Dracula had slipped and gone for his legs instead as the sun rose.

Meg's career in PR and Mark's lack of a career in anything meant it fell to Mark to walk Clarence early every morning. The scars were the result of failing in this duty two days running. His heartfelt plea to Meg fell on deaf ears. 'You know he gets grumpy if he doesn't have his walkies, Mark.' Grumpy! Jesus Christ, the scabby old twat should be destroyed and he'd happily to do the honours.

There were many drawbacks in this arrangement not least Mark's hatred of dogs and Clarence in particular. He also hated walking, getting up early and the outdoors. The only consolation he could think of was the bacon roll he always had in the deli in Highgate Village. This particular morning it was badly needed, having hit the Jameson's too enthusiastically as he surfed the endless delights of his digital TV. Settling on a Best Nude Beaches feature on the Travel Channel he had poured a generous measure of the Irish magic to savour such a televisual feast. Then another, then another…

Meg was always on her last legs by half nine, usually with the mutt dozing in her lap. The adverts would wake her suddenly, and she would retire to bed with Mark uttering his usual 'I'll be through in a minute' and then 'not that you'll notice' under his breath to a glare from Clarence. The usual routine was for an uneasy truce to develop as man and beast became engrossed in the compellingly bad fare that our broadcasters served up for the Great British public. Mark always lamented the amount of time focussed on old men's' cocks and senior saggy tits. The occasional hard body would saunter out of shot, and that was it. Utter shite, as deep down Mark knew it would be. The final part of the routine involved Mark falling asleep and spilling his beloved dram all over his shirt. The net result was that come 'walkies' time, Mark felt awful, and Clarence didn't.

Clarence ran ahead of Mark, stopped on the shore of the pond and went down on his stomach to take a drink and snap at some flies buzzing around his round black head. Mark took the opportunity of having a hardly earned breather on a bench. Mark wondered about Clarence and thought he envied his life a touch. This dog had a beautiful woman fawning over him, was fed heartily and generally treated like a king. He even had some lackey to take him for a walk every day. Not bad. Not bad at all. Mark really needed to get a job. A dog's life eh? Bollocks to that, he thought.

His reverie was shattered as a pop and splash disturbed the peace. Clarence's head slumped into the water. Mark ran to the dog and was startled to see a small bloody hole in the top of the dog's head. He pulled Clarence's body out of the water, heavy and lifeless. Mark didn't know what to do; he felt like laughing, he felt like screaming. Fear quickly kicked in. Would he be next? Only one thing for it, he sprinted to the public toilet and rang the police on his mobile.

A man quickly got down from a tree and disappeared into the brightening morning.

2

Jack Love acquired the moniker of 'Happy Jack' within days of starting his police career. His positive and, some would say laid-back approach to his work hid a steely determination to do the job properly and well. It wasn't that the awful cases didn't affect him. Far from it. It was just that he was able to switch off better than most when he left the station for the day, whatever case he was working on. Annie Love knew the pressures of the job only too well but didn't allow him to wallow or become too pre-occupied. She was a perceptive creature, Jack could talk through complex cases with her and many a Friday night in Maddens had seen a case clarified or reassurance gained on the direction of his thoughts. As a teacher, Annie had enough on her plate, and the couple took great delight in escaping the rigours of their jobs.

They had concluded early in their marriage that their jobs were just that - jobs and there was a life to lead as well. They hadn't tried to have children or not tried either. They seldom thought or fretted about it and used their income to spoil their black Labrador, Earnie, and enjoy socialising. The moniker suited Jack; he *was* happy, and frequently he was asked by gnarled colleagues after a few glasses in the Clissold 'How do you do it, Jack? What's the secret?' Well, there was no secret. Jack reckoned 'Lucky Jack' was more suitable but always answered 'the love of a good woman and no bloody kids.'

The second dog murder sent shock waves through leafy North London. Muswell Hill Police Station was ablaze with the shrill ringing of phones and detectives reeling off the questions to all and sundry, groping at anything that might give them a lead. Jack led a meeting, but there were more questions than answers and much scratching of heads. The jokes that flew round the station after Prince's murder were fading now that Clarence had suffered an identical fate. They had the local media on the case, and Jack knew it would only be a matter of time before the national media picked up on it. These were wealthy areas populated by powerful people, it was a potential nightmare for the police, and they were getting nowhere fast. Jim Ryan, a detective constable only six months into his CID career, broke the brief silence, his harsh South Yorkshire dialect filling the room. 'Sir, I don't think we can rule out that tosser Mark Shilling having something to do with it. He was a right surly bugger and clearly hated Clarence. He were more worried about his missus going ape than the poor bloody mutt.' There were murmurs of agreement, but Merton pointed out that arranging a hit on his girlfriend's dog was perhaps a touch too elaborate for Shilling. Would he really take out Albert's dog as cover?

Jack agreed but asked Ryan to question Shilling again. 'I've also asked uniform to step up patrols in the area, we've put up an incident board and posters up in Muswell Hill, East Finchley, Hampstead and Highgate Village. This won't go away, the media are getting a sniff, and the beautiful people of Hampstead won't abide their dogs being shot.'

Jack returned to his desk and wondered how and when the next dog would be killed.

Aidan Buchanan woke around midday in his usual fog of booze and fags. It had been a heavy night. A long groaning noise emerged from a throat that felt to Aidan like it was paved with sandpaper. It had been a good night though he thought. Mind you, he had no recollection past 9 o'clock. His band, Mile High, had been rehearsing most of the day for their American tour and as usual had repaired to the Well in Hampstead for a session of a different and in Aidan's opinion, much better kind. He had been in the mood for strong lager instead of his usual Jack Daniels, and Stella was his poison last night. Lots of it.

As his head began the long process of clearing, he became aware of two other creatures in his huge bedroom: a woman he didn't recognise lying naked in a deep sleep and a large Alsatian lying in front of the muted widescreen TV looking warily up at its owner. Moira was a patient dog. She needed to be - Aidan was an erratic dog-walker, so she would go weeks without a proper walk. Sometimes Aidan's housekeeper would let her out to chase photographers down the East Heath Road, but that could be it. A lot of her day would be spent lying on Aidan's bedroom floor looking wanly at her owner sleeping, drinking, taking illicit class 'A' drugs, having sex and most commonly channel-hopping from Sky Sports to MTV and back again shouting 'wanker', 'twat', 'shitbag' and 'wehey, that's more like it eh Moira?' at the giant screen at various intervals.

Moira learnt quickly that certain phrases like 'Ok Moira, you've persuaded me, I do fancy a pint', 'come on then you sack of fleas, don't want me pride and joy getting fat do I?' and 'don't look at me like that girl, I'm dying here…ah fuck it, the air'll do me good I suppose' meant a walk was imminent or at least a strong possibility. Low groaning noises and 'fuck off mutt' meant Aidan was not partial to the idea of leaving the house at all and lying quietly was the best option all round.

Aidan's head throbbed like a turbine engine, and his throat was so dry that swallowing made him wince. There was no way he was going anywhere. No rehearsals were booked, and he could do exactly what he liked today. He relaxed and thought about nothing in particular, that wonderful jumble of gentle thoughts that precede dropping off to sleep. This reverie was rudely interrupted by a faint, but unpleasant, aroma of sweat and stale perfume and someone mumbling something incomprehensible.

All thoughts of sweet slumber evaporated. Aidan scratched his stubbled chin, ran his hand through his long dark unkempt hair and looked down at Moira. 'Think it's time for a walk Moira, a long one' and put his finger to his lips conspiratorially. He carefully extricated himself from the nameless woman and quietly stood up. For a man in so much pain, he moved with the grace of ballet dancer. Moira tilted her head as she realised an excursion was in the offing and padded down the long wide staircase to the kitchen and her trusty lead. Aidan meanwhile had put on his fashionably ragged jeans on complete with fag burns and lager stains and grabbed the nearest shirt, a black Fred Perry polo where the stains weren't so evident.

He was almost clear of the bedroom when he walked into the stainless steel bin making a clatter. 'Shit,' he hissed as he grabbed his big toe and hopped on the spot. 'Fuck it,' he growled as the shape in the bed moved and moaned lightly. The shape turned its back on Aidan, broke wind and began snoring loudly. 'Classy, fucking classy love, nice one' he whispered and sped out of the room, down the stairs to the kitchen and an expectant Alsatian. Ellen, Aidan's ruddy-faced housekeeper, old beyond her 38 years had Moira all prepared. 'Ellen, do us a favour love…' 'Don't tell me, *give that silly tart upstairs a bacon butty and get shot of her, tell her I'm flying to fecking Venezuela tonight or something*' said Ellen, her soft Irish brogue giving way to a near-perfect impression of Aidan's cockney accent.

'Eh! You're getting too fucking cheeky you are!' laughed Aidan.

'Go on with you, take that beautiful dog of yours out for a walk; watch it, though, the usual maggots are out there.'

16

'Ah bollocks, what's new? See you later gorgeous. Come on Moira,' beamed Aidan as he opened the kitchen door and a blushing Ellen went back to her chores.

Moira followed her usual routine of barking wildly at the motley pool of photographers while Aidan sauntered past flicking v-signs in their direction as the flashes spat their light all over the street like an electrical storm in fast-forward. Because of the dog, the snappers rarely followed unless Aidan was in the news for a particular reason like the time he was romantically involved with a minor royal. Today he was left to go about his business once he'd left his own street. He breathed a sigh of relief and started strutting along. Here he was, Billy Fucking Big Bollocks, free as a bird, not a care in the world, storming along the road like he owned the gaff. They turned left and headed up Haverstock Hill towards Hampstead, the sun finally burning off the early morning cloud that had lingered so long. Aidan felt fresher by the minute and relished the walk and pint that lay ahead. When he was in the mood, Aidan took Moira for a real stretch. He would take her over the Heath and up to Highgate, stopping in the Wrestlers for a pint, of course, and heading back over the Heath, looking in at the Well for a pint naturally, on the way back through Hampstead. Lovely.

The emerging sunshine flooded Hampstead with bright light that brought alive all the colour in the village, Aidan felt like the whole place was pulsating and flowering an inch from his nose. The time was approaching 2 o'clock, and he realised no food had passed his lips since yesterday afternoon (that he could remember). Coffee was a much greater priority, however, and he stooped as he entered a cafe for a double shot espresso and a panini. Bagging a seat outside, Aidan tossed bits of cheese and ham to Moira and slouched in his metal seat watching the world go by. He flicked on his phone and saw he had 16 messages and turned it off again muttering 'bastards' to himself.

Fortified further, they set off again cutting through the lane past the Flask, off Hampstead High Street and down the tree lined streets to the Heath. Moira bounded ahead, occasionally stopping and looking behind to check Aidan was still with her. He resisted the very strong urge to pop in the Well for a livener but somehow managed to get past the place, silently justifying it on the grounds that he preferred it before the refurbishment. That hadn't stopped him last night of course. The lunchtime aromas bursting out of the open windows nearly got him, but he carried on manfully, feeling pretty smug and righteous. Two o'clock and Aidan Buchanan hadn't had a drink yet. Easy!

A warm breeze hit Aidan and Moira as they stepped onto the Heath and the strong sun was producing a haze over the distant trees towards Highgate. Determined kite flyers were trying to squeeze every drop of life out of the gentle thermals on Parliament Hill as a giant 747 banked and continued its approach to Heathrow. The glory of the scene was not lost on Aidan.

'This is the life, eh Moira?' he said to his dog as she struggled to carry a large branch along the path. They veered off the path at the top of Parliament Hill, BT Tower just visible in the haze directly south, Canary Wharf's towers to the east less so. Aidan crashed out on the grass and looked up to the sky soaking up a brilliant blue sky and vast clumps of fluffy white clouds. Moira was off exploring, taking this rare opportunity with boundless enthusiasm.

The languid rhythm of the day saw no suspicion in the wiry shaven-headed man walking into the trees, fishing equipment slung over his shoulder.

3

Jack met Annie at Southampton University. Deeply committed to the less academic aspects of college life, he had scrambled through his first year of a social sciences degree, needing to submit half a year's work to be able to sit his exams. He began his second year determined not to bomb out, and that remained the limit of his ambition as Annie Griffiths hovered into his consciousness.

Psychology students were sharing various modules, and Annie interested Jack straight away. She was attractive, cool and had a drive to her. She wasn't there for the beer and took part in seminar debates with gusto. Respectful until driven mad by someone who couldn't see her point, she then deployed an armoury of savage put-downs that never failed to make Jack laugh.

She also had big brown eyes, long legs showcased in tight jeans and Dr Martens. Jack started feeling unusually motivated to attend public policy lectures and even discovered the library. Seminars became unmissable when he knew Annie would be there, a phenomenon that wasn't going unnoticed by his tutors. He found himself joining in the driest of debates, frequently backing up Annie's point of view and making her laugh. 'You're quite the double act, aren't you?' their tutor once remarked.

Jack tried and failed to force away a blush while Annie just sighed, but he was convinced there was a hint of a smile there too. He was trying to be cool when bumping into her and saying hello to each other, but he knew he was gone. The sick anticipation of entering the library, the crushing disappointment when she wasn't there… He couldn't fathom how she felt, and it was getting more infuriating by the week. He had to do something.

A night of drinking and profuse sweating on an indie dance floor proved the unlikely turning point for Jack.

It was when he was giving it the 'full Morrissey' to *This Charming Man* singing all the words at the top of his voice wishing he had a bunch of daffodils coming out of the back of his jeans that he noticed Annie at the bar watching him. It had been a great night of pool and booze with the lads, which always led to a massive sing-song on the way to the union. So euphoric was he that when he spotted Annie, he just gave a little wave and carried on, a little voice in his head saying 'balls, this is me.'

The climax of the track was morphing into New Order's *Blue Monday* provoking bellows of approval from the packed dance floor, the distinctive stuttering beats enticing more students to fill any remaining gaps. The long intro finally gave way to Bernie asking 'How does it feel?' joined by a joyous throng bellowing the same question. Jack quickly became lost in just having a brilliant night though a familiar scent was drifting up his nostrils amid the beer, fags and sweat. There was Annie, moving rather well, beside him.

She had a bottle of lager waved aloft and belted out every word. Jack watched Annie, a world away from her college persona, with her long brown hair very much down, and knew he was in love. He was sweating, drunk and very happy.

Blue Monday gave way to The Fall's *Mr Pharmacist* before a blast of hip-hop punctured the indie blanket with NWA, Public Enemy and Run DMC taking the night towards 1am. Annie raised an eyebrow at the gusto with which Jack attacked these tracks but remained where she was. The feeling of total comfort and familiarity settling between them was what Jack remembered for a long time.

As revellers made their way out, Jack realised they hadn't even said hello to each other, and as his mates dragged him towards a burger, all Annie said was 'see you next week.' Jack nodded, held her gaze a second and drank in a smile that said so much more.

The first date was a curious mix of excitement and a feeling that they'd known each other for years. Jack often reflected on the easy familiarity between them from the off, though he also remembered trying really hard not to get drunk. It's fair to say Jack liked drinking and though never actively seeking to get drunk, finding it was the consequence all too often. Meeting his mates in the union at lunchtime with a lecture-free afternoon ahead led to impromptu all-day sessions that Jack loved. That feeling of utter freedom and zero responsibility was intoxicating, but even at the callow age of 22, he didn't want to be seen as a drunken bum.

He needn't have worried. Annie was also fond of a drink and drank pints of proper bitter with him as they talked non-stop and munched their way noisily through several bags of crisps. Her soft Manchester accent beguiled Jack as she talked about her upbringing in the North West, born to university lecturer parents that still lived and worked in Manchester. Her parents were both renowned in their fields, with father Matthew travelling all over the world lecturing on international relations and mother Alison, an expert on molecular biology.

She talked at length about her own academic ambitions in the social sciences, her passion for psychology and her longing to teach. Jack, the king of aimless drifting, admired her clarity of purpose and more than once wished he was more like that. You can't manufacture that drive however and once asked by Annie, it poured out of him how he could never think clearly about next week, let alone the rest of his life. The look on Annie's face betrayed her inability to understand this approach to life and Jack teased her for her bafflement.

Annie looked at her watch and said she needed to go. Four hours had flown by, and she reminded Jack she was presenting at a seminar in the morning. Jack couldn't help sighing as they finished up their drinks. They walked the half mile to Annie's house arm in arm, continuing to chat, before Annie finally said: 'I think you need to kiss me, now.'

When time and circumstance allowed, their perfect Friday evening these days involved Jack getting the tube down to Camden and meeting up with Annie in the Oxford Arms before refuelling in Pizza Express. This had happened all too infrequently recently, Jack lamented as he boarded the Bank branch train at East Finchley on a brilliantly lit afternoon. The rapid heavy shower that had drenched Jack on the way to the tube had quickly given way to strong sunshine again, and the streets seemed electrified, as if a lightning strike had frozen in time. Today though, with local journalists briefed and very few leads coming forward, Jack had left for the day to meet Annie and ruminate on the last few days.

As usual on Friday afternoon, the southbound train was half-full, affording the rare luxury of a seat on the tube, but Jack stood to let the surplus water drain onto the floor of the train. He smiled to himself thinking of Annie's many rants had about the tube and thanked his lucky stars he rarely had to travel at rush hour, one of the perks of living near your place of work and indeed, being a policeman.

A copy of the Ham 'n High newspaper had been left on the shelf of the train and Jack had a quick look to kill the ten minutes or so to Camden. As he fully expected, the first shooting had made it onto the front page with the headline of 'Pensioner's Pooch shot on Heath'. A shiver went through him as he ran his hand over his closely cropped salt and pepper hair. Two dogs already dead and the media already on the trail meant trouble. An animal hitman with an unerring shot popping adored pets in one of the most desirable areas of London. It didn't bear thinking about. There were too many questions. Why? What? Who? Jesus, why? Jack always came back to 'Why?'

He came out of his thoughts in time to realise he was at Camden station and jumped through the bleeping doors onto the platform. Jack walked the long escalator to ground level sighing loudly as he pushed past the inevitable person standing on the left and out into the seething mass of activity that is Chalk Farm Road. The smell of food that assaulted his nostrils made Jack realise how hungry he was.

Annie was already nursing a bottle of Beck's talking animatedly to two friends from her school. Jack's heart melted a little when her face lit up as she noticed him at the bar, his tipping hand gesture met with a beaming nod and a raised bottle. The bar was doing brisk business but, as was usually the case here, service was prompt. A tiny girl with far too many piercings for Jack's liking served up his orders with a radiant but metallic smile and Jack made his way through the Friday evening crowd to join Annie's table.

Jack had met Magda before, she was a Hungarian English teacher, and he couldn't deny she was very attractive. Her large round blue eyes and masses of long black hair were striking, and she reminded Jack of a witch, a very beautiful one at that. Annie teased him about Magda but as she often told him and others, 'we don't do jealousy.' Her otherworldly presence was topped off by a tendency to dress exclusively in black, and she always cut a striking figure particularly when her lithe six-foot frame carried her to the bar. Jack kissed her on both cheeks and offered his hand to a guy who must surely be a geography teacher, regulation brown cords, a check shirt, sensible shoes, bit of a pot, dishevelled hair and a ruddy, weathered face.

'Hi, Jack, Annie's husband.'

'Hi, I'm Brian, I'm the new head of maths.'

'Really? Good to meet you, Brian.'

'Likewise.'

Jack kissed and briefly hugged his wife and sat on a little stool next to her.

'So, how was it this year, discharging a new generation of criminals onto our streets?' asked Jack to the table.

'Oh Jack, it's a heavy burden, but hey, at least we have you to catch these newly honed villains, is that not right my Annie?' replied Magda.

'Oh yes, London's finest keeps me safe in bed at night,' cooed Annie.

'Not that safe I bet' replied Magda, winking at Jack's wife and stroking his knee. Trying and failing not to blush, Jack looked away and surveyed the scene. There was the usual after-work crowd mingling happily with the regulars and those arriving for the beginning of a night out. His thoughts again returned to his stomach and the joy of pizza when he noticed a crowd developing under one of the TV screens. As is the nature of rolling news channels, they were constantly flagging up the Breaking News graphic. Jack ignored it in the main, but the gathering crowd alerted his interest.

There were loud hoots of laughter and shouts of 'twat' and 'idiot' from some as Jack pushed his way to the front. His phone rang as he caught a full view of the TV showing a distraught looking Aidan Buchanan with a Sky News Breaking News graphic saying 'ROCK STAR'S DOG SHOT DEAD ON HAMPSTEAD HEATH'.

Jack glanced at his phone, saw Merton waiting, answered and said, 'I'm on my way.'

'You're joking!' snapped Annie, a veteran of many ruined evenings out, 'Say hi from me and get me a signed photo.'

Jack grunted, kissed Annie, and said goodbye to the table and his night out. In the urgency to go, he'd forgotten Annie's fondness for Mile High and Buchanan's waspish vocals. They'd bickered over the band, Jack berating her for liking what he regarded as predictable rock -Annie slating him for his musical snobbery and 'rehashing everything the Guardian says'.

Buchanan's soap opera of a life repelled Jack, and he stiffened as he contemplated the circus he was walking into.

Safely in a cab heading north to East Finchley, Jack asked for Radio 5 to be turned up. The story was all over the station with police refusing to comment at this stage. Jack knew he'd be on TV later giving a statement or even accompanying Aidan Buchanan in a press conference appealing for witnesses. Twitter was ablaze with rumours and jokes, Jack admiring the speed in which they appeared while #ripmoira was trending around the world.

Merton was waiting, as the cab pulled up outside the station on Fortis Green. Jack got a receipt, jumped in the station Mondeo and headed for Hampstead Heath. Merton filled Jack in on the basics.

'So, in broad daylight, while the overrated Buchanan lies on his dirty arse enjoying the sunshine, some maniac shoots his one redeeming factor in the head?'

'That's about it, Sir. What's going on?'

'Christ knows.'

They parked on the south-eastern corner of the Heath and walked up Parliament Hill. A sizeable crowd had gathered including a bank of cameras and reporters, many conducting pieces to camera. The pair silently pushed their way through the reporters and their relentless questions. A SOCO team were at work combing the area for evidence as a burly middle-aged man with thinning hair and a goatee beard comforted Buchanan.

'Jesus, what the hell is he doing here?' Jack shouted as they approached the dog.

The stricken furry lump that was once Moira lay at their feet. Jack nodded at the uniform and knelt to inspect the dog's body. He could see a small entry wound halfway up the bridge of the nose, right in the centre, so intricately placed that before he knew it, he'd said 'what a brilliant shot,' too loudly.

'You what? You taking the piss or what?' bawled Buchanan and lunged at Jack. Merton and the uniform quickly stepped in and restrained him.

'I assure you I'm not taking the piss at all Mr Buchanan.'

'So what you on about, "brilliant shot", that's what you said? A "brilliant fucking shot."'

The singer focussed his wild blue eyes on Jack's and held his gaze. They were bloodshot, and Jack could have sworn he was holding back tears.

'It occurred to me, Mr Buchanan, that whoever shot your dog and two others this week is a very good shot indeed.'

Buchanan's head shot from side to side looking about him as if the other dogs' corpses had just been shot and were nearby.

'There's been others? What the fuck is going on copper?'

Buchanan, after umpteen drunken run-ins with the law, didn't have much time for the police.

'That's what we're trying to find out, Mr Buchanan.'

'Too late for my Moira though innit?'

'Mr Buchanan, is there somewhere we can go and where I can ask you some questions?'

'Ask me questions? You should be out trying to catch the bastards who shot my dog you daft twat.'

Jack said nothing and looked away.

'Okay copper, my gaff is just off the Heath' said Buchanan at last.

His 'gaff' was indeed just off the Heath. Jack, not having been to a bona fide rock star's house, before didn't know what to expect. A roller in the pool, naked groupies draped over expensive furniture, Keith and Mick popping in for a cup of tea…No, he had no idea. The media scrum, cameras, reporters and satellite vans gave away which house it was immediately. What lay beyond the scrum was a beautiful three storey house with dense vegetation and an abundance of trees behind giant wrought iron gates at the front painted black.

'Get me through these wankers copper, will you?' barked Buchanan.

Jack nodded and pushed through the throng shouting 'no questions, let us through please.'

A camera banged Jack's head, and he swung round and pushed it away and still the questions kept coming. 'What effect will this have on the tour and album sales?' made Jack laugh out loud and Aidan swing a meaty fist at the reporter. An ugly melee broke out as Jack pulled Aidan Buchanan through his opulent gates to safety.

They hurried to the door, and Aidan closed it and stood flat against it, his unkempt brush of dark hair flashing like a fairy light as the cameras kept shooting pictures trespassing light all over the large, imposing hallway. He looked up slowly and looked for Ellen.

'Oh Ellen,' he said.

The diminutive housekeeper rushed into his arms, and she virtually disappeared in his clutches, her head barely reaching his chest. Jack felt like an intruder in this very private moment. Finally, Aidan broke down, and Ellen quickly followed. Jack walked into the kitchen, took a stool at the huge island in the centre of the room and fixed his gaze on a muted portable as a smiling DIY crew set about someone's house.

'Are you a policeman?'

Jack turned and saw a svelte bottle blond leaning against the sink in what looked like last night's clothes, a short black dress but very crumpled and smelling of cigarettes.

'DI Jack Love, nice to meet you.'

'He's supposed to be on his way to Venezuela.'

'What?'

'Aidan, he said he's going to Venezuela, or at least that's what his housekeeper said.'

'I see, are you a friend of Aidan's?'

The woman looked at her hands. 'Since last night, yeah…'

'Ah.'

'Doesn't make me a tart,' she said looking up at Jack.

Jack shrugged and raised his hands as Aidan walked in with his arm wrapped tightly around the tiny figure of Ellen, both sets of eyes glassy puddles. Buchanan wiped his eyes with his bare forearm, sniffed like a snotty kid in assembly and barked, 'Who the fuck are you?' not for the first time that afternoon.

'Aidan, she's your wee friend from last night,' whispered Ellen, a modicum of composure returning.

'Oh aye,' a grin threatened to break out on his stubbled face but never quite made it, 'I remember. Please go home.'

The girl got her coat, went to give Aidan a peck on the cheek, thought better of it and headed for the door.

'I didn't get your number' she said.

'I know' Aidan nodded at the door.

There was quiet as the door slammed. Ellen and Aidan sighed at the same time.

'Not going to be the new Mrs Buchanan then?' Jack asked.

'Not if I have anything to do with it. Never mind, you'll be able to read about it in the News of the Screws on Sunday, the *wild* night we had together and all that shit. Now, are we going to talk about Moira or what?'

'Yes, of course.'

Ellen made some tea as the two men headed for the living room.

Jack couldn't deny Mile High had made an enormous impact on British popular music in a short time. Loaded with self-confidence and telling anyone who'd listen they were the best band in the world, they swaggered onto the scene dominated by boy bands and X-Factor contestants and grabbed it by the balls. People loved it.

The band's *fuck you* attitude backed by searing guitar riffs, a nod and wink here and there to the Beatles and funny and often moving everyday lyrics that appealed to young people fed up with being spoon-fed slickly produced music. The band shot to super stardom in a blink of an eye.

Buchanan's appetite for excess in all its forms meant the media also lapped it up. Gigs were cancelled, photographers punched, lovers taken and left like rented DVDs and drugs snorted, injected and smoked like they were the only life-force that would sustain the band. They fought everyone and everything like rutting stags, and the public read every word in lurid detail.

The first album *US and Them* sold millions in the UK, the follow-up *Are you listening?* so eagerly awaited that pre-orders destroyed all previous records and broke the band to a worldwide audience. The albums were heavy on the malaise of growing up on working class estates in London, the dreams and the nightmares of trying to escape.

A Beatles influence ensured they had melody, the Stone Roses influence meant super tankers of attitude and Buchanan's love of Led Zeppelin meant their songs were underpinned with intense power and energy.

If you stepped aside from the relentless panto in the tabloids, the band had developed a fanatical fan base, and critics from all sections of society clamoured to be seen with them.

Jack had been a fanatical Led Zeppelin fan after cutting his teeth on AC/DC and Deep Purple before he was a teenager. Zeppelin accompanied Jack throughout puberty, Robert Plant's Viking wailings helping Jack lose his virginity, rather too quickly to a seventeen year old sixth former when he was 15. The two year age gap, enormous at that age, made her seem mysterious and rather wonderful to Jack.

He then negotiated his late teens with the help of New Order when he wanted to dance, the Smiths when he wanted to wallow, and like millions of middle-class white boys, he fell in love with Public Enemy's noise-filled fight against racism, an intoxicating mix of rebellion set to a beat that got you on the dance floor with minimal effort.

When Mile High came along, Jack understood how they had caught the mood of the moment, liked the energy of the music and the igniting of a very British musical moment. Yet Jack tired very quickly of the band. The omnipresence of the music grated as did seeing Buchanan's mug on the front-pages in some altercation or 'tryst' with some other celebrity.

Jack found himself sitting in Aidan Buchanan's obscenely large living room looking out on to Hampstead Heath as Mile High were about to go on tour to promote their 'difficult' third album *Back to the Future*. A decentish single *Where were you?* headed up the release but Jack laughed out loud after catching the video late one night on a cable channel. With a sprawling council estate and hideous tower blocks as a backdrop, the band snarled their way through a four-minute rant against a music press that had not yet deserted them apart from imagined sleights from certain journalists who had tired of the Mile High panto. Jack had turned it off halfway through and went to bed. Jack thought of the grim backdrop in the video as he surveyed the surroundings. Where were you indeed?

Ellen brought a bottle of Becks for Aidan and a cup of coffee for Jack.

'Sir, I know…'

'Call me Aidan for fuck's sake.'

'Right, Aidan, tell me what you were doing prior to your dog being shot.'

'Why?' Aidan took a long swig of his beer, near emptying the bottle.

'Why?'

'Yeah, copper, why? Some twat shoots my Moira and you want to know what I had for breakfast.' Suddenly, Aidan's up on his feet. 'Ellen, Ellen! Get me Bergerac on the phone, I need a proper copper in here.'

Jack sighed, sat back and concentrated on a tree on the Heath, watched a pair of parakeets settle on its branches and quickly fly off again. He took a sip of his strong black filter coffee and looked at Aidan standing in the centre of the room.

Standing at well over six foot, Aidan cut an imposing figure. Despite the ravages of his lifestyle, he was looking good, if a bit weathered. His unshaved face was warmer and fuller than publicity shots allowed, framed by a mop of unkempt hair. His round blue eyes rarely made full contact, and he couldn't sit still. He lifted his arms over his head occasionally revealing a very lean and sinewy torso. He was all nervous energy wrapped in anger and contempt.

'Aidan, please sit down.'

Knowing a fictional detective from Jersey was unlikely to roll up anytime soon, Aidan shrugged his shoulders and fell back onto his settee. 'Ok, copper, I'm all yours.'

Aidan recounted his day with a barrel load of expletives as it was clear he was relishing a day of relative freedom, out and about without a care in the world. It was also clear he had no idea who would do such a thing, and Jack knew that he could rule out a personal hit. With two other dogs shot that week, Aidan acknowledged he had plenty of enemies and that Jack would have to look at that angle.

The energy suddenly drained out of Aidan Buchanan, and his cockney accent faded to a more classless tone lending weight to those who pointed out he was born in Swindon and only properly moved to London in recent years. He sat motionless on the settee looking at the ceiling as Jack finished his notes.

'So what happens now?' he said eventually, his eyes not leaving the ceiling.

'We're gathering all the evidence we can at the moment, Aidan. He'll be caught quickly I'd have thought' Jack lied.

'So, let's get this straight, there's a geezer out there popping mutts. Like a serial killer, but with dogs not people? What the fuck is all that about?'

'I don't know Aidan, I really don't know. Rest assured we'll be doing everything we can to catch this man.'

'Man? You sure it's a man? There's some mad birds out there you know, I should know.'

The door buzzed as Jack nodded at Aidan.

'That'll be Rosie.'

It was indeed Rosie, a PR who handled the affairs of the band. Rosie Ballard, famous or notorious for planting stories about her list of famous clients and defending them like a mother Polar Bear defends her young. She was a regular face on news bulletins, chat shows and in the press. Her reputation as a ferocious man-eater was curious. She was short, very slim and had a sweet round face with big kind eyes. She wore black rimmed non-prescription glasses and let her long blonde hair fall over her face, self-consciously sweeping it away at any opportunity.

The clues were in the voice and the eyes. Her voice was not exactly deep, but it was even and never wavered. It remained even, betraying a slight northern tinge whatever situation she was in. She had instant authority, and the beguiling eyes had steel lurking just beneath their surface. The word was you never, *ever* messed Rosie Ballard around. There were plenty of casualties with war stories to tell.

'Hi Aidan, and you are?' asked Rosie, turning to Jack.

'DI Jack Love, Metropolitan Police.'

Rosie introduced herself curtly and turned to Aidan.

'DI Love just leaving?'

Before answering, Jack cut in. 'I was as a matter of fact.'

'It wasn't really a question, DI Love.'

'Now Aidan, the tabs are fighting for the exclusive interview on your dog heartbreak. I've gone for The Sun of course as we need maximum exposure. NME want you for next week, and I've got Radio 1, Virgin, LBC and Heart waiting for slots. We've got to get sorted. I can't believe our luck, it's August, nothing's happening, they're all over it. Absolutely exquisite timing.'

Jack paused at the living room door waiting for Aidan to explode in a volcano of righteous anger about the Murdoch press and put this heartless woman in her place. Instead, he nodded and grunted his agreement. He towered over Rosie but looked like a wee schoolboy being told off for wetting his pants.

'Oh, DI Love. Naturally, we'll be blaming the state of the world and poor policing in London for letting gun crime spiral out of control. Nothing personal, just letting you know' Rosie said evenly.

Jack looked at Rosie who held his gaze too calmly for his liking then looked at Aidan. The big man looked down for a moment then snarled, 'Yeah copper, find the bastards who shot my dog, ok?'

'I'll see myself out,' said Jack as he headed through the gates into the burgeoning throng of cameras and reporters.

Jack eventually got home just after 1 o'clock in the morning. Back at the station, the team were no further forward, and during an impromptu meeting, he told them all to go home. They looked shattered, bewildered even. By this stage, there was often something to go on, but there was nothing, nothing at all. Forensic reports would be back by morning, and Jack told everyone to be in by 8am.

He slipped into his chair, poured a nip of Talisker into his glass and put the television on. He allowed the aroma of fire to linger in his nostrils before taking a sip. He closed his eyes and savoured this one moment of comfort in a surreal day. On opening his eyes, Jack was startled to see an image of himself emerging blinking from the Buchanan house. He watched intently as he answered a few rudimentary questions and ignored the daft ones. Terrorist rumours? Must have been The Star. No one mentioned the other dogs, this was all about Aidan Buchanan.

Before going to the weather, the newsreader took a look at the coming morning's papers. The shooting even made the front pages of the some of the broadsheets, and the tabloids jumped all over it. The Sun did indeed get the exclusive interview. *MY DOG HELL ON HEATH* was the front page accompanied by a huge photo of Aidan and Moira in happier times. A separate story speculated on why this happened, and various farfetched theories were given a run. Jack made a note to buy all the papers in the morning. A lead might just emerge from the nonsense. You never know thought Jack as Earnie wandered in and put his head on Jack's lap and looked up at his owner.

'Hello boy. Are you a sight for sore eyes or what?'

Earnie sniffed his glass and instantly recoiled like he always did when Jack was enjoying a single malt. Earnie whimpered ever so quietly and lay at Jack's feet as he began to nod off.

Jack woke with a start and poured his single malt over his crotch. This was a common routine. After a night out, Annie would go straight to bed exhausted. Jack would linger in the front room, opting for music more often than not on YouTube or MTV. After a few drinks he regressed to being a sixth former, he relished every tune he listened to, developed an uber-appreciation of a band's work. Sometimes he was even moved to tears by what he heard.

Without fail he fell asleep with his glass in his hand and never spilt a drop. It was the waking that did the damage. Invariably, he would get cold and wake suddenly. Result – soaked crotch. He loved his Talisker and resented the waste. He called himself a tit, patted Earnie and climbed the stairs to bed. He hadn't stayed awake long enough for music tonight. The clock on News 24 said 5.41, and he sighed as the image of him leaving Aidan's house rolled again. He'd been out for some time and would be on his way back down Fortis Green in no time in another attempt to break this most perplexing of cases.

Jack crept into the room and heard Annie breathing evenly, the hint of a snore now and again. The scent of sleep drew Jack into the bed and to avoid waking Annie he undressed in the dark. He slipped under the covers and couldn't resist moving his arms around his wife's waist. Her naked midriff was the perfect antidote to a day that confounded all logic. Annie barely stirred as he spooned into her back and bottom. He could smell red wine and pizza, the faint smell of garlic and cigarette smoke in her hair. He remembered the sweet expectation of a meal with his wife, precious time where they would have chewed through the case so far.

With breakfast on the go and Earnie let out to the garden to relieve himself, Jack picked up the paper and contemplated the day ahead. He sighed, turned the bacon on the grill, savouring the aroma and begged no one in particular to give him a lead, any kind of scent to pick up and follow. The sun was already strong, reaching into the east facing kitchen and adding to the warmth of the cooker. Radio 5's weatherman predicted a heatwave for the coming weekend and nannied the listeners about the strength of the sun.

Moira's demise made not page one of the Guardian but page three, including a now familiar image of Jack answering the media's questions. He read the lengthy piece with interest, but little light was shed. The other shootings were mentioned, and the paper speculated that having a dog serial killer on the loose could be the perfect silly season story to rival Big Brother while the real world (i.e. the Westminster village) took a breather, particularly now an A-List mutt was among the victims.

A dog serial killer? As Annie joined him, Jack thought of the ludicrous names the tabloids would come up with for the killer. Canine Killer? Mutt Murderer? Dr Dog Death? Mmm, they need work, thought Jack.

Annie saw to the neglected bacon, poured herself a cup of strong coffee from the cafetiere and sat down. She reached for the paper as the phone's shrill tone erupted.

'Hi Merton, fine ta, yourself?' asked Annie as she passed the phone to Jack.

'Ok, I'll be there in 10 minutes,' said Jack.

He took a huge bite of his bacon sandwich, swilled it down with black coffee, kissed Annie and marched out.

Another dog had been shot.

Hampstead Heath was steadily becoming a killing field for dogs. This time, like Albert Johns and Mark, it was an early morning kill. A young woman named Maria Spoke was walking her beloved two-year-old golden retriever, Whisky, west up Parliament Hill. She barely heard the shot as a gusty breeze had pitched up from the south, but it appeared to come from a group of trees north of Parliament Hill.

Maria Spoke knew of the other dogs' deaths but openly admitted she was in the 'it'll never happen to me' brigade, like most people. Merton reminded her that the Met had not warned people off the Heath, but to be vigilant instead.

She often took an early morning stroll with Whisky from her flat opposite the Wrestlers on North Road over the Heath to Hampstead with Whisky. As a freelance illustrator, she had the luxury of dictating her own day and found a morning walk got her energy and creative appetite pumping. It was also a great way of bolstering her decision to give up her banking job to illustrate full time after favourable responses to her work.

Jack nodded as Merton recounted Maria's dire story. She was completely devastated, Whisky was her 'best friend' and a better companion 'than any man.' A rueful smile came to Jack's lips but not his eyes. Annie had said the same of Earnie when cases had consumed him and his life with Annie. Jack knew too many blokes where whisky was their best friend too.

Merton rubbed his face with both hands and looked at Jack. 'Like the others, no enemies to speak of, no warning and one shot to the dog's head.'

Aidan Buchanan had plenty of enemies, and they would be questioned as a matter of course. But Merton was right, this was a highly skilled operator with a distinctive MO aware that CCTV was virtually non-existent in the Hampstead Heath area. He appeared to move without attention, leaving the scene of his chaos with such stealth that not a single sighting of any kind had been reported at the time of the shootings. One of the tabloids had called it correctly in its screaming headline, 'Police draw blank in hunt for dog killer.' They obviously hadn't found a snappy title for the perpetrator of these crimes but were keenly aware that the investigation was no further forward than when Prince had been shot and killed four days ago.

The fresh kill had ratcheted up the urgency and desperation another notch in light of Moira's demise the day before. This was now a national story, indeed an international story thanks to Aidan Buchanan. A meeting called by DCI Stephanie Wallace for that afternoon would address all the questions.

Jack didn't relish his meetings with Wallace. She had chided him on more than one occasion for his relaxed approach. She even asked him how he got such good results, 'as you seem half asleep most of the time.' His answer of 'I'll have to sleep on that,' got a laugh from the meeting but a searing glare that could have welded gold from Wallace. This meeting had the potential to be every bit as uneasy as previous occasions.

DCI Stephanie Wallace was a headmistress who'd taken a wrong turn in the wrong era. Her glasses magnified small brown eyes that almost disappeared when she took them off.

Her permanent scowl petrified the most hardened of coppers, yet the top brass loved the results she got with her incisive mind and attention to ever decreasing budgets. Fiercely proud of the police, she'd back her officers while ensuring they always kept her in the loop.

Jack felt he got on quite well with Wallace, aside from his perceived attitude problem. He had confounded her time and time again by getting his man, and she appeared to be warming to him, at last. She almost got above freezing with him on occasion, though he wasn't expecting a dinner invite anytime soon. Thank god.

Her husband, Graham, universally known as PB (Poor Bastard), was also a policeman, serving in Berkshire as a DI.

'Brainstorming, my arse,' moaned Merton drawing a gaggle of laughs around the table as they waited for Wallace. It was fair to say Love's team wasn't keen on Wallace's idea of brainstorming. Meetings happened all the time as a matter of course in an investigation. Wallace seemed to imply that they didn't, and she was doing something different to move things on by applying the brainstorming label.

'I don't like it either,' said DC Natasha Wright smoothing her tightly braided hair and grinning.

'What?' replied Merton.

'I don't like brainstorming…or your arse,' she replied.

More laughter followed. Merton had a barely concealed soft spot for DC Wright and laughed, but the blush on his face betrayed his embarrassment.

DC Wright hadn't been with Jack's team long but had made quite an impact. She was bright, learned quickly and critically had that slice of confidence in her convictions that often made the difference. A graduate on the fast track scheme, Jack had high hopes for her.

She shared a large gappy grin with Jack and had an infectious laugh with a wiry frame and long, rangy legs yet rarely wore clothes that flaunted her body. Her attire on starting in Muswell Hill was more akin to a lawyer in the City, all black business suits until Jack stepped in and suggested she looked a little bit more casual on duty. She readily complied but still looked immaculate. Being black and from south London meant she had an edge over the normal graduates they received, who depressingly remained overwhelmingly white, middle-class and male. She would know about the street, its rhythms, its characters. She was no tough cookie from the ghetto of popular cliché, but she was smart and undoubtedly streetwise. Jack liked her, Merton *really* liked her, the whole station did.

Except perhaps DCI Stephanie Wallace.

'Care to share the joke, DC Wright,' said Wallace slapping a file on the table and shutting the door.

'No ma'am,'

Room 10 wasn't big enough for 10 bodies, but it was the only room available on this bright and very warm August morning. The weather forecast predicted a heatwave for the weekend, and Jack reckoned it had come early, especially if the film of sweat on Wallace's upper lip was anything to go by.

'No? Well, that's a shame. Now, let's get on. Jack, where are we?'

Jack gave a brief summary of events so far and rather limply concluded that they had no firm leads. No leads at all, in fact, firm or otherwise.

'All pretty dismal, wouldn't you say Love?'

'Yes ma'am, this case is extremely unusual.'

'Unusual it may be Jack, but what are you doing about it? What are your ideas, man?' She sighed deeply. 'Well, come on. Anyone else care to enlighten us? Merton, tell me something about our man, it is a man isn't it?'

'Probably,' stammered Merton.

'Probably! Jesus Christ, what's wrong Merton, can't a *bird* shoot a gun properly? Come on tell me something about our suspect.'

'He or *she* is an extremely good shot, Ma'am,' said Merton quietly. There were sniggers round the room.

'Wallace looked quickly around the room. 'What's so funny? We're actually getting somewhere now.' Wallace got to her feet and moved to the flip chart and wrote *S/he's a very good shot* on the blank piece of paper.

'Good, what else?' she looked around the table.

'He or *she* moves around largely unseen,' said Jack.

'Largely? I'd say completely wouldn't you, Jack?'

Jack had to agree, not one sighting to date of anything or anyone remotely suspicious. Wallace wrote *Moves around without arousing suspicion* on the board. 'What is this telling us? I think it would be fair to guess our man and despite the admirable care we're all taking not to rule out a woman, it's reasonable to assume for now it is a man, is a professional gunman, ex-army would be my guess. What else?'

'He appears to have no motive ma'am,' said Merton, the perspiration increasing on his reddening face.

'Good, no motive, yes Sergeant, that's true.'

'Also, he has no interest in killing humans,' said Natasha.

'Yes, at the moment.'

The flip chart started to fill up with what they knew and assumptions created as a result. Jack saw the value of the ex-army line of enquiry. The forces were not always massively helpful to the police when tracking down criminals with a forces background. Not good for the image, Jack guessed. Nevertheless, it was a road they had to go down. Gun clubs were another angle to be explored as was the unlikely suspects of Aidan's enemies.

Jack went back to his office, put on a pot of coffee and looked out of his window. Another beautiful day was passing, thick white cumulus clouds were bubbling far to the north with their suggestion of a late shower the only threat to a perfect August day.

As Jack's mini coffee filter bubbled and gurgled into action, Wallace popped her head round the door. 'Smells good, got enough for two?'

'Yes ma'am, how do you take it?' Strong and black, Jack guessed, just like him.

'Milky, two sugars, please. Bad for you, I know, but what the hell?'

'Indeed ma'am,'

'Now, I thought that was a very useful session didn't you, Jack?'

'I…'

'The point is we've got to act on it now. Brass is becoming very jumpy, and they want a result very quickly, and so do I, Jack,'

Jack poured the coffees, the bitter-sweet aroma taking his mind off to pastures more pleasant for a blissful second.

4

Jack Love always rose early when a big case was on and today was no exception. The early rising sun had pierced the gloom quickly, and he rose gently to avoid waking Annie. He threw on last night's clothes and tip-toed down the stairs, waking Earnie and marvelling at how awake and eager the beast was in an instant. He didn't bark though - as a pup he'd quickly learned that waking 'mummy' was a truly terrible idea. 'Daddy' had learned that too, in record time.

Jack and Earnie made their way along Fortis Green to East Finchley to get the papers and a heart-starting coffee in Gino's where Fortis Green meets the High Road. Gino welcomed them in.

'Good morning my friends, how are we today?' The genial giant bent down to lavish attention on Earnie. 'It's a beautiful day, no?'

'Certainly is Gino. It'll be even better with one of your lovely Americanos inside me.'

'Ah, never fails eh? What is it with these fruit teas? Since when did bloody chamomile tea put lead in your pencil?' Gino busily moved to his magnificent coffee machine and ground the beans.

Jack couldn't help but agree. Annie loved 'herbal infusions' and had eventually got Jack into them, but good grief, only a fully loaded coffee from Gino could get you going, first thing.

'How is your lovely wife, sir?' Gino shouted over the din of the machine.

'Fine, I think, Gino, fast asleep last time I looked.'

'Like Mrs Schillaci eh? Must never wake early eh?' he laughed loudly.

'Too right, unthinkable Gino, unthinkable.'

Gino laughed loudly again.

They sat outside and watched the day unfold, men and women with wet hair heading for the City, guaranteed a seat on the Northern Line this early, some strutting ahead, others languishing behind wishing they were still in bed. Like sheep heading into a pen, they all stopped, stooped, grabbed a Metro and headed into the station. So begins another weary day.

Gino brought the steaming coffee, and Jack inhaled the gorgeous bitter-sweet aroma. Jack was his only customer, so Gino joined them outside.

'Terrible business this dog shooting, no? Are you getting anywhere? I saw you on the bloody goggle box last night with that Buchanan idiot.'

'Not so far, I'm afraid. Not a fan of Mile High then Gino?'

'Me? You must be joking! What a bloody row they make.'

Jack nodded and looked at his pile of papers. After days of the media failing to come up with a sharp moniker for the killer, The Mirror had at least christened the Heath with no little genius, *Houndsdead Heath*.

'Oh, very good, very good indeed,' said Jack aloud.

Gino grunted and went off to serve an impatient looking young woman in a black business suit.

With Earnie transfixed by the traffic, Jack waded through the papers. The coverage was extensive, up to seven or eight pages in some of the red tops. The broadsheets were naturally more sober with less attention on Aidan Buchanan, but they were hooked like everyone else. The Guardian focussed on the old man, homing in on his distinguished army service fighting the Japanese in Malaya. To Albert's credit, he didn't bang on about the youth of today.

What he did say crushed Jack. 'You wouldn't believe the things I witnessed in Malaya, men having their heads chopped off, people dying of starvation while working. But to me, randomly shooting my dog in my dying days is the cruellest blow of all.'

Jack looked up from the paper and shivered. In Albert's case, a dog really was a man's best friend and a companion beyond value. To have that completely destroyed in a case of such random cruelty defied belief. Jack felt shame that he and Merton had joked about it before and after questioning Albert. The dignity of the old man shone like a beacon compared to their snide comments.

Jack wondered how he'd feel if he lost Earnie in the same manner. Or any manner for that matter. He looked down at him and Earnie looked up instantly, full of expectation, ready to bound off to the next place, wherever that would be. Jack took a moment to give him a good stroke.

'You look after that dog, Jack, don't want to hear no rubbish about Earnie getting plugged as well, you hear?'

'I know, Gino, makes you think doesn't it?' replied Jack.

'It does, you bringing that little fella in here always brightens my day,' said Gino tossing a biscuit to the lab with the shiny black pelt.

The next kill was the most brazen so far. An author and his wife were sat on a bench watching their three-year-old spaniel sniff everything in sight and jump in and out of Highgate Ponds.

'We heard a whoosh sound just to our right, and Casper let out the briefest of yelps before going down,' said Alan Wild, back at Muswell Hill Police Station. A tall elegant man dressed in navy cords and white Oxford shirt, he sat with his head bowed.

'We'd been for lunch at the Flask and headed down to the Heath for a stretch to walk off the food. It's such a beautiful day, and we thought it'd be safe seeing as it was the middle of the day and plenty of people about. We've taken to avoiding the Heath in the mornings and evenings.' He paused and for the first time, his eyes moistened.

'I don't think we'll be going back anytime soon,' he added, his voice barely audible.

Merton was poised to dive in with another question, but Jack raised his hand to give Wild a chance to compose himself.

'Mr Wild, did you see anyone fleeing the scene?' asked Jack eventually.

'Well, that's just it. I did, I mean we both did though my eyes are better than Trudy's. It's just I can't think of anything distinguishing, and he was gone so fast. It's maddening, as a writer, I can't adequately describe him to you.'

Alan Wild had written four novels, three of which had been published to reasonable critical acclaim. His last book, *The Fire Within* had been nominated for an award or two and he had made enough to give up working as a local authority press officer. His wife, like Annie Love, was a teacher and continued working. Wild taught creative writing classes between books. Jack knew his name was familiar but had not read any of his work and made a mental note to ask Annie later.

'It's ok, Mr Wild,' soothed Jack, 'this must be a terrible shock for you. Take your time and just tell us everything you can remember.'

So Alan Wild took it from the top and went through the whole episode. Both he and Trudy had rushed to Casper on instinct, but Alan had looked up and saw a man sprinting silently away up the hill towards the toilets. His head appeared to be covered in a balaclava, but he had blue denims and a black t-shirt on. Wild guessed that the man was aged somewhere between twenty-five and thirty-five years of age.

'He just moved so fast and so quietly, he was gone like that.' Wild snapped his fingers and shook his head in something approaching wonderment.

Trudy Wild relayed the same story but with less detail as she had concentrated on their stricken dog.

Uniform were out taking statements on the Heath, and they would go through them in detail for anything that would give them any hints on the killer's identity. With that duty in mind, he took Merton down to the Heath, despite the building heat.

'Our man's getting cocky, sir,' said Merton as they passed the Old White Lion, a smattering of reddening punters sitting contentedly outside enjoying a refreshing lager or glass of white wine.

'He certainly is, which can only be good for us. I'm sure some of the witness statements will throw something up. He ran past quite a few people, for god's sake.'

Deep down, Jack wasn't so sure. Something in Alan Wild's story told him they were dealing with someone very elusive. If a decent author couldn't adequately describe the killer then what chance an ordinary Joe Schmoe?

They continued in silence taking advantage of the shade on North Road, the shards of sunlight throwing fingers of light along their path. The temptation to pop in the Wrestlers was just fended off, but the real danger lay in Highgate Village. A finer collection of pubs, cafes and restaurants you couldn't wish to find in such a small area. The two detectives were overwhelmed by the aromas and sounds of a city winding down for the weekend.

If they thought there were more people around than usual, then they were right. The place was crawling with journalists. Knowing he'd be recognised, they turned right, past the Gatehouse pub and headed to the Heath. Apart from gaggles of media and police officers, the Heath was eerily quiet; word had spread quickly about the latest shooting and no one was running the gauntlet there anymore.

Jack and Merton had a brief chat with a PC, batted away questions from journalists and dipped under the tape onto the Heath. The two detectives walked in silence as they gathered their thoughts.

Hampstead Heath was Jack's favourite place in London. As a wide-eyed young man, everything about London fascinated him; he loved the landmarks everyone knew like Big Ben and Tower Bridge, the obvious places. That had dimmed only slightly over the years he had lived there though he feigned indifference like any other decent Londoner. But he did start to look out from town to the surrounding areas and was equally captivated, mainly at first because he could look down on central London and admire the view.

As a boy, he had seen Terry and Arthur in *Minder* sitting on a bench in parkland with a knockout view of St Paul's Cathedral and made up his mind there and then to find that spot one day. A guide book persuaded him that view must have been Parliament Hill on Hampstead Heath, but he didn't get there until he moved to London to join the Met. Sleeping on a mate's sofa in East Finchley reminded him the Heath was only down the road and soon he was the proud tenant there himself, the rental prices less hysterical than Muswell Hill and Highgate. Surprisingly friendly with a tube station to boot, East Finchley fitted the bill perfectly, particularly when he was assigned to Muswell Hill Police Station.

Blessed with more excellent pubs than he could ever remember seeing before in one area, Jack still regarded his early days on the force as his happiest days. The unique camaraderie the job engendered helped Jack through the difficult cases and the umpteen mistakes and bollockings. Jack quickly understood if the sergeant slaughtered you, it was for your benefit and forgotten the moment you went next door for a pint, though the drinks were often on you.

Like most police officers, he had his ghosts, and Cheryl Goodrich was never far from Jack's mind. He'd been off duty enjoying a night out in Camden and, having missed the last tube, had decided to walk the three miles back to East Finchley. The warmth of a good meal and more than a few drinks was still with him as he put his headphones on and headed for home. Jack never felt fear walking in London despite the numerous incidents he'd had to deal with as a policeman and saw no problem in taking a short cut through a park as he approached Tufnell Park with Cypress Hill rapping infectiously about getting high in his ears.

A young woman dressed stylishly in black was coming towards him as he was leaving the park, Jack instantly processed her as attractive, noting a not unpleasant mixed aroma of perfume and cigarettes, the tiniest of shared smiles and just as instantly forgot her. As he powered on, the music prevented Jack hearing her frenzied screams as she was dragged into the scruffy bushes that characterised the drab patch of parkland. Jack noticed lights going on in top floor windows but as he quickly turned a corner didn't give it another thought, looking forward to a lie-in as he was on the late shift the next day.

It was only as he listened to Radio London's news bulletins that his stomach began to churn with dread as it dawned on him what had happened. He phoned the station, and his sergeant ordered him to come straight into the incident room. It didn't occur to him that he may be considered a suspect and as he was watched CCTV of himself walking out of the park past the woman, the sergeant, Billy Armstrong, told him residents had heard her yelling 'Please, please help me' and her last words, 'Oh my god', just moments after they had passed each other.

'We can rule you out, then,' Armstrong had noted grimly, but Jack was transfixed by the two dark shapes

with the distinctive silhouette of a woman clearly screaming, the sight of Jack walking quickly away the last thing
Cheryl Goodrich saw in her young life.

A mentally ill man, Paul Stokes was quickly apprehended in the days that followed as it emerged he had
stopped taking his psychotic medication, slipping under
the radar of the authorities. A young Jack had played his
part with diligence, and though he was pleased this brutal
stabbing was quickly resolved, Stokes' tragic story deeply
troubled him while Cheryl Goodrich's face never left him.

Happier memories of that time centred around drinking in the Clissold and Maddens and walking the Heath to
Hampstead on a Sunday or whenever he had a free afternoon. Jack never tired of the Heath and was thankful Annie Love felt the same. He assumed their black Labrador,
Earnie, loved it too judging by the tugging on the lead and
the haste with which he sped off once released.

Jack felt deep comfort he had found somewhere to
live that suited them so perfectly. His reverie was shattered
by a news chopper appearing over the trees towards
Hampstead and lurching towards Parliament Hill like a
giant dragonfly buzzing a river bank.

This wouldn't go down well in Highgate. Due to the
cemetery, it was well known but less so than its neighbour,
Hampstead. Jack got the feeling Highgate liked it that way.
A few 'anytown' chains appeared, like Costa Coffee and
Pizza Express, but it still retained its character. It felt a
place apart, the pubs excellent, uncrowded and colourful.
Whenever Jack roamed through en route to the Heath, the
residents always appeared familiar, but not celebrities such
as those you often spotted in Hampstead. In Jack's mind,
he assumed they were authors or media figures of one kind
or another. He always felt it was their haven from the
bubbling media monster that sat below them in town.
Now there were news choppers and journalists everywhere. You could almost feel the collective unease at the
intrusion.

'We need a result, Merton,' said Jack as the two men took in the boiling vista of the city, a sultry haze muffling the sirens and roar of the traffic. The detectives looked up as two parakeets flew over them.

'Are they…?'

'Yes,' Jack quickly fired back. The parakeets were always a surprise to people new to the Heath, but Jack wasn't in the mood to explain now.

'The services link is nagging at me, Merton. This bloke is far too elusive to be an ordinary taxpayer. He must have special training, maybe SAS, Special Forces, what do you reckon?'

Merton nodded, 'I agree, it's uncanny how he moves about and he's a brilliant shot. I've read about people who have the ability to move about unseen but thought it was fiction, seems like a load of bollocks but that author…'

'Yes, exactly, but say it is services, ex-army, why is he shooting dogs? Christ Merton, I always end up back at "Why?"'

Merton was a good detective but didn't dwell too long in the whys and wherefores. He was practical, interested in catching criminals only later wondering why, a strength and a weakness in Jack's view. He knew he pondered the motivations too deeply but felt that getting an insight could open up the more mysterious cases.

'Jack, I say we pore over the CCTV in the area again and don't discount anyone barring the obvious, like someone in a wheelchair, young kids etc. The more innocuous, the more suspicious we should be.'

'Ok, Merton, put Jones on it will you?' DC Derek Jones hated getting on the streets but had a good eye for detail, so it was right up the lazy bastard's street. Meanwhile, it was time to call on their friends in the services.

Jack sighed as another news chopper banked over Highgate Village for another sweep across the Heath to show evening news viewers live feeds of enchanted parkland bathed in red evening sun unwilling to yield its mysterious secret.

The MOD cooperated when it came to investigating military suspects but, they didn't exactly fall over themselves to help, and Jack wasn't relishing the meeting he'd arranged with Major Bradley Wilkinson. He'd sounded slightly cold on the phone but Jack was hoping the general nature of his enquiries would help proceedings, and he was cheered when the clipped military accent, flavoured, ever so slightly with a West Country lilt, suggested meeting for coffee. Jack readily accepted his suggestion, and they settled on an early morning meeting the following day.

August had thus far been sultry, making sleep difficult and Jack brought a number of methods to try and remedy this most annoying of problems. The humidity definitely had a positive impact on Jack and Annie's love life. From a breathless goodnight, the pair would lie naked on top of the sheets trying to nod off. The thought of Annie's slender frame lying naked and sweaty beside him. He could feel the heat from her body and coupled with her aroma, fresh from a late cool shower meant he couldn't help but reach over and kiss her.

For Annie's part, the giddy sleepy high, lovemaking with Jack never failed to get her off to sleep, and she couldn't deny she sometimes 'used' him for that very purpose, which he loved. Though sleepy himself, he didn't quite make it so plan B was deployed – 5 live. The case and next morning's meeting with Major Wilkinson were keeping him awake in addition to the oppressive heat.

Jack was blessed that Annie never minded the radio being on in the middle of the night. Indeed she sometimes awoke and enjoyed *Up all Night*, revelling in the BBC reporters checking in from their various posts around the world. Jack would put the radio on *sleep* and he was usually away.

Not tonight. The heat and the case had defeated sex and 5live with ease, so Jack got up and sat naked in his chair watching the news channel. Earnie woke and joined him before conking out again before the weather bulletin. Jack watched mesmerised as shots of Hampstead Heath were played on a loop, bathed in hot evening sun as reporters reported on the latest developments, such as they were. The Mirror persisted with the excellent *Houndsdead Heath* angle without adding anything of substance. The Sun ran Aidan Buchanan 'exclusives' of the 'my hell' variety while the Star gave the woman Jack had met at his Hampstead pile a run, giving lurid details of the 'torrid' night they had spent together. Jack made a mental note to read that later in Gino's. He snorted as he saw the sub-headline 'there was a real chemistry between us.'

Yep, that'll be the cocaine thought Jack, and the Stella… and the knowledge that Mr Aidan Buchanan could pretty much sleep with anyone he chooses. Jack thought of the person behind the tabloid bullshit and remembered his genuine horror at losing Moira and sighed. He hated resorting to thinking the world had gone mad but in the early hours, sitting naked in his armchair watching himself on the news hunting down a man who was shooting celebrities' dogs in his favourite part of London; it was difficult not to come to that conclusion.

Major Bradley Wilkinson raised an eyebrow at the policeman chuckling over a copy of the Daily Star. He walked to the table, 'DI Jack Love? You look more like a Guardian reader to me.'

Irked that he read him so easily but pleased he knew he wasn't a Daily Star reader, Jack got to his feet and shook Major Wilkinson's hand. At just over 6 foot, Jack was no pygmy, but Wilkinson was taller and thick set. His closely cropped hair hinted at ginger and his large blue eyes presented a kind but weary face. Jack guessed he was in his late thirties and felt a twinge of jealousy at how well he looked, pale but very healthy in his civilian suit. The firm handshake and formalities dealt with, Jack bought the Major a skinny latte and inwardly laughed at the unlikely choice of coffee.

The two men swapped professional moans, budgets, staffing, the same things any two workers might be moaning about at 9 o'clock on a Tuesday morning over coffee. They paused and looked through the window out onto the embankment, tourists already heading for Big Ben and the Millennium Wheel.

Bradley shook his head gently.

'Tourists?'

Bradley nodded.

'Bloody tourists,' this time, Jack whispered it conspiratorially.

They shared a smile and continued to contemplate the scene before Bradley eventually turned to Jack. 'It's odd, but I felt at home immediately in this city.'

'Where was home?'

'A small village near Taunton.'

Jack nodded, the West Country burr just about discernible in the clipped military tones.

'It was the same for me, I loved it straight away too, still do, actually. I came over from Cardiff, a city obviously, a lovely city actually but…'

Bradley nodded. They shared London war stories, tube woes, great pubs, restaurant tips and tales about their neighbourhoods. So convivial was the company that Jack was almost beginning to forget why he was there. Almost. A tourist on a neighbouring table had a copy of the Standard and on the front page was a full-length photo of Danny Koumas sporting a t-shirt with the legend *I shot Moira* emblazoned on it. This would be Danny Koumas, lead singer of Whoosh, sworn enemy of Mile High and participant in innumerable drunken spats with Aidan Buchanan.

Bradley nodded towards the front page, 'Is that helpful?'

'Not terribly, it's enough of a circus already.'

Jack couldn't worry about that for now, he was interested in what Bradley had to say, and they hadn't touched on the subject yet. Probably close to the only two who hadn't that morning in London.

'So, if I've got this right, Jack, you think the bloke running round popping sniper rounds at dogs is army or ex-services?'

'It has to be a possibility, the aim of this man is quite remarkable, and his ability to move around unseen is uncanny.'

'I see that. I also see that there are hundreds of legitimate gun clubs around the London area let alone the illegitimate ones. There must be crack shots in every one of them.'

'True, and we are checking them don't worry.'

'Big job. Does the Met have the resources for such an extensive round of *checking*?'

'Granted, it's a big job alright, but we're doing what we can.'

You could almost see the ice forming in the air around them.

'So some grunt of a DC is ringing gun clubs, 'Hello, can I speak to Mr Smith & Wesson, ah hello, got anyone there who might want to shoot dogs? No? Ok, sorry to have troubled you.'

Jack resisted the urge to laugh. 'No need for that, we have to look into all angles as I'm sure you'll appreciate. You have to admit it's a possibility there is a services link.'

'It is a possibility, but we have over 100,000 service men and women.'

'But surely we can narrow it down somewhat, most are based out of town and overseas. And what about men who are discharged, surely we could see a list of those who have been discharged in the last two years for example?'

Bradley nodded slowly, 'Yes, I'm sure we could. Definitely a man you say?'

'Definitely. The author who lost his dog said it was definitely a man, though bar his gender he couldn't tell us anything else. This man has an elusive air to him; he seems to move unseen and unheard. I'm no expert, but I can't help thinking Special Forces. It's starting to nag at me the more I think about it.'

Major Bradley Wilkinson made a bridge of his hands and rested them on his jaw. 'Ok, I know people who work in the tribunals who will give me access to the men discharged, where they live and the reasons for their discharge. If you're getting hunches like this, I bet people who are experts are too. I must warn you, DI Love, this won't be easy and may lead nowhere, but I give you my word I will look into this for you.'

'Thank you, I appreciate it.'

The Major finished his latte with a gulp, leaving a touch of froth on his immaculately shaved face and left.

Jack ordered another black Americano and sat back down. He felt a bit deflated after the encounter, disappointed it had taken a frosty turn after such a pleasant start. He didn't blame the Major too much for that, he knew he wouldn't appreciate a similar approach from the Military Police for example. In truth, he knew the scale of the task was mammoth, and that was the main reason for the slump in his spirits.

The other was the untimely intervention of Danny Koumas. The tourist had left the Standard on his seat, and a new tabloid war between the stars was about to unleash all its fake fury and bile. Whoosh and Mile High had been at each other's throats in a battle that had ignited as soon as both bands had come to prominence.

It was a perfect media storm as bright, successful and feisty rock stars went toe-to-toe at award ceremonies or festivals. Jack felt Whoosh were a bit more sophisticated and interesting having had the art school moniker attached to them in contrast to the hard-edged and one-dimensional rock of Mile High.

As if living up to increasing critical acclaim and a broadening range of projects, Koumas had gone quiet on Buchanan as if he was playing the statesman to his rival's thuggish appeal. Jack wondered why he chose now to stick the boot in. He had to admit it was funny, though. Oh Danny boy, you've done it now.

Jack made his way along the river to Westminster station, gasping at the heat before making his way underground and back to Muswell Hill to the strangest case he'd ever worked on, desperate for a breakthrough.

Emerging out of Highgate Station into the blinding sun, deafening traffic and increasingly frantic voicemail messages from Merton, Jack smiled at the news Aidan Buchanan had rocked up at the station with his publicist demanding blood, his as well as Danny Koumas's. He knew what the front page of the Sun would be running with in the morning. Jack returned the call.

'Have they gone? Yeah, I know, but have they gone? I'm not coming in until those pricks have left. God help you if you're bullshitting me, Merton.' Jack picked up his heels and made for the station actually really hoping Aidan Buchanan and his wretched side-kick/babysitter/bloodsucker were still there.

Disappointed though he was by the absence of Aidan Buchanan and Rosie Ballard, Jack felt relief on his arrival at Muswell Police Station because the humidity had virtually melted him, he had the chance to catch up with his team. The news wasn't good.

'Sir, you'd better come and have a look at this,' said Merton after Jack had freshened up. He joined the throng underneath the TV in the incident room. With Britain getting gently steamed in the humidity, it appeared people liked the idea of shooting dogs. The news channels were reporting dogs being shot in areas from Humberside to

Devon, a Scottish dog had been shot and killed in Dumfries, and a poor schnauzer had been taken out in Enniskillen.

'Jack, can I have a word?' DCI Wallace tapped his arm.

'Of course.'

'My office, 10 minutes, bring one of your nice coffees and get one for yourself.'

The attempt at humour fell flat, she looked agitated with the stifling heat not helping. Jack went to his office and billowed his shirt to create any kind of breeze to make a tiny dent in the lack of air-conditioning. He boiled the kettle and got the mugs ready. He ran his fingers round the collar of his shirt feeling the perspiration on his neck. He was loath to moan about the weather, but let's face it, the British are terrible in the heat, especially the Celts. We look awful and it makes us miserable he thought to himself then laughed out loud. We're also never happy, he always riled against the 'too hot, too cold' brigade but they were bloody right, the bastards.

Wallace took a sip of her coffee and sighed. She looked at Jack expectedly, 'so, what have you got for me? Please tell me you've got a solid lead and this will be wrapped up in no time.' Jack sat and returned the look, 'I'm afraid not ma'am, we are where we are.'

'What the bloody hell does that mean?'

Jack hated the phrase himself, 'Sorry ma'am, what I mean is that we have nothing, I'm drawing blank after blank and so is the team.'

'Now, we've got these idiots doing copycat shootings all over the place. I've had colleagues from all the country ringing and asking about our progress like that would suddenly stop this madness.'

'With all due respect, ma'am, we are trying our best, I'm following the services line, I've got a nagging feeling that's where we should be looking, huge task though it is.'

'And what about Johnny Koumas…?'

'Danny.'

'What?'

'It's Danny Koumas.'

'Whatever his bloody name is, Buchanan comes in with some assassin of an advisor making all sorts of arch threats, he's shouting the place down, and she's saying calmly, 'of course, you'll pay for this, you'll pay heavily for this,' and walks out, Buchanan following like a little puppy. I won't have it, Jack, what the hell is going on?'

'Well, we need to ignore Ms Ballard and her threats, such that they are. She can only mean she will make sure we're heavily criticised, but it will be small beer compared to the media war between Buchanan and Koumas. That'll be brutal for sure, how much of a distraction it will be for us is debatable. The sniper might get complacent for a start.'

'What do you mean?'

'Well, we have to assume he's getting some gratification out of this killing spree. If the attention turns to the reigniting of the war between Koumas and Buchanan, that might upset him, and he might get sloppy.'

'Ok Professor Freud, I see what you're saying, but this worries me. What if he ups the ante? What if he starts shooting humans? Brass is jumpy but I can sense their attention is elsewhere and why wouldn't it be with the various maniacs still looking to blow our beloved tube system up and all the rest of it.'

Jack knew she was right, you don't get to her rank without having a strong nose for how the human psyche worked.

Wallace let out a sigh, pinched the bridge of her nose. 'So how did it go with the Major?'

'Ok, we got on well, he seemed a good bloke to me…'

'For god's sake Love, it wasn't a date, or I hope for Mrs Love's sake it wasn't.' Wallace was reminded what irritated her so much about Jack, his tardiness in getting to the bloody point. Jack survived a severe urge to laugh by the skin of his teeth.

'Is he going to help us, Jack?'

'Well, he was a bit reluctant at first and baulked at what he thinks is a massive task. He's also not convinced we're able to thoroughly check gun clubs and suchlike. I got the feeling he thinks I've come to a lazy conclusion. But he did promise he'd look into it. So I was grateful for that. We'll be seeing each other again for sure.'

'How sweet.'

5

Jane Harkness woke and immediately her eyes were full-moon open. This was the case every morning, she was one of the few people who actually did live each day as if it was her last, and all those other hoary old chestnuts that sound good but which are very difficult to put into actuality. While it would be unfair to say she didn't care about her appearance, she certainly wasn't vain. It just didn't occur to her. Her weight bothered her a tad but she wasn't going to agonise over it like too many people she knew, some professionally. She would as soon turn up in trainers inspired by her youngest son, with a long flowing colourful dress. Eccentric you might say, plenty did, but it was never affected, never studied. She was far too focussed on making the most of the day to worry if her outfits were coordinated.

As a counsellor with a formidable track record and some highly respected books to her credit, she percolated intense energy for her work. She was committed to her clients with a fervent passion that could not be manufactured. She was always shocked at conferences to hear her peers moan about clients, how so and so bored her, or how Mr X had driven him to distraction. True, you couldn't always like your clients, it was impossible actually, but what was undeniable was that everyone had a story and it was your duty to explore that story in the spirit of helping them deal with whatever issues are troubling them.

In Jane's case, she very nearly did like all her clients and worried about them all. She built relationships with them, listened, soothed and ultimately loved them. Her clients loved her right back, felt comfortable in no time and talked and talked and talked.

Not that it was ever easy. The stories, peoples' lives, were all unique, and often contained excruciating pain, abuse, violence and emotional torture in all manner of ways. The resilience always amazed Jane, human beings were tough and could withstand horrors that in normal society would be considered unbearable.

She often wondered when she saw an X-Factor contestant go to pieces on a Sunday night because of the pressure of how real it was and guessed that in 'real' adversity that person would find the strength. The cheapening of ordeal in the media, as she saw it, made her deeply uncomfortable. The collective loss of composure when Diana died she suspected underpinned or played a part in this process.

'On the ground', she knew it was different, she worked in the real world and ignored the media as best she could. This made her joyously naive and a total delight to her husband, Ray, at dinner parties. Topics that would be discussed all week in offices and factories would rarely make it onto her radar.

In truth, she was uncomfortable at first, but in time she developed a thicker skin and almost enjoyed the notoriety she'd acquired for her news blind spots. Almost. Professionally, it could be tricky, especially with younger people where it could be handy to know a bit about what they were doing or listening to, but she got by with stuff gleaned from her two teenage boys, Ryan and Paul.

These days, she embraced a very wide range of clients. From drug and alcohol addiction to self-harmers and sex-offenders, it was endlessly fascinating and challenging. However, the MOD had approached her after she gave a paper on counselling post-traumatic stress disorder at a nationwide conference in London. The MOD was at the conference seeking ways to improve their care for soldiers returning from Afghanistan and Iraq, both medical and psychological.

The Ministry, despite publicity to the contrary, had made great strides in caring for their troops, past and present. The fact remained that too many soldiers ended up homeless and suffering a variety of mental illnesses and conditions, chief among them post-traumatic stress disorder. Since armies were deemed necessary, soldiers had witnessed horrors most people would never have to. It was what they signed up for, but that didn't lessen the impact when war's grisly consequences kicked in.

The enemy had changed in the recent wars in Iraq and Afghanistan. The coalition forces swept through Iraq with minimal resistance from a ragged Iraqi army. But once settled in their garrisons and in occupation, the enemy was insurgents from abroad and well organised tribal warlords. This had lessened in Iraq though casualties were high in the three years following the overthrow of Saddam Hussein. In Afghanistan, the Taliban were resurgent and represented the antithesis of a conventional enemy. They were organised, committed and critically, knew the terrain. They used weapons that chilled every soldier's bones, Improvised Explosive Devices, or IEDs as everyone in theatre and at home now knew them.

Everyone except Jane Harkness, it seemed. Until now. The two Gulf wars had largely passed her by, not through anything other than innocent ignorance. She took no heed of the news and rarely read a newspaper though of course knew the wars were going on.

The full horror was revealed to her exactly two weeks after the MOD witnessed her speaking at the conference. Major Liam Collins turned to his sergeant, Chris Price, at the conclusion of the day and simply said, 'we need her onboard, see to it will you, sergeant?' Major Collins left Price to speak to Harkness and seal the deal.

Being something of a celebrity on the psychotherapy circuit, Harkness was becoming accustomed to the gaggle of people who wanted to speak to her during and after conferences. This was no different, and she enjoyed chatting to colleagues and breezily agreeing to lunch appointments and other speaking engagements. All the while she was aware of a stocky young man in green army uniform standing at what she took to be 'at ease' around twenty yards away. Naturally, in a sea of civilians, he stood out readily enough, but something in his posture said he was waiting for her and was going to escort her somewhere. She felt thrilled and ever so slightly unnerved. She thought he had a kind face, roundish with big brown eyes but perhaps it was the uniform, she found his gaze intense, a look accentuated by the low slung angle of his black beret, like he wasn't used to waiting.

Emboldened by the adrenaline of public speaking and slightly giddy from all the attention, she excused herself and walked up to the soldier.

'Hello sergeant, my name is Jane Harkness, you look like you want to speak to me?'

'Yes ma'am.' His soft north-eastern vowels surprised her, why, she couldn't tell.

'Ma'am, my name is Sergeant Christopher Price from the Ministry of Defence…'

'Jane please,' Harkness had no time for formalities, in stark contrast to Price. 'Very good to meet you Sergeant Price, can I call you Christopher? Or Chris even?'

'Of course, ma'am, Jane I mean, that would be fine.' His eyes twinkled and melted Harkness's heart in a thrice. His quiet tones belied the fact he was no wallflower. 'Major Collins and I were very impressed with your speech…'

'Major Collins?'

'My commanding officer, Jane, he had to leave I'm afraid, but we think you would be just the job for our new counselling initiative for returning and injured soldiers.'

'On the basis of that speech?'

'Yes, well, you do have an excellent reputation as well, we came especially to see you, in fact.'

'Well thank you very much, Sergeant, that's very nice of you to say, but I'm not sure my expertise fits the bill for the military. I deal with alcohol, drugs, abusers, self-harmers, suicide risks, eating disorders.' She looked at her watch. 'I'm flattered, but I'm not sure I can help you.'

'Jane, we're sure you can. We feel you fit the bill perfectly actually.'

'Really?'

'Really.' Sergeant Price visibly relaxed. 'Look, I warned Major Collins you might not go for it straight away. All we ask in the first instance is that you attend, a week from now, an informal seminar with some of our military psychotherapists and doctors. If you decide not to after that, then fair enough. I should add you would be well remunerated for your time.'

'Money isn't an issue,' she lied, 'but I will happily come along and have a chat with your people.'

They swapped contact details, and Sergeant Price left the auditorium.

Harkness slumped into a seat in the front row and exhaled loudly, the slight echo causing her to quickly look round and check she was alone at last. The tidal wave of fatigue that hit her after such days kicked in and she started fantasising about a glass of wine and a hot bath. She knew that was some time off, there was the northern line to Balham to negotiate, the boys to feed and most crucially, her debrief of their respective days. It had become the highlight of every weekday, the hour post dinner when they chatted eagerly about what each of them had got up to that day. She never tired of it, and it was due to the enthusiasm her sons recounted their capers and the earnestness in which they enquired after her day.

The thought of it seemed to energise her again. She made for the door and strode for the tube, the best of her day yet to come.

Through bitter experience, Jack was certainly of the opinion that you should never meet your heroes, footballers in particular. He appreciated that it must be a pain in the arse to be approached in the street but showing good manners wasn't really a chore when you thought about it. One famous centre-forward he had to interview said to him, 'why don't you fuck off?' Sure, his attitude quickly changed when he saw the warrant card and realised the nature of the approach, but Jack seethed about it for days and gave the man an unusually torrid time over something relatively trivial.

Jack pondered this as he sniffed and enjoyed his first Americano of the day at Gino's. The case meant he was up early and not for the first he thanked the heavens that Gino chose to open at 7am. He never fathomed why as punters rarely rolled in before 8 at the earliest, but self-interest meant he never brought it up. Such early morning chill as there was had long dissipated, and he sat outside with Earnie enjoying the sun on his face and the tantalising smell of bacon and eggs from the local greasy spoon. It was going to be another hot day, but he felt up to the challenge. The more difficult the case became, the more energised Jack seemed to get. And difficult this case was, possibly the most difficult and perplexing of his 17 year police career, a nutter popping celebs' dogs, copycat shootings breaking out all over the country and a freshly ignited rock star war. Nice work if you can get it.

The culmination of his chat with Wallace was his boss suggesting he goes to speak to Koumas. He questioned the value of this but couldn't help relishing the task too. As he listened to Whoosh's early stuff the night before with Annie, he realised all his questions would have nothing to do with the case. Wallace essentially wanted Jack to warn Koumas to stop his antagonism of Buchanan and to rule him out as a suspect given the t-shirt (though thousands were already wearing them too) and longstanding enmity with him. So Danny boy, art school rock star, writer of plays, fulcrum of rock super groups and now deadly dog assassin. Was there no end to his talent?

Curled up on their sofa, Annie guessed he'd be 'cool' and asked if she could come, 'you know, to help, like.'

'Yes, you'd be invaluable, 'Can I take down your particulars, Mr Koumas?' That would be so helpful.'

Annie giggled but couldn't deny that while she was a definitely a fan she also really fancied him.

'I'll take this assignment solo if you don't mind. Thanks and all that.'

'Think about it, when he caves in to the inevitable, you will have a free run at Magda.'

'That's outrageous!'

Jack smiled at the memory at what followed next and felt like popping home and grabbing her all over again. The mountain of work that awaited him calmed his ardour, and he ordered another Americano to take out.

As Jack made his way to Ladbroke Grove, Merton called to update Jack on the case, ending the call with 'Overrated.' 'Peasant,' muttered Jack, checking the info Merton had provided on where he needed to catch up with Danny Koumas and smiling at Merton's one word opinion of the star. He was straight down the line in his tastes, thinking Coldplay were a bit edgy and marooned himself in the likes of Keane and Travis. Mind you that was a bit edgy compared to many in the station, and Jack's tastes were considered 'out there', which never failed to amuse him.

Koumas's 'people' told Merton he would be in his studio on Ladbroke Grove in West London and that he could see Jack for half an hour 'tops.' Merton with considerable indignation told the assistant that the duration of the 'chat' was up to them. She simply said, 'yeah, course it is' and put the phone down.

Which all added to a growing sense of unease in Jack's stomach. He couldn't tell if it was star-struck nerves or just the dread fear he was totally wasting his time. How ludicrous that someone would feel anxious when he had broken the news of someone's child dying to loving parents, had questioned vicious murderers and rapists and had raided drug dens with firearms.

Jack was running unfashionably early, so he got off at Shepherds Bush and strolled the rest of the way to Ladbroke Grove. The aromas of every type of café you care to mention gnawed at him as he made his way along Shepherd's Bush but he wasn't hungry and was still buzzing from two of Gino's finest Americanos first thing. Another coffee would leave him gibbering uncontrollably, so he avoided all distractions as he made his way through the crowds and heat to the shade and partial relief from another steaming day in the capital.

Jack was still ten minutes early but pressed the buzzer on the unprepossessing studio in a mews just off the grove. No one would have guessed this shabby exterior would hold one of the foremost musical talents of his generation, and Jack was sure that's exactly how Koumas would have wanted it. Jack was stopped from pressing the buzzer marked No Way Productions by the door swinging open, and a mix of icy air con and cigarette smoke as a unfeasibly skinny middle-aged man in a leather jacket greeted him with a quick but polite 'alright, mate.'

Jack managed a surprised 'hiya' and walked into the reception area. A startlingly attractive young woman with long jet black hair was sat behind a glass and chrome table talking on the phone.

'Yeah, Dan just left. Oh yeah, cool...cool. Dunno, some policeman is coming in or something. Dunno, something to do with dogs. Yeah, dunno, look, I'll speak to you later, yeah?' Her East London accent could not have sounded more bored, and she still hadn't laid eyes on Jack. She was tapping something into her Mac as it dawned on Jack the exiting skeleton was Dan Jonson.

'Ah Dan Jonson, right?'

'What?'

'That was Dan Jonson…the bloke who just left?'

'Yeah, don't tell me, you're a big fan?'

'I am actually.'

'They all say that.' She still hadn't looked up. 'He knows you're here.'

'Right, great.'

Ten minutes turned to twenty minutes then thirty minutes, Jack took the many calls he received with an increasingly loud voice, to annoy his new friend. Mainly it was updates at the lack of progress from the team and the odd DI from the growing number of other forces affected by the case.

Merton's name came up on his iPhone. 'He's a twat, isn't he? Kept you waiting, has he? Oh dear.'

This time, Jack hushed his voice and walked to the window. He could hear the team laughing in the background, and then a rendition of his most famous song 'To be lost' broke out making Jack laugh out loud. They then shouted 'Overrated' in unison and hung up.

'What's so funny, copper?' What was it with rock stars calling you copper? A tall and rangy man was leaning over the bannister of the narrow staircase. The tall man being Danny Koumas, tall and perfectly formed Jack had to admit. Famous people always looked different in the flesh, and Jack was drinking in the familiar and unfamiliar aspects of his face. His slightly unkempt mop of black hair chimed, but his flawless complexion jarred a touch as did the large light blue eyes. 'So, what were you laughing at? Share the joke, man.' Jack hated the trend for Brits to add 'man' at the end of sentences that had crept in, from America undoubtedly. Yeah, yeah, language was fluid, ever changing, he knew all that, he just didn't like it. In fact, the Americanisation of language was a bugbear he bored Annie with regularly, especially when it snuck into her speech from school. But that was for another time, he *generously* let it slide with Koumas.

'Ah, just a bit of banter with the team, spirits could do with a boost at the moment, frankly.'

'Banter, god I hate that word. You hear a lot about *banter* these days. Some dick gets caught being a racist twat, and he says it's only banter. Banter this, banter that, drives me nuts. Some no-neck from the rugby club brays about the great banter at the bar, give me strength. Know that channel that shows Top Gear and QI on a loop? *Home of witty banter* apparently.'

'Right, sorry.'

'Don't apologise, Jack.'

Jack was embarrassed but honest enough to admit that Koumas calling him Jack completely disarmed him. In fact, even though he'd just had a rant it was done with a tired smile and no little charm.

'I know what you mean, though, white British blokes saying 'man' all the time is one of the many linguistic tics that drive me mad,' said Jack, emboldened.

'Ha, nice one, Jack, right back atcha eh?' Koumas's famously slippery accent was pure mockney today. Probably because Dan Jonson was 'in the house' earlier. 'Thing is, you kinda pick these tics up as you go along you know?'

Jack nodded as Koumas reached for some cigarettes. He groaned as he stretched, which heartened Jack given he was doing it more and more himself these days. Or so Annie told him.

'So, as much as I'd love to hang out and discuss the ebb and flow of linguistic tides, I'd also like to know what you're going to do for me?'

Jack raised an eyebrow.

'You know, the death threats? The reason you're here in the first place.'

This was news to Jack though given the fanatical nature of some fans, not a massive surprise.

'What station did you report this to?'

'Paddington Green. You're not here about the death threats are you?' Koumas lit his smoke and exhaled loudly,

'I thought you were quick, I only called an hour ago. And that was only because my manager went on and on about it. Just kids probably, happened a lot in the 90s.'

'Pretty unpleasant I'd imagine?'

'Well not great I suppose, don't want my kids to hear about it but I guess the tabs will hear about it soon enough. It's all internet keyboard warriors, let's face it, Mile High attracted… shall we say… a boisterous following?'

This was certainly true, their high-octane form of rock led to wild gigs and plenty of crowd hysteria and trouble.

'What was with the t-shirt?'

'You sound disappointed?'

Jack shrugged.

'Dunno really, I was at a gig for a mate at the 100 Club, and one of the backstage crew had it done. Christ, he really hates Buchanan, and he said I should wear it on-stage if I did a number for the band. I sometimes do an acoustic song while they take a break, just for a laugh really. You're never off duty at a gig I find. So…' A slight grin morphed into a beaming smile as he ran his hand through his hair. Despite himself, Jack couldn't fight the urge and smiled too. Koumas rocked back in his chair and gazed at the ceiling still playing with the memory.

'Thing is, this is a bloody circus already, and your untimely intervention hasn't really helped matters, Mr Koumas.'

'Danny, please.'

'Ridiculous though it is, I have to ask you your whereabouts on the day Moira was shot.'

'Mmm, last Thursday wasn't it? Really hot day, the odd thundery shower in the vicinity if I remember rightly?'

Jack nodded.

'I was yomping through Hampstead Heath, it's how I keep fit these days, now I'm clean. Had some of that army fitness training, you know, I even carry a sniper's rifle these days for a full authentic army experience.'

Jack held his gaze unsmiling.

'Ok, I think you can safely rule me out of your enquiries. I wasn't even in the country if you must know, been in Iceland for a few weeks, I'm not mad on English summers if you must know. You can check with Sasha if you like.'

'I will.'

'Well, good luck, she doesn't like visitors much, she hid that well in the interview it has to be said.'

'Bit of a flaw in a receptionist's armour really.'

'Shit, whatever you do, don't call her a receptionist.' Koumas blew out his cheeks, and the two men shared a smile again, the earlier warmth returning.

'Look, I know Buchanan's a dick, but he's actually ok when you scrape beneath the bullshit, you know, if you've got the time and inclination. You've met him I presume.'

'Yes, and his PR, a formidable lady.'

Koumas pumped himself up and launched in a pitch perfect bumbling toff accent, 'Quite, Love, a very, very formidable lady indeed… quite sexy though don't you think?'

Jack shrugged again. The worlds they inhabited couldn't be more different, he wondered if they all mixed and laughed at the great unwashed and their febrile interest in their nocturnal capers. Did they meet and cook up all these stories to keep their profiles high? Did Koumas and the indefatigable Ms Ballard meet for torrid afternoons of coke infused lust?

'Christ, Jack, where are you?' Koumas was waving him out of his reverie. Jack blushed and thought to himself that he must get out more. Fat chance.

'Fancy a beer?' Jack ignored his vibrating phone and nodded. 'I'd quite like a tour of the place if you don't mind as well.'

'Yeah, why not, I'll sort you a beer, and we'll do exactly that.'

Koumas returned with a champagne bucket with four bottles of Heineken. The icy cold clean hit of the lager was a wonderful moment on a boiling day, and Jack took a huge draft and just about suppressed a belch. He was embarrassed to see that he had virtually drunk over half the bottle in one gulp.

'Simple pleasures, eh?'

'Indeed.' Jack felt a bit giddy and took a moment before taking another sip.

'It's why I brought four, a day like this, one is never enough.'

'Must be nice to take a beer break when you fancy it, one of the many perks of the creative life I'd imagine?'

Koumas nodded slowly and thought for a moment. 'There's so much excess in this game, though, you don't even think about it really, I can have a snooze and work til the early hours or whatever, no deadlines or routines, a blessing and a curse I guess.'

More a blessing Jack thought.

As is if reading his mind, Koumas said, 'There's a lot of bollocks, to be frank, I'm lucky now, I've reached a level where I am master of my universe but to get here I had years of playing shitholes with 11 people watching, interminable hours in a van and getting done up the arse by the record company. He's a dick, but all Buchanan was doing was taking some time out of the shit with his dog. Like I say, simple pleasures, Mr Love, simple pleasures.' He mumbled something about the t-shirt that Jack couldn't quite catch but imagined it was a small utterance of regret.

A quick but enjoyable tour of his studio with the second bottle and a warm farewell and handshake and Jack emerged into the heat of the city thinking maybe it was ok to meet your heroes after all.

6

Jane Harkness woke early, and the day ahead immediately filled her head. A sponge for new experiences and learning opportunities this was really too good to turn down. She was impressed and flattered that the MOD had sought her out and she was relieved that the itinerary involved talks from soldiers past and present about their battle experiences. Endless academic presentations would have driven her nuts. One of the reasons she was so popular was that she cut out all the nonsense that the counselling sector was prone to, and entertained and inspired her audiences.

So free of vanity and ambition, she still felt like a child inside whenever she was being feted for some speech or piece of work and that feeling very much prevailed that morning. Jane also felt a bit anxious as her ignorance of anything war-related would be obvious and she couldn't help feeling she might embarrass herself. She sat on her patio with a mug of coffee and let the peace of her garden envelop her, the gentle birdsong dancing on the already warm breeze.

She closed her eyes and thought how uniquely blessed she was. She was thankful every day for the life she led. Friends and acquaintances were always struck by her love of life, seemingly natural and not carved out by a life changing experience. She lived every minute of every day, and while her enthusiasm was a shock to a lot of people, her sheer warmth and love won the hardest heart. In a cold and cynical world, Jane Harkness was the perfect antidote, and without seeking it, highly marketable.

Unusually early, she allowed herself a walk along the Thames, looping over Waterloo Bridge through the tourist throng at the London Eye and back across Westminster Bridge enjoying the cooling breeze off a strikingly blue river, noted that she was a little out of breath, put it down to another fiercely hot August day and entered the Ministry in good time.

Used to speaking at large auditoria she was pleasantly surprised to be shown to a meeting room with mercifully efficient air-conditioning. Major Collins and Sergeant Price were present, and both quickly got to their feet to greet the counsellor warmly but with formal handshakes. At the end of the room stood a tall white-haired gentleman, very trim with a waistcoat and bowtie fiddling with a laptop and projector.

'That's Colonel Dominic Waterstone, he heads up all our care services for military staff, if he ever sorts the laptop out, he'll be giving you an overview of what the army has introduced and how we work with other organisations.' Major Collins then offered Jane tea or coffee. 'Also, I'm afraid we'd like you to sign these papers, standard stuff to ensure all our visitors don't nip down the Iranian Embassy afterwards with key battle strategies.'

'I really…'

'I'm joking, of course, like I say, standard procedure, have a look through while you have an awful coffee and a stale biscuit, we'll be ready in a minute I'm sure.' Major Collins went to assist an increasingly flustered Waterstone.

The coffee was indeed awful, at public sector appointments that was a given, but Jane never minded and was astounded at the level of moaning that went on wherever she went. Her top tip for rank coffee was lots of milk and two sugars or to just stick to black tea. She felt silly for even having a strategy for this, it really didn't matter in the wider scheme of things. The biscuits were fine and not remotely stale she was relieved to note as the hot dog vendors and their onions on Westminster Bridge reminded her she was too excited to eat breakfast that morning.

Finally, Waterstone coughed and announced he was ready to start. Jane looked around. It was just the four of them.

'It's just you, Jane, we're not expecting any other visitors, civilian anyway,' said Major Collins noting the surprised look on her face, 'is that ok with you?'

'Yes, of course.'

'Ok, excellent. Colonel Waterstone, everything under control?'

The Major nodded and introduced himself properly and thanked Jane for coming. He ran through an overview of the measures and programs they had put in place in the last three years, the criticism in the media and the issues they still faced. Jane was fascinated from the start and sat rapt throughout. She was struck by the commitment of the team and their genuine desire not just to be seen to be doing something but actually doing it. She was appalled by the number of ex-soldiers who ended up on the streets and the numbers with mental health issues. In a period when soldiers were increasingly portrayed as heroes for their bravery overseas, too many seemed to be falling through the net.

The man you shunned on the street for being drunk or homeless or both could easily have seen action in one of the Gulf wars, the Balkans or Afghanistan. Waterstone shone a very bright light into the attitudes of the general public and widespread double standards. Tear-laced ceremonies and proud marches through towns, but no thought to the strange young man talking to himself on the street outside McDonald's.

Jane Harkness felt ashamed as she had done exactly that on occasion and while you can't go and hug every person she knew she had to have a long hard look at herself. Maybe this was the reaction the military wanted. Everyone had a story, remember? She had deep wells of compassion but definitely felt uncomfortable when approached in town by homeless people. The meeting was barely half an hour old, and she knew this an area of work she would be involved with. Her mind crackled with questions, but she held fire for now as it was so early in the day.

Whatever she felt about the plight of squaddies on the street paled compared to the section devoted to those who had lost limbs in IED explosions or those who watched comrades die. She was reminded of her parents constantly running her profession down, with the help of the Daily Mail. She knew a common view pervaded that we were nannying people to the point of rendering them hopeless. *No one needed counselling after the great wars of the 20ᵗʰ century, why were we bothering when people had a drink problem? Oh dear, daddy shouted at you when you were young did he? No wonder you can't function.* Her dad would often end his particular rant with 'they should grow a bloody backbone and get on with it.'

Jane was always struck when her folks would say in hushed tones about an old man they knew that he never spoke about the war and what he saw. The fact he was lonely and never formed solid relationships was conveniently ignored, and Jane would be shouted down if she suggested that some sort of intervention was overwhelmingly required. Visiting her husband's uncle in North Sydney, who had been a pilot in the Pacific during the Second World War, was also illuminating. Very gregarious, he was the most genial host. Who wouldn't be, happily married for over 50 years living in Manly, a goal kick away from one the best beaches Jane had ever seen?

When Ray had mentioned on the flight over that his uncle was a pilot, Jane knew she'd ask him about it. Such was his congeniality, she assumed he would be full of tales of stirring dogfights with the Japanese. After a particularly enjoyable lunch at their yacht club, talk turned to the war and how he ended up in Australia. Jane asked about his experiences as a pilot, and his face immediately turned ashen, and he looked down into his glass of red wine. His swirled the blood-red liquid and didn't look up bar a quick sideways glance at his wife. Ever the jolly sort, she remarked how nice the food was and wondered what we had planned for the rest of the day. It hadn't spoiled the visit, but Jane never forgot it and was always reminded whenever her parents launched their latest tirade against her 'mumbo jumbo.' Everyone had a story, indeed.

Listening to Waterstone talk about the intensity of friendships forged in the heat of battle reminded her again of Ray's uncle. He must have returned from missions having seen a close mate shot out of the sky. He must have landed every time and wondered who would also return. Every single time. The 'clients' this time faced different but just as challenging situations. A routine patrol in a Land Rover could easily end in personal catastrophe, when you least expected it, you hit an IED and one of your mates can be literally blown apart. As so graphically illustrated by one of Waterstone's slides, a young man of 18 could lose his legs in the blink of an eye. Corporal Wayne Tomkins lost both his legs below the knee to an IED in January last year. He had been in the army for just 18 months.

Waterstone outlined the medical scenario from the moment of the blast, how he very nearly died and was only saved by a quick thinking medic as the chopper scrambled to get him out was delayed by rocket-propelled grenades. As Waterstone went through the painstaking treatment and the tortuous rehabilitation process, Jane of course, already knew that the main battle would be raging in his mind. How the hell would he even begin to recover from the mental trauma he had suffered?

She was about to find out. There was a knock on the door, and Corporal Wayne Tomkins walked in. Jane's initial look of amazement quickly gave way to tears, not torrents but enough that it was impossible for them to go unnoticed. A rash of thoughts flooded her head, how is he walking? Why is he smiling? Is this a joke? A very sick and awful joke? What Tomkins did next amazed her; he walked over and embraced her. Jane stood up, and the boy who she had just seen skinny, boyish and hideously injured now enveloped her completely, thicker set and every inch a man. She noticed tears in his eyes and saw how the other men looked on, not a hint of embarrassment on their faces. These were truly marvellous people she thought.

Jane gathered herself, there was so much she wanted to know. Without prompting, Tomkins showed his prosthetic limbs to her, took them off revealing the stumps and the treatment regime still required in that area. He put them back on and walked around the room.

'Took me a while Mrs Harkness, thought I'd never walk again, killed me, no football, running, swimming…' His North West lilt trailed off, cleared his throat and looked at Jane. 'Thing is, I could never sit still, was always told off by my mam, hated books, just wanted to move, you know?'

Jane nodded. It wasn't something she could admit to but her youngest boy, Ryan was like that.

'So essentially, you had to learn to walk again?'

'Not essentially, that was exactly the position. I couldn't even contemplate it for months as the pain was unbearable, and then there were the flashbacks, the nightmares…' He looked down, clasping and unclasping his hands.

'Ok, lad,' said Waterstone gently, 'there's no end point here, Jane, no end of the road, care of some description will be required to a greater or lesser extent for life.'

Jane thought of the soldiers who had nothing, who had been left to deal with the horrors alone and felt tears welling up once more.

'We should take a break,' said Waterstone, clicking off his laptop and popping on his blazer.

Jane followed the men out of the room, accompanied by Tomkins who was walking, well, normally really. She thought about the massive impact on his recovery that being able to move around normally must have had on the young man. Of course, playing football was out of the question, but she'd seen paralympians running and imagined Tomkins doing something similar.

'Sorry I made you cry, Mrs Harkness.'

'Jane, please. Well as long as I can call you Wayne, anyway. I'm not big on formality, to be honest. And don't worry about the crying at all, please. I've never understood the social horror of crying in public, bloody go for it, I say. Not like that in the regiment eh?'

'Christ no, you get slaughtered, forfeits and everything, only seen it a coupla times and it's not pretty, never in combat, though. Is that odd?'

'I don't know, you tell me. I'd imagine that in an extreme situation you dig deep into your wells of resilience and make no mistake, Wayne, humans are bloody resilient beings, you're living proof of that.'

'I suppose so, never thought of it like that, really.'

'I can see the massive distance you've covered in your life already, it's remarkable. Hence the tears really, the determination to come through adversity, to beat the sheer bloody awfulness of your situation. And look at you, you're in great shape all things considered.'

'I'm a lot better, thought about killing myself all the time, I just couldn't imagine life being normal, it made me horrible Jane, really horrible, even lost my girlfriend over it. I was a pig to my family, especially my mam, my dad couldn't even look at me. We're sorting it, though, getting there you know.'

Jane nodded.

'I spend so much time at the rehab unit they've almost become like family now. They get it you see, no one outside does. It's safe, Jesus, I'm even seeing one of the nurses. I will have to leave, I know. Just trying not to think about that, though, at the minute.'

Colonel Waterstone was spot on, this was a lifelong battle for Wayne. While wildly different circumstances the healing processes drew parallels with people she dealt with who had suffered the traumas life could throw at them. It never really ended, that was the first thing you had to realise.

The rest of the day consisted of a talk or two from counsellors who worked for the unit and another soldier who came in to talk about witnessing your friends dying in battle. It was fascinating stuff for Jane, but she'd known from the moment Tomkins had walked into the room that she wanted in on this type of work and knew she'd make a bloody great job of it. She was so impressed with the approach of the staff, who seemed so removed from her stereotypes of military men in every way.

When the day concluded, Major Collins took her aside.

'So, what do you think? Is this an area you feel like taking on? We would totally understand if it's not for you.'

They shared a smile.

'When do I start?'

7

August was a tricky time for the media traditionally known as the 'Silly Season,' news editors had a hell of a job chasing enough copy to fill papers. The tabloids chased ever-more salacious stories from celebrities, the mid-range titles ranted about favourite hobby horses like immigration or benefit cheats while the broadsheets seemed to struggle the most while the Westminster village closed down for a spell. Sometimes, like the great Ashes series of 2005, sport made it onto the front pages but barring some natural disaster or a catastrophe overseas the papers were considerably thinner.

All of which made the Houndsdead Heath killings a gift as the Great British public broiled, boiled and roasted in a very hot summer. The tabloids sent 'intrepid' reporters onto the Heath walking dogs in bulletproof coats (The Sun) or with a trained marksman in tow (The Mirror.) The Star posted a man up in a tree near Merton Lane, and Sky News continued to use choppers to buzz the area daily, driving the good residents of Hampstead and Highgate to demand they stop.

The Mail and the Express bombarded their readers with 'proof' the world had really gone to hell in a handcart and that morals were at an all-time low, especially when reporting and commenting on the copycat shootings around the UK. The Guardian, boasting a considerable readership in the area, provided a wry commentary on the shootings and the subsequent media frenzy with more serious straight reporting. It was the only story in town when you considered the newly engaged hostilities between Aidan Buchanan and Danny Koumas.

Apart from threatening all and sundry at Muswell Hill Police Station, Buchanan had given another double spread exclusive to The Sun threatening to knock Koumas out; the glowering hero photographed with a raised fist. Mile High fans were tweeting and blogging all sorts of vengeful ripostes to Koumas as well as inundating his message boards with threats. Retaliatory t-shirts bearing the legend 'Wanted – Danny Koumas' were selling well and seized upon by the media. Anti-Koumas Facebook pages were springing up all the time and the most popular, 'Danny will Pay' had registered over 150,000 'likes' popular with Mile High fans, dog lovers and animal rights campaigners. Furious cyber confrontations broke out and were distorted to war-like reverence in the tabloids.

On Jack's request, Koumas had kept a low profile in the days after the story broke but as the frenzy intensified he used his Twitter account in a way that only served to fan the flames, delighting his fans and seemingly outraging everyone else. One tweet, presumably a few drinks into a session, announced late one night that he might dig Moira up and shoot her again to calm things down, propelled him onto the front pages again, The Sun somewhat ludicrously proclaiming him 'Britain's most hated man.'

More serious columnists were genuinely wondering if the country had taken leave of its senses. Some compared it to the hysteria that gripped the country when Diana, Princess of Wales died in 1997, though the Prime Minister didn't deign to declare Moira or any of the other slain pets, 'The Peoples' Pooch,' noted one commentator.

The copycat killings had resonated in their areas and parks, lakes and beaches were eerily quiet even in the middle of the day. Local radio phone-ins barely bothered with any other subjects as they were jammed with listeners complaining about being 'trapped indoors' as their beloved pets were going mad being confined to gardens and living rooms. Councils, police and the government were all blamed in one way or another. Cricket and baseball matches were cancelled, bowling greens were deserted, and everyone considered themselves at risk.

On a Norfolk beach, a cocker spaniel got shot in the leg by from an air-rifle prompting Stephen Fry to boldly declare on Twitter enough was enough and that he was not going to be intimidated and forced indoors. He tweeted that he was going to the beach that morning and promptly got shot in the arse, presumably by the same marksman. He took it well and was soon joking about it but didn't venture out after that in daylight or certainly didn't announce his intentions.

Police patrols were stepped up in the capital with a highly visible presence on Hampstead Heath. If the intention was to increase public confidence in the vicinity, then it had palpably failed. Jack garnered a front page picture in the Mail for taking Earnie for a walk on the Heath one evening, the paper clearly believing it was a PR stunt by the Met. The headline, 'Is that a good idea, sir? Desperate DI in dog stunt,' causing great mirth in the station and a carpeting from Wallace.

The truth was Jack, and more pertinently Earnie, were going a bit mad due to cabin fever and with so much uniform about didn't feel the risk was that high despite Annie advising caution due to his rising profile. Claiming Earnie's scalp would be a major coup for the marksman. In the event, his fantasy of a peaceful walk was shattered by the press chopper and saying hello to a colleague every 20 yards or so, not to mention the whir and chatter of the snappers and cameramen. His beloved Heath had turned into a surreal landscape occupied only by police and press. Was this what the dog killer wanted? If so, what would he do next? He had not shot a dog for three days. Maybe, he was done with it. Was he bored? It always came back to why? Did he even know himself? These were the questions everyone was asking.

Things moved swiftly for Jane Harkness after she'd attended the meeting at the MOD. Two days later, Major Collins called and said that had an office had been set up for her at a rehabilitation unit in Barnes Bridge and would she like to see it and have lunch with him afterwards in the White Hart. Never shy of mixing business and pleasure, she immediately agreed and given the early hour he had rung, with military precision at 0900hrs, they settled on that very day. Jane often kept Wednesdays clear for research and admin and sometimes a fat afternoon snooze, a guilty pleasure she never admitted to Ray and the kids. So it was no problem meeting the Major.

The MOD meeting had made such an impression on her that she would've cancelled any number of appointments to have made it. Factor in a pub lunch on the river and there was very little to think about. Showered and dressed, she made her way to the tube on another cloud-lessly roasting day, butterflies using her stomach as a summer meadow as she wondered what horrors she would hear in the weeks, months and years ahead.

The 'unit' turned out to be a huge Victorian asylum, all tall windows, angles and a magnificent phallic chimney on the banks of the Thames with large rambling but well-kept grounds. The shade of the ancient trees with the aid of a little breeze from the river brought relief to Jane as she entered the grounds. The bustle of Barnes faded quickly as she crunched up the gravel path. She felt like she was entering another world and even took a peek behind to make sure Barnes was still there. With the entrance another hundred yards away, she took a deep breath and slowed her pace breathing in the unusual surroundings. To her right, a nurse was wheeling a man who could not have been over thirty towards a patch of sunlit grass by the river. She could just make out the sing-song of a chat on the breeze, but as they slowed to a halt, there was silence, and the nurse just held his hand. She briefly let go as she sat on the grass beside him but quickly offered her hand again.

Jane stopped and noticed a number of similar scenarios unfolding in this peaceful haven. Approaching the entrance, she noticed the imposing figure of Major Collins in a first-floor office at the window. He gave a quick wave and disappeared.

She made her way into a dimly lit reception where Major Collins quickly joined her.

'Reminds me of school, that weird mix of mass made food and disinfectant,' she said and offered her hand which he firmly shook.

'Yes, it's a bit overpowering at first, but you won't notice after a while. Takes some cleaning a place like this I can tell you.'

'I wouldn't fancy it.'

'No, nor would I. Spooks people a bit too, being an old mental asylum but that's all in the mind, as it were.'

'All in the mind. Interesting phrase to use here,' said Jane following the Major up the rather grand wide wooden staircase thinking she'd stayed in hotels that had this air of faded grandeur.

Her office was a different matter altogether. They swung through double fire doors down a long wooden tiled corridor, their steps echoing as they walked. She was deeply impressed to see her name already mounted on the door and even more impressed at the calming interior of her office. It even had a couch and a comfortable armchair, tasteful brown leather too. Pastel coloured décor and large mounted paintings of landscape and seascapes all pointed at the thought that gone in to providing a serene atmosphere for the clients. She also noticed with interest the panic button and was already thinking of little changes she would make.

For a start, with a large bay window at her disposal, a pair of chairs both facing out of the window but slightly inclined to each other could work well. Being a fourth-floor office, the views were delightful over the grounds and the river as well as the whole of south London. Through the intense haze, she could just make out the Crystal Palace transmitter and the lumpy skyline of Croydon. Yes, having gained the trust of the client, this would be an excellent alternative to the couch/armchair combo behind her.

'Well, I'll leave you to it, Jane, feel free to add or re-arrange anything as you see fit. We have a few empty offices around the place as you can imagine so you can pilfer or dump stuff as the mood takes you. I'll rustle up a kettle for you, but you might want to get a cafetierre, the coffee is dire around here. I'll stop by in a while, and we can grab an early lunch.'

Jane thanked Major Collins, gave a little salute and walked back to the windows. The faintly musty feel to the room hinted at little fresh air for some time, and she soon found out why. After a couple of failed attempts and feeling very feeble indeed, she gave one last heave, and the window shifted with an almighty groan. Relieved not to have to bother the Major, she enjoyed the breeze tickling cream curtains that on closer inspection perhaps needed a wash. The distant sound of children playing and relentless traffic drifted in as she surveyed the view once again feeling at ease immediately. She had a really good feeling about this place as Major Collins stopped by to take her for lunch.

They walked into the White Hart, and the dark wooden interior formed a cooling contrast to the relentless heat outside. Being midday, they'd just avoided the lunchtime rush though the shady river terrace was filling up rapidly. They grabbed the last table and took their seats, and Jane felt a twinge of relief the Major was joining her in a glass of rose, a bottle in fact. After some initial pleasantries and the ordering of their lunch, the pair got into the detail of how the arrangement would work. Jane, of course, had private clients and did stints for other public and third sector organisations that were non-negotiable.

She was relieved to hear other counsellors were being recruited and that given a bit of manoeuvring, she could agree to two full days a week. Working long days and weekends was commonplace for Jane, but she didn't want her home life to suffer unduly, so it was an easy decision to sacrifice her admin time and perhaps finally take Ray's idea up of hiring a part-time PA. She could definitely afford it now, and the prospect was becoming more appealing as time went by.

'Jane, we're delighted to have you on board, the Unit consider it a real coup.'

'Thank you,' she blushed but felt very proud. 'I am intrigued, though.'

'Go on.'

'Well, I've done some preliminary reading, and there are plenty of references to soldiers saying they can only talk to people who can directly relate to their experiences, in other words, people who've been in combat situations. So, why me?'

The Major took a sip of his rose and sat even more upright in his seat if that was possible. His army posture was immaculate.

'Well, it's a very fair point, commonly expounded as you say. There are a couple of things here, though. The demand for our services is such that we simply can't provide a counsellor for everyone who has that direct experience. It's not a well-worn route at present, combat soldier to trained and qualified counsellor. Secondly, every patient is different, in my experience, some favour talking to someone who is far removed from the situation they have experienced, some don't. We aim, as far as possible, to accommodate those concerns. It's by no means as clear as the literature you have read would suggest. I've a question for you.'

'Go on.'

'You counsel child abuse victims, alcohol and drug addicts, correct?'

'Correct.'

'Are you addicted to crack cocaine?'

'No.'

'Are you an alcoholic?'

'No, not by common comprehension anyway.'

'So, how can you relate to the problems these people are suffering?'

'Very good point, Major, though I could easily have had those issues, it's a much more well-worn route, victim to counsellor, in my sphere of work. I suppose I'm relating to the unique and extreme nature of the experiences soldiers have in battle situations. I do wonder if an overweight woman is an ideal person for soldiers to open up to. I've another question for you,' Jane was enjoying this immensely.

'Ok, go on.'

'You said, 'In your experience,' is that professional or personal? Or both? Are you one of the rare soldiers who went from combat soldier to counsellor?'

Collins looked out onto the river, as a four-strong rowing crew powered by, their foreheads and biceps shiny with sweat. His face clouded momentarily before looking evenly at Jane. He took a sip of his wine, looked down and slowly clasped his hands. His smile was slight and forced.

'I was an officer during the first Gulf War, Desert Storm as it was known. I was leading a tank battalion in the desert south of Baghdad, we were encountering very little resistance, and spirits were very high. In fact, some of the boys wanted some action, they were trained, had done endless drills and training exercises and understandably wanted to get stuck in.'

Jane nodded but didn't understand.

'There were abandoned trucks and tanks everywhere, motorbikes too. We were curious to look at their equipment for real, rather than in briefings and a few of the boys started bombing around on the bikes riding up and off sand dunes, that kind of thing. Fair to say it didn't feel like a war at all. Felt more like a training exercise, not a very disciplined one at that.'

Jane got a sense of how Collins must've been as an officer, she was thinking hard but fair with a real love for his men.

'Actually, the bikes were brilliant, couldn't resist a go myself as I had a thing for bikes back in the day, we got into teams and raced each other, it was brilliant to see the lads let off steam, great for me too I can't deny. Blowing off steam in the army usually involves shed loads of alcohol.'

Collins' accent changed from his clipped classless tones to gentle Cumbrian, like he was right back in the moment, back in the desert, twenty years ago.

'The 'procession' as it became known amongst the officers went on like that for days and days. The much-vaunted Republican Guard failed to show but the closer we got to Baghdad...well, there was a change in the atmosphere. It was definitely more tense and there was more activity in the skies. There was always the faint drone of planes, but now they were flying straight over us, F15s, I remember how deafening they were. Lots of the lads would wave at them, but I doubt the pilots would see at those speeds.'

Collins paused, filled Jane's glass and his own, and took a gulp this time, a faint tremor visible in his hand. He looked at the river again then up at a 737 following the Thames into Heathrow, the sun reflecting sharply off the silver panels of the fuselage before disappearing from view.

'Anyway, this particular morning, the skies were quiet, and I thought this was unusual given the previous activity. I led a small battle group of tanks ahead of the main procession to scout possible enemy positions. We were about 5 miles ahead of the main group in fact. I could hear a faint drone to the west that was getting louder and louder, and I don't really know why, but it made me feel uneasy despite the negligible Iraqi air threat. Maybe it was the change of pattern, I don't know, but I didn't like it. The drone turned into a roar, and when I saw through my binoculars the angle they were approaching, I knew we were in trouble. They had locked onto us as a target, and they were 'friendly', American F15 fighters who, with their technology, don't tend to miss.' Another pause.

'Are you ok?' asked Jane lightly brushing his hand, 'you don't have to do this if you don't want to.'

Collins nodded and took a deep breath. 'It's ok, I think about it every day but as you know, verbalising it is different.' He cleared his throat. 'I started yelling into the radio that friendly fighters were attacking us, to call them off, over and over again while my sergeant gave the order to take cover, all completely useless of course. In my mind, everything stopped for a second before a screeching noise like a wailing banshee pierced the silence and the tank 50 yards to my right exploded. In the top of the tank was my close friend, Captain John Miller, the missile blew him to bits in front of our eyes, and when I say bits, I mean bits, Jane.' His voice faded away to nothing. Jane reached for his hands, he didn't recoil.

'You really don't…' she started.

'No, it's fine, you need to know I think, though, this isn't what I planned at all.'

There was a silence as their meals arrived, bangers and mash for Collins, chicken burger for Jane. They looked down at their meals, then at each other before eating their meals in comfortable silence punctuated only by genuine expressions of how good the food was. Jane wanted more, though. She was grimly compelled by what the Major was telling her. She had admired him from their first meeting, his impeccable manners, his palpable empathy, strength and undeniably, his vulnerability. She found his openness about his vulnerability equally admirable. He'd experienced things most people could not even contemplate; struggled through to the other side, acknowledged the pain he still suffered and held himself in a manner that transcended mere dignity. Best of all, he was resolved to help others in similar circumstances. In Jane's eyes, that made him a total hero.

'Where were we, Liam?' His face darkened again, he dabbed his mouth with his napkin, took a sip of his wine again.

'You don't hang around,' he muttered. Jane thought she'd overstepped the mark. She looked out at the river, full and brown with the tide in, its powerful currents pulling debris this way and that. A tug pulling waste barges made light of the current, churning up the surf with ease towards Battersea, its throbbing diesel engines reverberating through the clammy stillness of the day. The table next door seating 'ladies who lunch' as Collins speculated, were now loudly discussing amid gales of laughter, the horror of a wardrobe malfunction at a dinner party. Jane wondered how Collins saw the world every day, through what prism did he view the trivialities of everyday civilian life. Just how did you go from watching your close friend end up all over your army fatigues to sitting on an idyllic river terrace listening to idle chatter of popped buttons and a flash of bra? She would ask him eventually. But for now, she wanted Liam to talk. He didn't let her down.

'I remember silence, but it couldn't have been quiet, two F15 were buzzing us for a start, but it was like the world had stopped for a moment, like we all had to freeze-frame the picture to absorb what had happened. My shirt and vest were wet with John's blood and worse, I was aware of various body parts, was that his leg on fire over there? I couldn't tell, and then there was the screaming of his mates in the tank. While John had taken the brunt of the blast, his two mates were literally on fire. They emerged like figures in the worst horror film you'd ever seen. But the sound was far worse than the sight. *Screaming* didn't come close, this was something far more fundamental, primaeval even, and I hear it every day, Jane, every day… We did what we could, of course, blanketed them, rolled them, all basic stuff but we lost one and well…'

'Did he make it?'

'We got him back to base, the lads were brilliant, held his hand, told him he was going to be fine but he was black and the look in his red eyes… he knew he was going to die, the burns to this throat meant that speech was beyond him, every swallow sounded like an immense effort, like a cartoon character when scared. We gathered round him, sang regiment songs, he was Welsh, and one of the other Welsh lads sang their national anthem. I've never been more proud of a bunch of people. They say everyone dies alone. Well, Corporal Riley didn't, we held him and looked into his eyes til his last breath in the tent just after midnight.' His eyes were moist, but his voice remained even.

'We left the medics to do what they had to do, and I ordered the men to bed. I wanted some quiet to think about John and the rest of that dreadful day. I had no chance. I was aware of a commotion in the next tent, frantic whispering and wailings. One of the lads was completely freaking out, full on fit as it happened, foaming at the mouth and everything. The medics gave him a shot, and it calmed him down for a while, but he was a basket case.' He smiled.

'What?'

'Basket case. Terrible phrase, you hear it a lot, or bonkers, barmy, nuts and mad. I hear it in the young, almost a badge of honour to be 'mad.' He shook his head slowly while another gust of laughter blew over from the next table, the rose really beginning to flow.

'So, did you know then that you had to help? Did you realise that was the path you would take?'

'Not straight away. It's odd, but my rank meant I didn't think of myself. I grieved for John of course and meeting up with his wife and family was every bit as hard witnessing his death. So many questions... I was there, you know? But ultimately, the welfare of my men came first. The first inkling came when I had R'n R. My CO ordered me to take a long break, and the thought terrified me. I didn't want to leave Iraq, I didn't want to leave my men. I got home to Barrow, and everything seemed preposterous to me. I'd be in pubs listening to everyday moans and groans, and all I could think of was getting back to Iraq, the heat, the flies, shitting in a hole in the ground. I love football but couldn't concentrate on any game I watched, it just didn't matter.'

'Does it matter now?' Jane had never understood football.

'Carlisle United meant everything to me at one time but does it matter? Not really. Living in London, I catch up with them when they play Leyton Orient or Brentford, and it's nice to see some of the lads who go away. You have to have hobbies and interests.'

Jane nodded and smiled, *hobbies and interests* made her think of stamp collecting or train spotting, but not Major Liam Collins.

'Anyway, the upshot was I couldn't wait to get back to Iraq. You can imagine how that made my family feel. They didn't get it, and I'm not blaming them at all, I knew a couple of blokes at home who were ex-army, and they were like me, couldn't get enough of talking about our experiences, a blessing and a curse in retrospect.'

Jane thought she knew but asked anyway. 'How a blessing?'

'Well, just talking to people who relate to what you're saying you know, people who've been there and done it, they've seen things on the same level as you have. I started hanging around the Legion, talking to old vets, one who had even survived the Great War, Les, no longer with us sadly. The older boys were different, though, more reluctant to talk, much more removed from the adrenaline rush.

That planted seeds for me I must admit. Les, in particular, would only go so far, it would totally disturb him. I ended up sticking to the younger blokes, still serving or recent discharges.'

'Curse?'

'Well, drinking too much primarily, getting maudlin and resentful, blocking out my family, sticking to the army boys like barnacles til I got back out there, where I thought I belonged. It was very tough, there were arguments with my dad, he tried so hard to understand but I put up a wall and the look my mum used to give me breaks my heart now, I couldn't look at her. My dad found me one night very drunk crying my eyes out and shouting sitting on a wall 100 yards from the club, people just hurrying by on the other side of the road.'

'That must've been very tough indeed?'

'It was, I was drunk, and he shouted at me, and I pushed him away, he came again, and I went to hit him and… I'll never forget it, the horror on his face. He just held his hand up and quietly said, 'I'm your dad, I love you,' and I collapsed, he caught me, and I cried and cried, thought I'd never stop.'

The Major paused, his eyes glistening, his voice, however, again, remained even.

'But you went back?'

'I did and oddly, or perhaps not when you think about it, that meltdown had helped me. I left the family on much better terms and put them at the forefront of my mind. I was still relieved to get back though and be with my men.'

They declined the offer of dessert and ordered coffees falling into a comfortable silence once again. The Major excused himself, and Jane enjoyed the respite to take in her new surroundings. She loved the pub, her new office, Barnes Bridge, she never lost that childlike excitement at new places and felt very grateful indeed. When it came to Major Collins, she just felt privileged he shared these deeply intimate experiences with her. He was an amazing man and for him to share these deeply intimate experiences with her was incredible. She also felt that in a sense, it was part of an induction and she was grateful for that too. Maybe he was testing her, seeing how she reacted especially after she had been reduced to tears at the MOD. She knew that wasn't held against her, she wouldn't be here otherwise. By the same token, it wouldn't do to break down in tears in every session where souls were being bared.

Collins returned to the table as the coffees arrived. His phone rang.

'Excuse me, Jane, I need to take this.'

She smiled and nodded. Unlike so many people he didn't leave the table, so Jane had a front row seat of a different part of his life as it was clearly a lover who had phoned him. He laughed and teased the woman, and all the horrors he had shared seemed to fall off his face. He kept it short, though, organising dinner later and before signing off said, 'Yeah, I'm fine.'

He sipped his coffee, 'you look thoughtful.'

'Yes, I don't know where to start really.' Collins just nodded.

'For a start, I'm struck by your need to be with people who 'got it' after your experiences in Iraq. I'm still concerned that lads won't sit down in front of me and do what you just did.'

'And lasses.'

'And lasses, of course.'

'I know but trust me, they will. I certainly did when I finally gave in and started this whole process.'

'I'm loving 'gave in' but tell me about it, when you turned to the Army for help.'

'Well despite the macho culture of the forces, the welfare officers have always been brilliant, and thing is, I assumed because I came through a horrific incident, I would be in better shape the next time something happened. Big mistake.' Collins slowly shook his head as if reprimanding himself again for such an obvious error.

'Well that's the 'common sense' view, "what doesn't kill us, makes us stronger."'

'Indeed, I fell for that one hook, line and sinker. I had it disproved within days of my return to combat. I led a patrol into the desert, a 'routine patrol' so beloved of our friends in the press. Believe me, there's nothing *routine* about being on patrol anywhere. There's a reason you're on patrol, anyway…' Jane assumed he was counting to ten.

'Anyway, I was out of the tanks this day leading two land rovers, four men in each when a dust cloud started gathering about 3 miles to our right-hand side. This wasn't unusual in the desert, you saw all sorts of weather phenomena. Through the binoculars, I could see two land cruisers racing towards us creating the cloud. They were pick-ups and there were men, insurgents, packed into the back of both vehicles. I could clearly make out their RPGs.'

'RPGs?'

'Rocket Propelled Grenades, not that accurate but lethal if on target and a favoured weapon of the various groups of insurgents. They were very handy with them indeed. There was no prospect of getting away from them as our vehicles are hideously slow. I radioed for air cover and told the lads it was time for some action. There was no point trying to outrun them so we stopped, took what cover we could, set up the two machine guns and took the fight to them. It was a straight firefight at first, but their RPGs got in a good position and took out our machine guns killing all four men in the process. One cruiser stayed out of range while the other came close and their men charged us. We had a slightly elevated position which helped us a bit, we took out at least four of the men who charged us but in the chaos I didn't realise it was now just me and an 18 year old lance corporal, Rhys Daniels was his name.'

Jane shook her head, as clearly as Collins described the battle, the more unimaginable it became, this would be work that took her out of her comfort zone by a considerable distance. Was she up for that? Damn right she was.

'Daniels and I fought hand-to-hand, bayonets drawn. I got stabbed in the leg, and Daniels sustained a stomach wound but we bloody did it, we fought them off, killed the men who charged us but we were hurt. We were lying in the sand face to face, I turned and saw that the other cruiser was coming towards us, I heard a roar, some sort of commotion. I looked into Daniels' face, his eyes full of fear and yearning. It's the last thing I remember.'

Jane held both his hands across the table. The other table fell silent again, as if in reverence to the harrowing tale he had just told. The truth was they had momentarily run out of tittle-tattle though a couple of the lunching ladies were paying more than a passing attention. Jane braced herself for Daniels' death and the unbearable burden for Collins, not to mention his other comrades who had fallen that dreadful scorched morning in the desert.

'Daniels?'

'Daniels, well he survived.' She was so gripped that gave a little yelp of relief. Immediately embarrassed she gestured for Collins to continue.

'Don't worry, it was the first thing I asked when I came round. The worrying thing from my point of view was that I completely blanked out, not unconscious as such, just absented myself completely. Daniels said my eyes were open, just nobody was home if you know what I mean. He said I was rocking back and forth mumbling incoherently. The roar I mentioned was the air cover arriving and a tank battle group who were in the area. Apparently I watched a F15 chase the land cruiser and destroy it, but obviously, I was just facing in that direction. The medics took us to a field hospital, and while Daniels made a quick recovery, relatively anyway, I basically didn't come to for two weeks. When I did, I was back in England.'

'That must've been a shock?'

Collins laughed, 'It really was. I was in a special facility in a hospital for servicemen. I had to be put in isolation as I was yelling and screaming in my sleep disturbing the others. I made a run for it one night, too. I had no idea at all until the doctor told me. I was mortified but more than anything I was relieved I was back in the real world whatever the hell that is. Coming to didn't give me any respite from the nightmares, unfortunately, they were brutal. Night after night, afternoon snooze after afternoon snooze,' he grinned, 'they kept me in isolation. Well, when it came to sleep anyway, I dreaded going to bed, but some of the drugs knocked me out.'

Jane nodded, she often wondered about the drugs prescribed for traumatic cases, she was no expert but felt science was only scraping the surface in this notoriously difficult area.

'How long were you there?'

'Just over three months.'

'Did they send you back to Iraq?'

'Oh no, that was very over for me. As I got better, the staff told me to rest as much as possible and I did, though relaxing isn't easy for me at the best of times. So I started to take an interest in the work they were doing, on me and the rest of the men in the facility. The talking therapy, psychotherapy and counselling, I found particularly interesting. I talked about it to the doctors and nurses, eventually leading the group sessions and becoming a sort of de facto patients' representative. The thing that struck me most was that it definitely seemed to help the men. And, my god, some were in far worse shape than me, dreadful physical injuries as well as the psychological impact. They all reacted differently of course to what had happened to them, but the talking therapies definitely helped virtually all the men.'

Naturally, Jane wasn't surprised to hear this though the extremity of their experiences did make her wonder sometimes. 'You said virtually.'

'Yes, we did suffer two suicides, and though the staff reacted with great professionalism, they were completely devastated. I was really struck by that. Actually, from the moment I came round, I thought their commitment and dedication was incredible. Through the horror it ignited something in me I completely didn't expect, a huge urge to help. When I was finally told I wouldn't see combat again, I was terrified a medical discharge would be the logical next step.'

'Was it that unthinkable?'

'Completely, I loved being in the army, it was my life. Civvy Street didn't even remotely appeal, the army seeps into you, it becomes you. I still feel that despite being away from the frontline. So I got more and more involved, probably drove the staff mad in truth but what I had seen, what others have experienced drove me on, helping people like me is my mission, my life's work if you like.'

Jane had seen it in other 'victims', she preferred *survivors*, a compelling desire to help, using their experience, however dreadful, to help others come through the other side. That aspect of the human condition electrified her.

'It didn't happen straight away, I was posted to various desks around England, Germany and Cyprus. I enjoyed it, Cyprus was fantastic actually, and the longer I was away from combat zones, the more I realised it was for the best. I got involved in designing training and tactical exercises but couldn't face supervising them or being out on the field, it was still too much, and my superiors understood, most of them anyway. All the while, my interest in the welfare side grew and grew. I took courses in counselling, did a degree in psychology and became a course junkie really. I worked closely with the army chaplains and became an official counsellor eventually, six years on from combat in Desert Storm.'

Jane tried hard not to gush, 'that's fantastic, Liam, truly. What an incredible story. You should write a book. Do you still counsel the men?'

'I dip in to keep my hand in, a couple of men a week generally. I get involved in the extreme cases mainly, as part of a specialised package we developed. If we were a football club, you'd say I was 'Director of Football.''

'I wouldn't, I know nothing about football.'

'Well, someone who has responsibility for the overall direction of our service, I'm charged with improving everything we do. We, well, the army anyway takes a lot of stick for not caring for our men and women. Hope I've proved that at least isn't true.'

'You certainly have, though I hadn't given it any thought until you approached me, not one for the news, I'm afraid.'

'What's wrong with that?'

'Makes me a bit ignorant, comically so if you listen to Ray.'

'Ray?'

'My husband. He's a total news junkie, frustrated the hell out of him at first, and just makes him laugh now.'

'How does that make you feel?'

'Are you counselling me, Major Collins?'

'No, curious though, I must admit.'

'I'm fine about it, actually. Counselling young people can be a bit tricky if they feel you don't relate to them, just takes a little longer to win them round that's all.'

'You're confident, but not in a big-headed way at all. You're really confident in your ability, I really like that. It's one of the reasons we pursued you, I think our men deserve the best and you represent exactly that.'

'Thank you. I am, you're right, it's odd, I know I relate to people, I never worry about being cool or anything, I just get in there, seems to work.'

'You're not very self-conscious if I may say, definitely a good thing in this game.'

'Like you, Major, I love people, that's what it boils down to, and don't blush, it's true. I don't worry much about whether people like me, doesn't cross my mind, I'm too interested to care most of the time.'

Jane didn't want to the lunch to end but chose a natural lull in conversation to suggest they call it a day. The Major agreed and said Jane could head home and that he would like her to start next Monday. He would email her some background information on the clients he had in mind for her by the weekend. They parted with a firm but warm handshake. Slightly giddy with the wine and exhilarated by the conversation, Jane sat on a bench looking over the river towards the unit, aglow with the possibilities ahead as she traced Major Liam Collins crossing the river and making his way through the grounds back to his mission and life's work.

8

The lack of leads frustrated Jack and his team, but despite the media whirlwind surrounding the shootings, Danny Koumas and Aidan Buchanan, the copycat shootings, it couldn't be denied that their man hadn't struck for five days. The collective head scratching at team meetings showed no sign of abatement. Wallace was still feeling the heat to get a result which she duly passed down to Jack, though all he could give her was more questions. He felt the team was tiring of this investigation, a stage reached sooner by the fact the victims were dogs.

Other crimes in the area didn't conveniently cease either especially as hot nights led to drinking, lack of sleep and short tempers. Men were getting stabbed, domestic violence was spiking, and officers were gratefully being pulled off the dog killings to get their teeth into some pretty nasty crimes.

Jack emailed Annie to say he wasn't working to 'stupid o'clock' as she called it and would be back at a reasonable time, gasping for a pint, a pizza and her in no particular order. Her 'hello stranger' reply, full of vivid laments made him look forward to some rare quality time with his wife even more. They settled on a walk with Earnie up to Pizza Express in Highgate Village, calling in at the Prince of Wales for a cold beer en route.

As pleased as Annie Love was to see her husband, she was brimming with questions about Danny Koumas and the case generally. He'd missed their debriefs and her telling insights.

'Right, Mr L, I need a bit more than, 'yeah he was ok,' not just for me, Magda's been onto me.'

'Oh no, has she got a crush on Koumas too?'

'Makes mine look like indifference.'

'Blimey, that's a serious crush, fair play. God, even Magda eh? That's devastating, I thought I was her one true love. Whoosh big in Hungary are they?'

'No need for that, she's been here for 15 years.'

Jack laughed, 'I know that, how is she anyway?'

'Never mind Magda, tell me about Mr Koumas, the sexy, oh-so-talented Mr Koumas.'

'Well, you know I said you shouldn't meet your heroes? Danny Koumas proved to be a pleasant exception to that rule.'

'But did he shoot Moira?'

'No, I've decided to rule him out of our enquiries.'

'Well done DI Love, I think that's a good decision, will you be holding a press conference to announce this development?'

'Yeah, we're bringing Buchanan down and having them stand toe-to-toe for the verdict.'

Jack shook his head and looked out onto Pond Square and was heartened to see the odd person out walking their dogs. Normality was beginning to peek its head out ever so slowly. Jack recounted the tale of his encounter with Koumas to a rapt Annie that culminated in them discussing his music provoking an urge in both of them to get home and put his CDs on. Hunger overcame that urge, and Jack just delighted in being with his wife. They left the Prince hand in hand and headed for Pizza Express, the village still beset by clammy heat at 8 in the evening.

Jane Harkness snapped awake at 6am. Ray murmured something and was soon gently snoring again. She slipped out of bed, padded downstairs and put the kettle on. Truth was she hadn't slept much, couldn't keep still. She charged herself with being a bad mother after not giving the men in her life much TLC that weekend and smiled. Ray was used to it and so were the boys to an extent. When she 'got on one' with work as Ray put it, she would almost disappear. Ray was fantastic, made sure the boys were actively entertained and over-compensated if anything. She laughed when she heard the youngest, Dan, 11 say 'I love it when mum has work to do.' It hurts a bit too but it was by no means the norm, and they all knew it.

She explained to Ray that this was different; she was out of her comfort zone and needed to give it her full concentration. She knew it was unnecessary, he just raised his hands and said it was fine. He always did. Ray was a very busy man during the week as a building site manager and knew Jane went beyond the call of duty then. Luckily, he was free on weekends more often than not, and it worked well.

Major Collins had dutifully sent through some case notes on four clients she would be seeing that week, and Jane reached for them as the kettle rumbled to the boil. She poured her tea and had a flick through them again. She had been allocated a wide variety of situations to deal with, even over the breadth of four cases. There was post-traumatic stress disorder, drug and alcohol abuse, psychosis, domestic violence and eating disorders, all heavily intertwined of course.

Captain John Mackintosh caught her eye immediately, a new referral, not so much for his symptoms in the evaluation but the fact he was SAS. She couldn't pretend to know an awful lot about the SAS, but in common consciousness, they were legendary, mysterious and very tough indeed. His biography was gripping on its own. 'Black ops' in the Balkans, Afghanistan, second Gulf War and Sierra Leone. No 'routine patrols' here. It was full of operations under the radar, disrupting enemy regimes, rescuing hostages and hand-to-hand fighting the Taliban. This man was on a different plane to the other men she had met and read about. 'Horror plus,' Ray had described it. She felt flattered Collins had allocated Mackintosh to her. Perhaps it was the relative mildness of his symptoms – he had complained of nightmares and interestingly, 'losing himself' but he hadn't lost a limb, he hadn't been self-harming or attempted suicide like one of the other men. He was her second appointment and the one she was looking forward to most.

The tube sucked the life out of Harkness, or tried to. She was soaked and irritable by the time she got to the unit. The carriages were packed, all manner of humanity heading on their way to their destinations, some clearly deciding it wasn't worth showering judging by some of the armpits she'd encountered. The Metro front page she saw again and again was rattling on about some celebrity she'd barely heard of now the dog sniper had taken a break (or stopped altogether, nobody knew.) She rarely took notice of the news but realised that she should take an interest with the increasing breadth of her work.

It wouldn't do to not to have a working knowledge of some of the conflicts in the world and British involvement in Iraq and Afghanistan in particular in this aspect of her work. She cursed not bringing a change of clothes as there were obviously showers at the unit, but immediately felt cooler and calmer when entering the grounds, the breeze from the river and the shade of the ancient trees soothed her and took her into another world. Still early, a couple of patients and their nurses were already out on the fields with Jane wondering what was going through their minds this morning.

She fired up her computer, said a quick hello to Major Collins and awaited her first client. As was her want, she waited for her client to enter before sorting herself out with a drink so they could chat and feel comfortable with each other quicker. She found that clients would often be nervous and turn down a drink, offering 'tea or coffee?' instead of 'would you like a drink?' was far more successful in her experience. Given the heat, she also made sure a jug or iced water was on hand.

The drapes fluttered in the lazy breeze reminding Harkness they had to go. She would pay for it herself if necessary. A gentle knock on the door extracted her from curtains as a giant beast of a man filled her door, moving purposefully on crutches, Lance Corporal Andrew Barrington to be precise, and her very first military client.

What a way to start too. Barrington had been blown up by an IED, losing a close friend and comrade as well as both legs beneath the knee. A Highlander with the Scots Guards, he was lost, afraid and clearly in the throes of PTSD. The drink manoeuvre worked and disarmed Barrington, but he took a while to talk and despite his height and stature looked like a timid boy on his first day of school. He smiled a lot but fell to looking into the middle distance with increasing frequency. He couldn't maintain eye contact, and Harkness suggested they moved to the window seats in V formation. Barrington visibly relaxed and with frequent but comfortable pauses outlined his horrific story. It was his first tour to Afghanistan, and the IED blast happened just days into the tour. He was 21 and his friend, Sgt Colin Torrington, 24.

He gripped the arms of his chair so tightly, you could see the veins in the arms bulge, and at times he visibly shook. Finally, he collapsed into tears, huge juddering sobs that wrenched the heart. Harkness felt a cool tear run down her face and smiled when Barrington promptly fell asleep. She looked out on the sun-drenched grounds, then at the clock, 10 minutes til Captain John Mackintosh was due in the room. She felt a shiver of excitement and gently roused Barrington who wasn't quite sure where he was.

'What happened?' his Highland brogue twisted into a rasp.

Harkness smiled, 'Oh, you know, I was talking to you and you fell asleep.'

The young soldier rubbed his hand over his ruddy face, his pale blue eyes moist from a hearty yawn, 'I'm sorry.'

'What for?'

'For crying and falling asleep, done plenty of crying but never conked out like that before, weird. Maybe it's a good thing?'

'Maybe it is, but either way, it's fine by me, this is just the start, Andrew, I'm just privileged you are sharing this with me. I'm looking forward to seeing you next week already.'

Barrington looked down, sighed, nodded his head and eased himself up, 'The hour goes quickly, eh?'

'Does when you're asleep, yeah.'

A smile this time as he guided himself to the door and out into the cool of the corridor.

While making some notes, Jane listened to the clang of Barrington's crutches and him saying hello to someone without reply. A single rap on the door and Captain John Mackintosh entered the room and seemed to be in his chair before she even blinked. It seemed to Jane as soon as she turned her back he'd be somewhere else in the room in literally a blink of an eye.

His appearance was ordinary, Harkness could not get past 'ordinary' in her mind, black t-shirt, dark blue jeans, white trainers, slim, slightly thinning, closely cropped brown hair, maybe about 35. Ordinary. He opted for tea, but when she asked him if he took sugar, he was the other side of the room.

'No thanks. The old man…'

'I'm sorry,' Jane looked round stirring the tea not really sure where he would be. He was stood near the door pointing at a black and white photo of a rocky outcrop mounted just beside the light switch.

'The Old Man of Storr, place on the Isle of Skye, looks a bit gloomy for a shrink's office, though.'

'I'm not a shrink, Captain.

'I know.'

Jane turned, picked the cups up and turned again to take their tea to her table. She gasped as he was already seated again.

'Are you ok, miss?'

'Jane, and yes, I'm fine thank you. You move very quickly and quietly don't you, Captain?'

'Mac, and yes, so I've been told. I hadn't really noticed.'

'SAS, according to my notes, I'm guessing moving quickly and quietly is very useful in the SAS?' Jane was enjoying this already as Mac's face clouded then cleared, clouded then cleared by the second.

'Yes, I suppose so,' he offered eventually. Jane decided to let a silence descend on the meeting. His brown eyes bored into her but not in an aggressive manner; in fact, Jane felt very relaxed now. He was everything she had expected bar the elusive movement. A curious individual with the internal conflicts headlined on his face.

She followed with a few cursory questions about length of service and some of the tours he'd been on, impressing herself with her ready use of newly acquired army lingo.

'You know nothing about the army, do you, Jane?'

Jane put her hands up, 'No, I don't. Is that a problem for you, Mac?'

'I don't know, yet.'

'Well, let's see, shall we? You can always bin me and draft in a soldier if I'm just not getting it?'

Mac gave this some thought and after what seemed like minutes, slowly nodded.

'Good, what are you hoping to get from these sessions, Mac?'

Mac stared through Jane, beads of sweat spotting on his forehead. He sighed deeply and closed his eyes. Jane didn't push it and allowed another silence to settle in the room. She too closed her eyes. She could hear the persistent diesel drone of a barge heading for central London. The hot breeze blew aromas of food in from the river pubs and cafes, and she thought back to her lunch with Major Collins last week, remembering the sensation of the chilled sauvignon blanc hitting her tongue and instantly wanting one there and then.

Mac intrigued her, and she was unconcerned that he had barely said a word so far. She opened her eyes and started when she saw he had changed positions again. He was sat in the chair overlooking the grounds, and she joined him there. 'What are you thinking?' she asked.

'Are you my girlfriend?'

'No, do you have a girlfriend, Mac?'

Mac shook his head slowly, 'Nah.'

'So why did you ask?'

'What are you thinking? Can you see a camel in the clouds? All that bollocks.'

Jane had to laugh, she had done just that many times with various boyfriends over the years, the idle chit chat that imparts great meaning at the time.

'Nessie, actually,' she said eventually.

'What?'

'Look, that cloud looks like the Loch Ness Monster.'

Mac let out a laugh and frowned. He looked down and rubbed his hands up and down his forearms. Again, he shook his head slowly.

'What is it, Mac?'

'I can't remember the last time I laughed,' a smile attempted entrance onto his face and immediately became distorted into anguish.

'I'm glad I made you laugh, at least. That's definitely progress.'

'Can't remember much these days, truth be told,' drops of sweat gathering again on his forehead.

'What do you mean?' asked Jane quietly, 'long term memory or what happened yesterday?'

'Short term, I seem to lose blocks of time. I wake up on the kitchen floor for example, and I've no idea what's happened or how I got there.'

Mac was warming to his theme a bit, Jane noticed, the otherness had ebbed somewhat. There was fear, though, lots of it. He sat so still, like a croc on a river bank. She wondered what he had seen, what the real story behind the case notes was.

'How are you sleeping?' Mac grunted a laugh and sat forward shaking his head.

'What?'

'It's hard to explain.'

'Take your time, want another cup of tea? I know I do,' she said rising to put the kettle on again.

'Yeah, go on, thanks,' Mac nodded.

'I don't know why tea works so well on days like these, but it just does,' said Jane brightly.

'Yeah, when I played cricket, I drank gallons of it, nothing but sweet tea worked in the heat when we had an innings break,' Mac paused, 'same goes for Iraq. The lads would literally go mad if we ran out of the stuff.'

He was by her side again, surprising her rather than startling Jane this time. She was getting used to him.

'British solution to everything, a nice cup of tea, I like that about us actually.' Mac quickly rubbed his clean-shaven chin, 'never thought about it.' Jane glanced at the clock, only 15 minutes left already, the time had flown by.

'So, tell me about sleeping.'

'I close my eyes…'

'No, really Mac.'

'I'm being serious, I close my eyes, and I'm there again in a mashed up version of all the places I've served. It can

110

be a desert with a blizzard going on, it's fucked, completely fucked. My friends speak to me.'

'That's good,' encouraged Jane, 'it's always good to talk.'

'Not in my dreams it isn't, trust me. Given they're all dead.'

'I'm sorry, Mac.'

'They died, I survived. I wonder who got the best deal sometimes.'

He sat back, exhaled loudly and slowly, Jane thought his eyes were glistening a touch. He shook his head again, 'I don't know how I made it. In our game, there is a lot of waiting and watching, you have to remain completely fo-cussed, you can't miss a thing, or it will cost you your life, even then there's a good chance you will die. When you finally attack, it feels like it's over so quickly, we rarely get involved in long battles. They're quick raids, element of surprise, get in, get out. Or if you're sniping, you can wait over 12 hours and fire one shot and that's it.'

'What happened to your friends?' asked Jane.

'Well, people die in battles, obviously,' said Mac with-out spite. 'They die horribly, they get caught. Say the Tali-ban get hold of you, they'd think nothing of cutting your head off and later throwing it over the fence of the nearest coalition compound. Charlie Grey's head talks to me in my "dreams."'

Jane noticed Mac gripping the sides of his leather chair hard.

'Charlie Grey?' asked Jane, guessing straight away what was coming.

'One of the greatest, bravest men I've ever met.' They were sat down again, sipping their fresh cups of tea watch-ing the clouds billowing up to the east, a storm threatening to break the grip of the sultry heat. The wind had picked up too, and the drapes were jumping about like they were hiding street dancers. Jane and Mac relished the drop in temperature and cooling draught. They watched a nurse and a patient in a wheelchair near the river turn back towards the unit, there was definitely rain in the air.

'Two nice days and a thunderstorm,' sighed Mac.

'Been a few more than that, I've loved it after last summer.'

'Missed that one.'

'So… Charlie?' said Jane, refocussing the session.

Mac nodded, deep in thought. 'Drones had picked up what we assumed to be a heavily guarded Taliban comms unit, it looked like they could broadcast from there given the aerials on display. We wondered if bombing would be enough, a raid could seize vital intel as well as taking out an important source of info for the insurgents. We watched the site for two days noting patterns for the guards, comings and goings, that kind of thing. As a trained sniper, I took out a guard to see how they reacted. Would they all charge out like disturbed ants or hunker down? It was very much the latter which meant they were organised and disciplined. Prepared too, no doubt. It meant more reconnaissance after clearing the area for three days. Like I say, a lot of waiting and watching. Anyway, we decided that ten of us would rush the place after dark in night-vision gear and disrupt their comms structure and see what intel we could gather. Creating chaos is easy, but you have to time it right.'

The relish with which Mac referred to creating chaos added something to an already fascinating story. He actually licked his lips.

'So, with Charlie at my side we took out the guards to the south, cutting their throats, muffling any noise with rags and we entered the tent system. The boys attacking the north let off stun grenades, and the chaos began. With our bayonets drawn we slashed and cut anyone we saw moving from space to space. Like it had been stage-managed, we all entered the central space in the camp, an open air area. We were met by the site of at least thirty Taliban around a large fire. I actually laughed, and we were off shooting and slashing at speed. The numbers did for us, though. Charlie was captured, three of the others shot dead with six of us getting out alive somehow. A miracle if you ask me.'

Jane felt out of breath but not for the first time also felt privileged to be listening to these brave men's' stories. She couldn't deny it was exciting to listen to, she was actually on the edge of her seat. 'That's amazing Mac, how on earth did you get out?'

'Two grenades created enough chaos to get out. They've got good equipment but couldn't chase in the dark. They didn't have night-vision, or not enough of them did anyway. But my last sight in the camp was four of the bastards taking poor Charlie away. I wanted to get him, but the others said no, and we got the fuck out.'

'Must've been hard leaving him?' Mac just stared into the middle distance for what seemed like an age. Finally, he turned to Jane, 'yeah it was,' and looked out again at the fields, the river and the gathering storm.

Another pause, then, 'We thought they'd demand a ransom, but no, they cut off his head instead, put it on the fucking internet then threw his head over a neighbouring compound's fence. It's not like it is in the films either, it's very hard work cutting off someone's head, or at least it was in Charlie's case on the film they posted on the internet.' Jane put her hand to her mouth, failing to comprehend something so brutal and cruel could happen. She heard terrible things in her line of work but nothing that could match this. It stunned and grimly fascinated her in equal measure. This was just one of Mac's experiences. Her last thought as the clock ticked to the hour was god, poor Charlie Grey.

It was only Jane's second client, and she felt exhausted. She flopped back in her seat after seeing Mac out and closed her eyes. Thank god it was midday, her next client was 2 o'clock. Barrington was a relatively straightforward case despite the very tangible horror. It would take time, no question, but she felt strongly that progress would be made. He was young, damaged and had experienced unimaginable pain in his army career, but she had already mapped out where she wanted to go. She was so confident she had to warn herself against being too confident and made a remark to that effect in her case notes.

Captain John Mackintosh was something else, though. Where to start in summarising that session? She sat up and tried, feeling like a schoolgirl again, chewing the end of her pen. More tea was required and as she put the kettle on again, felt a surge of relief when Major Collins knocked on the door.

Looking slightly pale, he wondered cheerily if there was a spare cup for him. Glad of a potential sounding board, she pointed to the seats in the window and grabbed a clean mug. She grinned as he asked for a 'strong, milky tea with two sugars' while preparing a peppermint tea for herself.

'They always smell nice but never taste that great,' Collins said taking a noisy slurp of his tea pointing at Jane's mug.

'Bet you've only tried once?' Jane smiled, 'the trick is to let it brew for a few minutes, let it cool a bit then take a hearty mouthful.'

'If you say so, won't put hair on your chest, though.'

Jane laughed, 'I don't need any more, trust me. Anyway, I can't imagine a squaddie asking for peppermint tea after the heat of battle.'

'True, you could be court-martialled for less. Tea is very important on tour, stronger and sweeter the better.'

'Yes, Mac was saying very much the same thing this morning.'

'Mac?'

'Captain John Mackintosh to be precise, insisted I called him Mac,' said Jane with something approaching pride.

Collins took another loud sip of his tea, shuddered ever so slightly as an almighty crack of thunder followed sheet lightning that lit up the satanic blackness enveloping south and west London. Rain drops as big as marbles starting falling fitfully at first, loudly hitting the roof and trees about them. A deluge followed that rendered conversation virtually impossible, so the pair sat there watching the storm, swapping occasional glances at the loudest claps of thunder, neither willing to shut the window. In the teeth of the storm, it got so dark it felt like the end of the world, a feeling that aroused primaeval instincts in both of them. And then it was gone, an apocalyptic interlude that barrelled on through Mortlake, Richmond and on past Heathrow. A curtain of intense heat dropped back on the city as soon as the storm cleared, distant rumblings and the sound of pregnant gutters and busy drainpipes the only clues to the spectacular storm that had just swept over them.

The sky turned cloudless, the relentless drone of aircraft audible again and people were back on the streets wondering if they'd imagined the angry rain.

Mac had wandered out of the session into the coming storm. He knew he wouldn't make it to the tube and shinned up one of the great oaks in the grounds of the unit for shelter. As he waited in the pressure cooker heat for the downpour to hit, he wondered what benefit, if any, the counselling was to him. Despite his misgivings, he liked Jane Harkness and felt he could open up to her in time. Open up about what, though? He wanted to be truthful, but he wasn't sure what it was he had to unburden himself of. He genuinely lost time, genuinely felt confused and scared but then when lucid it all seemed so preposterous to him.

As the first thunderclap landed like an artillery shell, he felt such an idiot. How could he lose it like this? Where was his discipline? He was a disgrace to the regiment. As huge raindrops battered their way through the canopy, he resolved to attend all the sessions with Jane, it's all he could do for now, it seemed the only chance to make sense of this blurred and misshapen situation he was in. Another explosive dispatch from the sky reminded Mac he had to sit tight and get back to base without giving his position away to the enemy. He rested his head against the steaming bark of the tree waiting and watching.

With a gentle breeze once again tossing the curtains of Jane's room, Major Collins asked Jane about her first morning.

'Interesting, to say the least,' she said nodding gently, reliving the fascinating tales of the soldiers and their grisly experiences.

'Especially Mac, eh?' said Collins pointing to the grounds.

'What are you looking at?' Collins kept his arm straight, Jane followed the trajectory and just made out a lean figure jumping down from an oak tree 50 yards from the window. They followed his progress to the fence on the river bank like a hallucination, so quick and elusive was his movement. Jane gasped when he disappeared.

'That was like watching an old film, like my eyes were playing tricks on me, as if he actually disappeared for bits of that, that was uncanny, extraordinary.' Collins' face betrayed no hint of surprise at all listening to Jane's incredulity.

'He's a remarkable soldier indeed, Captain Mackintosh,' he said eventually.

'What was he doing up the tree?' Jane replied wondering why it wasn't her first thought.

'Your guess is as good as mine. I'm thinking it underlines why he needs help, though. His responses to events aren't what you would call normal and appropriate are they? The things that make him such a brilliant special forces soldier look like they are crossing over into civilian scenarios, and while I don't imagine he's a risk to others at this stage, he certainly has many issues to confront. It's why I assigned him to you. I felt he needed a fresh pair of eyes on him, non-military eyes if you like.'

Jane nodded, still absorbing what she had just seen and finding it was slipping from her memory already. She urgently made a note on the file. Later, she was to find she didn't believe her own scribbled account.

Collins nodded to her pad, 'What were your thoughts this morning?'

Jane took a sip of her tea, 'Well I was struck by his movement, he seemed to move silently. One minute he'd be sat down next in a blink of an eye he'd be the other side of the room remarking on a painting or a framed photograph, he was interested in the Old Man of Storr for instance.'

'Yes, some of the remotest country in the UK on Skye, he'll know it really well for sure, he'll have camped out in the Cuillin for nights on end in the harshest conditions. If you have a keen eye you will spot Special Forces in that neck of the woods, thankfully, not many do, or aren't looking anyway. Climbers and walkers will be followed, though, sometimes just to break the boredom. Quite rightly, they're on the lookout for eagles and taking in the scenery. Luckily for us, the Brecon Beacons are known for SAS training, they're not supposed to use anywhere else but you know, they don't take much notice of that really.'

Jane nodded but didn't dwell too deeply on military training, 'I was also struck by his otherness, his face was a constantly changing canvas, it scares me what must be going through his mind. He was reticent at first, but I actually made him laugh, and he opened up a bit, the hour flew by. I'm pretty sure he'll be back.'

'I'm pretty sure too, looking at his notes, he came back before as part of his discharge routine when he didn't think he needed it and didn't really give it a fair go. Things must be deteriorating quite sharply, I get the impression he's a very proud soldier, wary of weakness.'

'I don't imagine that's unique by any means in the military,' said Jane. 'What can you tell me about the man more generally?'

'He was an exceptional soldier…' Noticing Jane wanted more than that, he scratched his head and went on, 'He was popular wherever he went and not the loner you might expect. His COs said he was drawn to chaos, the causing of it and something of an expert at extricating himself from it, another characteristic that appealed to Special Forces. In regular units and the many nights of drunken bonding sessions, he'd seemingly get bored. It was if he'd wonder what would happen if he punched the biggest bloke in the bar or smashed all the optics so he'd do it and reap the whirlwind. He attracted mates in the units who loved trouble and hung around Mac wondering what he'd come up with next. His most legendary escapade was celebrating wildly at England's last penalty shoot-out fiasco in a pub full of sailors in Portsmouth. Took the Military Police hours to get it under control but Mac had walked out of the pub after a few minutes without a scratch. Unsurprisingly, he became more serious and withdrawn the more extreme his tours became, but he wasn't alone in that. The overwhelming and unsatisfactory phrase that keeps coming into my head is 'normal', he was really normal yet anything but, if that makes any sense at all.'

Jane bit on her pen, 'Yes, that's what I thought of his appearance, normal, unremarkable if you like. It's hard to remember what he looked like actually and yet there is so much to this man, I didn't want the session to end.'

9

DI Jack Love was feeling the heat, truth be told he wasn't great in the extremely hot conditions that gripped Britain and which showed no sign of abatement – he chose not to moan about it as so many around him did more than enough of that already. He soldiered on, relished how good North London looked in the evening when it was slightly cooler. Dogs couldn't talk of course, but he was sure Earnie hated it too. He was keen enough in the early morning to grab a stroll but essentially slept all day and reluctantly went out with Jack and Annie in the evening.

Annie claimed she loved the heat, but he wasn't so sure. The languid nights when they sort of rolled into each other in bed were great of course, but ill-ventilated class-rooms couldn't be pleasurable with 30-plus kids roasting away during summer terms; though, she never moaned either.

Heat of another, more fierce source was punishing Jack too. DCI Stephanie Wallace was desperate for a result and being one never shy to let rip at Jack's methods, was calling him in for 'a moment' to her office with irritating frequency. He understood that her superiors would be jumping around too, of course. A sniper on the loose was bad for business whichever way you looked at it. He was frankly making a fool of them, and their superiors were pondering 'escalating' matters - code for 'someone else needs to have a go.'

Sitting outside Gino's in the early morning coolness, such that it was, sipping an Americano, he was reminded that he needed to follow up a meeting he had with Major Bradley Wilkinson of the MOD. He surely would've been in touch if there was anything to report but felt it was courtesy to follow up their chat and he was genuinely interested in what, if anything, Wilkinson had done. His watch told him it was 9 o'clock, definitely a decent time to catch a military man at work.

Wilkinson picked up on the third ring and instantly apologised to the barista serving him in the coffee shop. He didn't ask who it was, simply saying 'hold on a sec, please.' Jack listened to him order his skinny latte and pay, punctuated with plenty of clipped politeness.

'Sorry about that, Bradley Wilkinson.'

'That's quite ok, Major, DI Jack Love, how are you? Sorry to interrupt your coffee stop.'

'Ah, Jack, good to speak to you again, how are things progressing? Pretty tricky I'm guessing.'

'Yes, that's one way of describing it,' said Jack quickly giving a brief resume of where the case was heading just about avoiding the phrase 'down a big fat cul-de-sac.'

Jack heard the scrape of a chair and the chatter of a cafe servicing the office workers arriving in Whitehall and the early and eager tourists. Wilkinson let out a sigh as he took his seat.

'I'm glad you called actually, Jack and sorry I haven't been in touch sooner. Not that there's much to report, but I have been asking around on your behalf. I've been thinking about the nature of the case and thought it might be worth going to see a colleague of mine who is running an army rehabilitation unit out Barnes Bridge way. It's a long shot, but given the behaviour exhibited in this case, it would certainly be worth a chat at the very least. I'm going down there at two this afternoon.'

'Thank you, Bradley, what sort of work do they do?'

The Major briefed Jack on the innovative work carried out there on soldiers traumatised by active service with as much emphasis on the psychological as the physical work. Interesting as it was, Jack couldn't help feeling it was another dead end. However, with a lack of a decent lead, he asked if he could accompany Major Wilkinson.

'Not this time, if you don't mind, let me see how the land lies, and I will gladly call you this evening,' said the Major, the tone slightly more terse, Jack noted.

'Of course, I'm very grateful for this, I'll look forward to hearing from you later. Good to speak to you again,' Jack hung up and felt brighter getting up to buy a take-out for the office. That quickly dissipated when his phone rang and he saw a call from Wallace waiting. He paused, pressed divert, paid Gino and made his way down Fortis Green, the heat coming at him from all angles.

Jane wondered if Mac would turn up for their next appointment, exactly a week after their opening session, as she sipped her tea looking out over the scorched grass of the hospital grounds. She needn't have worried as he was already sat behind her also taking in the view.

'Jesus Christ!'

'Sorry Jane, I did knock,' said Mac. Jane didn't hear it but recovered her composure quickly.

'No problem, Captain,' she said with a smile and put the kettle on.

She didn't turn her back on him while the kettle boiled but he didn't move. At all. She couldn't even hear him breathing, let out a sigh or clear his throat. Of course, after she poured him a sugary cup of tea, he was standing at the window not looking out but staring straight at Jane. She thought a moment and decided to immediately investigate the Captain's tree escapade during the short-lived violent storm last week as they assumed their positions in the window arm-chairs.

'Which tree was it?' replied Mac. Jane overlooked his apparent inability to remember the tree and pointed to the huge oak tree halfway to the river bank where a nurse had wheeled a patient with half his right leg missing and his left arm in a sling. Mac nodded slowly, assessing the tree Jane had selected.

'If you look carefully, the canopy is thickest in the centre of the tree and provides excellent shelter in a storm situation. When cover is the central consideration to staying alive on covert ops, this particular tree is exceptional for hiding from the enemy. They may seek shelter too, it pays to get elevated and out of the way.'

Jane nodded. 'Sounds like excellent military logic, Mac, but you were leaving this unit, no enemy here.' Mac looked at Jane evenly.

'Do you remember being up the tree, Mac?'

He looked hard at the tree for a moment then shook his head slowly.

'It's ok Mac, it really is. Do you remember the session with me?'

He frowned but said that he did adding, 'Was it the same day?'

'It was indeed. How did you feel after? Only your first visit I know.'

'Like climbing trees, apparently.' They shared a smile. 'Well, I'm back aren't I?'

'Yes, I'm very glad that you are, too.' Jane smiled.

Mac's forehead was beginning to glisten as if the exertion of remembering was making him sweat. His breathing was even though, and Jane was glad he wasn't getting distressed.

'Why did you join the army?'

Mac raised his eyebrows at the sharp change of tack but didn't hesitate in answering.

'One of my teachers thought it would be a good idea. He was a bit old school, Mr Rogers and saw my build and athletic ability coupled with what he called my "bravery and bloody mindedness" as perfect for the army. He thought I had a brain on me too despite only average marks overall apart from physical education. Didn't go down well with the "trendy Wendies" as he called them but I didn't care about them. I went to a few army recruitment events and signed up with the cadets, and I was away, signed up as I soon as I could leave school.'

'What did you like about it?'

'I just took to it straight away. I found life in the cadets very easy, sailed through all their endurance tests and exercises. Then when they put a gun in my hands, they quickly found I had an uncanny eye for shooting.'

'How soon was special forces a consideration?'

'My sergeant major mentioned it not long after basic training. He was really hard on me during those first nine weeks but everything he threw at me I took. If I got knocked down, I got straight back up. I think part of him hated that, but I could tell he was impressed. Towards the end, he eased off on me, and more senior officers started to turn up.'

'How did the other lads feel?'

'I got some stick, but because I helped some of the strugglers, I was seen as one of the lads.'

'And were you?'

Mac just shrugged, then, 'I suppose I was really. I was close to a couple of the boys in those days, we literally lived cheek by jowl.'

'Are you still in touch with any of them from the regular army?'

He shook his head slowly and sighed. 'Only when you stay in a unit for a long time do you really get close. I moved about a lot after training until I got to Special Forces. It was very different there, really I had only made acquaintances until then.'

Jane nodded, she had watched her own boys make best friends one year only for it to change the next year if they moved classes. It was a pattern that underneath the proclamations of friendship suited social creatures and the myriad of situations they found themselves in.

'And what about when you moved to Special Forces?'

Mac looked out through the windows, drapes suddenly all of a flutter as a welcome breeze announced its presence. He closed his eyes.

'Mac, do you want to have a break?'

Mac again shook his head slowly. 'It's very difficult to explain.'

Jane folded her arms. 'Try… But first, tea.'

Jane put the kettle on, quickly evaporating the slight dizziness she felt standing up. Must be the heat. She felt a slow trickle of sweat wend its way down her back as she reached for the milk. She'd enjoyed this session so far, Mac was definitely more relaxed and more willing to speak. She knew he could disappear at any moment however and was relieved to see him still sat in his seat when she turned around with the tea.

His expression had not changed as he stared through the window she noticed. Where was he? What was he thinking about or reliving?

'Here we go, Mac, you ok?' asked Jane as she passed him his milky tea.

A small smile developed but disappeared just as quickly as he answered, 'Fine.'

'Good,' she took a sip of her tea. 'Before the break, Mac, you hinted that the relationships formed in Special Forces were different to any others in your experience. In terms of intensity? What is it about special forces that makes you say that?'

He rubbed his hand hard across his face. 'The situations we face are so extreme, the danger so pronounced, I approached every mission as if it was my last, as it easily could be.'

Jane nodded, remembering the horrific story of how they had disrupted a Taliban communications camp and how they had to leave a close friend of Mac's behind. The thought of him being beheaded had never been far from her thoughts since the first session.

'You are literally dependent on each other to survive, and when you look into their eyes, you want to see that each man understands that. The bonds are unspoken but deeper than family. We would often link up with regular units and while the commitment was there and they'd always be well drilled, there was something missing.'

'What was it?'

'Intensity was the word you used earlier, and I've been trying to think of a better way of expressing it but intensity is it. We didn't need bonding exercises or massive piss-ups for morale, we were on a different level, and once I was there, there was no way I could ever go back.'

'How did the unit react to losing men?'

Like a faulty TV picture, Mac was suddenly up on his feet flitting all over the room to the extent Jane's dizziness threatened to return.

'Mac, please sit down, Mac please!' she cried.

He stopped at the window, and Jane detected a judder that suggested he was crying. She noticed that the clock had ticked round to the hour and knew another man would be waiting outside to talk about horrors civilians could only guess at. She reached into her purse for her card and said, 'Mac, please call me anytime if you're struggling before next week, I mean it.'

He looked at her quickly, shook his head but took the card and left the room. Jane took the two minutes before the next session to try and absorb her time with Mac. It was clear to her that the utter horror these men experience impacts on their lives to a degree that was almost impossible to comprehend. Hideous things happened in civilian life, and Jane hated grading experiences in terms of gravity, but this was terror and horror on a massive scale. As she gathered herself for the next hour-long session, she fretted that she wouldn't be able to get near them. It was almost impossible to understand, but she straightened in her chair as she realised it was the 'almost' that kept her going.

Jane did mean it about Mac getting in touch anytime. As she shambled through her front door with four bags of shopping, four new 'bags for life' acquired to add to the pile, it's fair to say she wasn't expecting it to be so soon.

She blew out heavily as she set the bags down and tried to muster a cheery 'hello' for the house. It was a bit breathless but her youngest boy, Sam, appeared at the top of the stairs.

'Hi Sam, how's your day?'

'Good, hot, though, I'm bored of the heat now, mum.'

'Still better than the rain though eh?' Sam looked unconvinced so asked what was for tea instead.

'Pizza. Where's Ryan and your dad?'

'On the patio talking to your friend.'

'Friend?'

'Yeah, someone from the army I think.'

'Ok, I'll give you a shout when tea's done.'

She picked up the bags and quickly made her way through to the kitchen where she could suddenly hear voices on the patio, convivial, laughter too, but an icy bolt hit her spine when she saw her 'friend' was Captain John MacKinnon. Mac was sitting with Ray and Ryan nodding as Ray was holding court about some issue or other, youth unemployment from what she could hear, a favoured topic for Ray.

She took a deep breath and joined them on the patio, the sun still high and hot above the surrounding terraces. Ray immediately got up and kissed his wife on the cheek smiling adding unnecessarily, 'We've got a guest.'

'So I see, evening, Mac,' she replied evenly before ruffling Ryan's dark bird nest hair and asking how he was.

'Sorry to intrude Jane.'

'Not at all, bit of a surprise that's all.'

'You did say anytime,' he replied, a beseeching look breaking out across his face.

'I did indeed,' Jane paused. 'And I meant it.'

Ray read the situation, 'Ok, Ryan, let's leave them to it and we'll sort tea, ok mate.' Ryan's eyes had rarely left Mac's face, but he nodded and followed his dad into the kitchen.

A blackbird was asserting its territory as Ray popped through with tea. She thanked him and immediately took a big sip, partly as she was so parched but also to gather her thoughts. It wasn't unheard of for clients to turn up at her house but it had been unsettling in the past. She did her best to separate work from home life and given the nature of her work that was definitely the right way to go. Ray and the boys were very aware of her work, and she liked to think they were very interested as well as proud. But on the rare occasion a client showed up at home, it usually meant delicate situations to negotiate.

They still talked about the time Natasha turned up late one night. As a girl, Natasha had watched her mother die of a heroin overdose. She didn't know who her father was and a long spell in care began leading to her own descent into heroin addiction. Academically bright, her school refused to give up on her, and after many battles, scrapes with the police and umpteen runaways, she was eventually referred to Jane.

Funny, sparky and beautiful, Jane liked her straight away and although the early sessions were difficult, punctuated as they were with outbursts, storming out and threats of physical abuse, there was something in Natasha's big brown eyes that captivated Jane. It was a mixture of grief, deep sadness and an almost cosmic need to be loved and understood. They weathered the early storms and built a trusting relationship. But no matter how many sessions they had chaotic lives breed chaotic situations, and one night in apocalyptically bad weather Natasha came to Jane's door.

It was late spring, but a strong westerly had blown in shower after heavy shower and Natasha had been out in Clapham and was extremely drunk and off her head on drugs. She had a black eye and blood caked her mouth and blood ran gently down her chin as she banged on Jane's door. Jane's mobile had run out of battery and not for the first time, she had forgotten to charge it.

Ray, a light sleeper, woke immediately and at first thought, it was a random drunk until he heard the frenzied cries of 'Jane, Jane' from the street. He roused his wife who shouted out as the cries and screaming had entered her dream. She quickly gathered her wits, put on her dressing gown and ran downstairs. She gasped as she opened the door at the pitiful sight that greeted her and the look in her eyes was never to leave Jane. Her fervent hope that the boys had managed to sleep through the noisy interruption evaporated as they called out for her fearfully before Ray got to them to calm them down.

'I'm so sorry to wake you all up from your perfect suburban sleep,' she snarled as she stumbled through the hallway brushing Jane aside to get to the kitchen. 'Got any booze?'

'I think you've had enough don't you?' hissed Jane, instantly regretting it.

'Oh do you, Mrs La-Di-Fucking Da? Who do you think you are telling me what I can and can't do? You're not my mother.'

'No, I'm not!'

'What's that supposed to mean?' she howled and Jane cursed as the load of glasses she meant to put away but couldn't be bothered and left on the dishwasher top were swept onto the floor by Natasha's flailing arms. The terrible smash of the glasses brought Ray tearing into the kitchen.

'Oh look, daddy's here to save the day, what you going to do? Hit me too?'

'Jane, shall I call the police?' shouted Ray as the crying upstairs intensified but Jane ignored this.

'Natasha, 'hit me too'. What do you mean, 'hit me too?' darling, tell me what you mean?'

'Jane… '

'Shut up Ray, sort the boys out… please.'

The wildness in Natasha was shifting to something altogether more unsettling. Ray quickly went upstairs to see to the boys as Natasha began to howl, gently at first before giving in and really letting go. Jane had never heard a human noise like it before or since and simply put her arms round her and murmured soothing noises in her ear. The smell of blood, booze, tears and rain filled the kitchen as Jane tried to calm this poor lost and shaking feral soul.

Jane had no idea how long they were in this clinch for, but the shaking gradually eased and the howling reduced to a whimper. She opened her eyes and saw Ray and the boys standing in the kitchen with towels and the kettle boiling. She scowled at Ray, but he simply shrugged and said, 'They wanted to help.'

Jane felt a sharp stab of love as she looked at her men around her all wanting to help, all wanting to make this wretched creature better. She became aware of a gentle purring in her ear and realised Natasha had dozed off. They wrapped her in a towel, and Jane eased her along the hall and upstairs as the door was knocked again, blue lights dancing through the glass porch.

Once upstairs, Jane undressed Natasha and put dry clothes on her keeping an ear out on the developing discussion Ray was having with two WPCs. Concerned neighbours had called the police with one swearing an animal was in distress. Ray explained as best he could before he agreed to one of the officers popping upstairs to speak to Jane. She politely explained the scenario, and while the officer was sympathetic, she insisted the police returned first thing to return Natasha to care. In truth, had Jane not been a registered counsellor whom Natasha had been referred to, they would have taken her there and then.

When the officer left the room, Natasha opened one eye and whispered, 'you said I could call you anytime,' just as Mac had done when he arrived at the house in very different circumstances.

Mac peered over at Jane. 'What are you thinking about?' he asked.

'Sorry, Mac, miles away, was just thinking of the last time a client turned up at the house.'

'Does it happen often?'

'No it doesn't,' she replied, with a hint of a stifled laugh.

'What's so funny? Did it get ugly?'

'You could say that but you know, we sorted it,' she shrugged.

'We?'

'Yep, me, Ray, the boys and the police eventually.'

'The police?'

Jane nodded.

Mac looked up and followed a 737 on its final approaches to Heathrow, its undercarriage engaging and realised he hadn't been on a plane since his medical discharge. He had just wanted to sleep when he left the army and did just that. It felt like he lost weeks. His GP had prescribed heavy tranquilisers, and in truth, Mac relished the sleep coated oblivion he fell into. He ate the bare minimum and had locked himself away apart from visits to his despairing and overworked doctor who tried various combinations of drugs but back he came time and again. He shivered as he realised he had essentially lost a year, and here he was sat in a counsellor's garden without really being able to tell her why.

'Do you mind if I ask you what you've been taking?'

Mac listed the anti-depressants and tranquilisers he was on, and Jane gently shook her head at the familiar roll call of pharmaceutical solutions to unknowable problems.

Jane nodded and was thankful Mac had taken notice of the letter he was sent by the MOD, quite an achievement given the symptoms he presented with. It heartened her that he was present enough to seek help and despite the intrusion, it was ok he was sat there in her garden on a very warm Thursday evening drinking tea. For the first time since they'd met, he seemed almost relaxed, at ease with his surroundings. He remarked how peaceful it was.

Jane smiled. She thought the same and had done since they had bought the house as an excited, freshly married couple. For inner London, it was peaceful. The sirens were muffled by the trees and shrubbery in the gardens, and even the planes didn't seem so loud. Birdsong was the prevailing soundtrack to mornings and the sultry dusk that characterised this heatwave.

'This place makes me feel relaxed,' he said and immediately seemed startled by the statement.

'That's good isn't it, Mac?'

He stared ahead into and through the dahlias. 'I should go,' he said so quietly Jane could hardly hear him.

'Are you sure Mac? You're very welcome to stay for dinner.' The smell of garlic and pepperoni had begun to waft through the windows some time earlier reminding Jane how hungry she was.

Mac turned to her and shook his head, mumbling his gratitude at the offer before leaving quietly.

10

Major Bradley Wilkinson had never met Major Liam Collins. He had heard of him and was intrigued by the work of the new unit since it opened. He had been slightly unsettled since meeting DI Jack Love though he wasn't quite sure why. Love seemed a thoroughly reasonable and likeable chap. Wilkinson put it down to a general dislike of other agencies poking their nose into their affairs. He remembered his sniffy reaction to Love and regretted it once again.

The usual 'too hot/too cold' office temperature was firmly set in the former, and he was glad of an excuse to go out. Leaving his jacket, he headed out to join the braised tourists heading for Westminster tube, looking forward to meeting his fellow major.

A stifling journey ended with Wilkinson gasping at the pitiful breeze afforded by a full and sluggish Thames. Sweat dripped into his eyes, stinging slightly as he tried to focus on getting to the unit. It was 11am and must have been 35 degrees already. Over the brown and turgid river, the unit appeared like a dream-like mirage through the haze. The tortuous tube journey and subsequent oven of a bus made him wonder if he'd ever make it to Barnes Bridge.

Pulling himself together, he made for the bridge, panted his way across and lamented his lack of shades or hat. Crossing the threshold into the leafy cover of some giant oak and horse chestnut trees instantly cooled and soothed him and the sight of a double leg amputee being wheeled to the river's edge put his battles with the heat into perspective. He relished the cool shade and felt a calm envelop him that he hadn't felt in some time.

The Major reached the dark wood panelled reception and before he could ring the bell as instructed Major Liam Collins appeared on the rather grandiose staircase.

'Major Wilkinson?'

'Ah yes, good to meet you, Major Collins.'

'Liam, please.'

'Liam, of course. I prefer Major Wilkinson personally…'

The two men paused for a second then laughed, an easy military familiarity instantly kicking in. Very firm handshakes exchanged and a cursory summary of his journey in London's furnace heat over with, Wilkinson followed Collins upstairs to his office. A large woman in her forties waved at Collins a little, how could he put it? Unmilitarially? Probably no such word he thought as he absorbed her odd garb, a perfectly serviceable long white blouse and hideous orange leggings. She said hello more formally to him, her round face and big blue eyes enquiring and kind, captivating Major Wilkinson.

Before he could say anything, Collins spoke. 'That's Jane Harkness, our new counsellor, quite a lady I can tell you.'

'Interesting outfit.'

'Well, she knows we don't employ her for her fashion sense, put it that way.'

The two men smiled but not unkindly, though Wilkinson checked what Collins was wearing again just in case he'd overstepped the mark. The neutral charcoal trousers and immaculate white Oxford shirt reassured him.

'Bugger to get to from Whitehall, Liam.'

'Sorry to put you out, thought a trip out might appeal, all that pen-pushing must be wearying,' said Collins with a smile.

'Ah it is, and it's no bother really, two oven-like tubes and a packed bus with hygienically challenged civilians was a bit of an ordeal that's all,' he replied looking at over the grounds as the nurses wheeled their patients here and there, seeking shade, peace and a haven from the hell raging in their heads. 'This place is a total oasis, though, you feel it as soon as you enter the grounds.'

'I don't notice now, or at least not very often but I certainly did when we first opened, there's a real calm here, it's hard to explain. A surprise too given its history.'

'A mental asylum I gather?'

'Googled it this morning eh?'

'Well, one needs to be abreast of one's subject matter,' said Wilkinson with forced comic formality.

The two majors swapped war stories, regiments, tours of duties, mutual friends, characters and acquaintances before a natural lull brought them to the business in hand. Collins was caught by surprise a touch. 'Of course, I've been following it in the news, laughed at the Isis speculation, the celebrity circus and all of those things, but what's it got to do with us?' His indignity surprised him, and Bradley noticed his Cumbrian accent emerging out of his classless tones when calmer.

'Well, the police have to follow all lines of enquiry of course. DI Jack Love contacted me, you might have seen on the television in press conferences, like that classic with that prick Buchanan.'

Collins nodded. He had noticed Love, how calm he looked when Buchanan was mouthing off and the slight but withering look of disdain he gave him towards the end of the now legendary press conference. Collins, despite all his training and ingrained self-restraint, was fairly sure he would have knocked him out. He remembered being impressed by Love bringing the conference to order with as much dignity as he could muster.

'The point is, Liam, this guy is an uncanny marksman and seems to move around North London unseen. A bloody author couldn't even describe him.' Liam could not help but raise a quizzical eyebrow at this, but equally, he had to admit it was a legitimate line of enquiry for the Met.

'I agree, but what do you want from me?'

'Just keep an ear to the ground that's all, anything unusual, any behaviours that may arouse concern…'

'Christ that's everyone here, even some of the staff, that's why we're here.'

'Think we can rule out Jane Harkness shinning up trees and popping mutts on the Heath,' laughed Wilkinson, bringing a smile to an increasingly defensive Collins.

'Point is, and you know this Bradley, we look after our own, confidentiality is king, the lads need to feel they can unburden themselves here.'

'Even if they're running around with a sniper's rifle, discharging live rounds into dogs?' Collins looked down at his clasped hands. A long moment passed, and he looked at Major Bradley Wilkinson evenly. 'It can feel like we're in a bubble here, the things these boys have seen and suffered are so extreme, we do exist in another world altogether.'

'But, we're not above the law, surely?'

Another pause. 'No, of course not.'

'Believe it or not, I'm not thrilled about the police sniffing around us either, I'm really not and made Love all too aware of this. However, he does have a point, and at the end of the day, it's just one line of enquiry that could well lead nowhere. I promised Love, and it is actually my duty to speak to the relevant people and ask them to keep an eye out.' Wilkinson held both hands up as if surrendering.

'I appreciate that, Bradley, and I will speak to all the staff here. You'll have seen already some of the boys on the grounds, there's plenty who can be ruled out immediately, we do take out-patients though, I'll get the word out, in fact, I'll write a memo this afternoon.'

'That's all I ask, no need to alarm anyone, no one is under suspicion or anything like that.'

Bradley thanked Liam, and they returned to more comfortable territory before Bradley's face darkened looking out of the window again at the parched fields and gently swaying trees. The journey back to Whitehall was waiting like a death row guard when all your appeals had been exhausted. Collins seemed to read his mind, laughed at his big sigh and simply said, 'Pint?'

The two men walked companionably over the grounds to The Ship on the river seeking refreshment and shade, Major Bradley Wilkinson content he had done his bit for justice and DI Jack Love. Major Liam Collins chewed his lip, mulling over his meeting with Wilkinson, dark clouds gathering all the while in his mind as shards of conversation with Jane Harkness about one of her clients came back to him again and again.

Captain John MacKinnon could barely remember how he had got back from Barnes Bridge. Come to think of it, he wasn't even sure why he had gone there or what he had done there. Actually, that's not strictly true he thought as he stared into his steaming hot tea. He remembered speaking to a lady, a large lady with an odd sense of dress. The colour orange kept suggesting itself to him and the feeling that it had done him some good. When did he go there? He couldn't really say.

He took a sip of his tea, sweetened with four sugars but no milk. He walked to the living room window and watched people struggling here and there in the street, many shorn of their shirts, tattoos proudly on display through shimmering skin. He put his tea down as a wave of dizziness hit him, he gasped faintly nauseous, sweat spotting his brow as he held an arm out to balance with the aid of the clammy wall…

… he looked out again proud of his men, going about their duties despite the fierce desert heat. He smiled. Special Forces never got bored, preparation was everything, that was drilled into them from the word go in the army but more especially in the SAS. The physical trials were relentless, but you soon realised every spare minute could be usefully spent preparing yourself mentally as well as physically. He saw it in his men now, fearlessly ignoring the heat and using their downtime for whatever mission was coming their way.

Mac thought of his next target, a lone mission, no backup, no air cover – just how he liked it. He received his orders, prepared and left. No fuss, no messing, get out there and get back – sorted. Sniping didn't quite match the adrenaline rush of surprise raids or rescue operations, but by this stage in his career he liked to work alone, he was getting a name for it now. He had mates of course and even felt love for his comrades, but he'd lost so many it couldn't help but harden you. This unit didn't drink that much, for a start their operations were based on tiny percentages, if you weren't quite on the money you weren't coming back. It was dangerous enough as it was for Christ's sake. Mac knew that booze made the boys maudlin and sentimental for lost comrades, and they learnt together the hard way they avoid that as much as possible.

Sure, on R&R, get pissed with your mates and family back home, talk about something else, football or their civvy street jobs, wonder how they go and sell cars or do peoples' accounts and all that. Have a few beers and talk crap. But here, in the desert, with men who know, conversations rarely strayed beyond ops they'd been on, great mates they'd lost, family even. Throw booze on that fire and it always ended badly, tears, fighting and bitter recriminations and the loss of your edge.

It still happened in the regular army and other Special Forces units, senior officers still talked about men letting off steam. But maybe Mac's unit had been together too long, they were a fiercely united team and let nothing get in the way of that. They were hungry too. Mac smiled to himself at the cliché, but they were literally lean, mean fighting machines. Not an ounce of fat on any of them, the camp cook quickly learnt the men wouldn't tolerate anything that would bloat or slow them down. It was all tacit, no histrionics, just how it was.

New additions to the team didn't have to be told, the unit had something of a reputation plus they would've come across team members in training where at first they feared them, then respected them then loved them. It's just *how it was*. With that platitude settling in his head, Captain John MacKinnon grabbed his kit and entered the late afternoon heat on his latest mission.

Jack ended the call from Major Bradley Wilkinson, a rather perfunctory call letting him know that he had contacted a colleague at a rehab unit over in Barnes Bridge and that the word was out to keep an eye out for any cases that may tally with his investigation. What was Jack thinking would happen? That the Major would line up five likely candidates so him and Merton could pop over and match the right candidate. He supposed it was his tone, a bit disinterested or distracted, hung over even. He probably had an old style army lunch having a good laugh at the rozzers. Jack was miles away in this reverie when his phone rang, Annie wondering if he was coming out to play later. The way this case was going, he certainly bloody would be. The frustration of the case was mitigated by time with Annie, who was now in the midst of her summer holidays.

He teased her about it but knew full well she deserved every minute of her summer break and slept most of the first week and preferred Jack to be busy. Some days he'd get in gone 6 o'clock, and she'd be curled up in a tiny ball on their sofa, Earnie looking decidedly unwalked but sat on the end of the sofa, his big black head resting on her feet. He'd always leap up and greet Jack with undiluted glee yet Annie would barely flinch, the slits of her eyes widening a touch then snapping shut again. 'Hmmm,' the reply to the news Jack was taking their poor neglected dog out.

Jack had made it to their end of term booze up, some cursory 'nibbles' on a table in the Oxford Arms courtesy of the head teacher lining their stomachs for a mammoth session. It was always his pet hate to arrive late when everyone was smashed, but here he was struck by how exhausted everyone looked; even Magda, radiant with her maths teaching new beau, looked in need of a long sleep.

Anyway, she'd had her week's hibernation and was ready to play again, and Jack allowed the warmth of that realisation to rush through him and mop up his current disenchantment. A meal in Nahling with their aromatic Thai food and a stroll up to the beer garden at the Flask was a great prospect later on. Just a day of banging his head against a brick wall while a crack sniper led them all a merry dance to get through.

Mac darted and squirrelled his way to the canal and crawled through dense undergrowth looking for his target. He came across a netted area and sniffed. Yes, definitely animal life, the sweet foul smell of monkey, definitely other animals too. He could hear the insistent nag of a chimpanzee, was that an elephant? A lion? He screwed up his face rubbing his hands hard over the stubbled contours desperately trying to work out where he was. Was that a macaw squawking overhead? He needed an elevated position and fast – when unsure of your position, get higher as soon as possible.

11

George Dingle strode through Regents Park enjoying the slight breeze that had crept in from the south-west helping the shade to cool him down even further after a roasting on Oxford Street. Shopping for his wife Pearl was the only blot on his otherwise blissful London life. He looked for all the world the bluff Yorkshireman he was, and he knew he played up to it too when it suited. He was 62 years old and felt nowhere near it though his bald head hinted at it. He was very fit and as an ex-army man, very disciplined. After a 15 year stint in the Army, he made a small fortune in electronics in Sheffield before meeting Pearl at a conference in London. A wedding followed a short romance, and with all and sundry raising their eyebrows, George sold up and moved down to London to live with Pearl in Belsize Park, George finally able to put an unhappy divorce behind him.

Pearl, at only 50, chose to keep working at her bank in the City, and it worked really well. George never took her or their marriage for granted and knew people back home hadn't fancied his chances, but here they were 10 years later very happy indeed. No one thought he'd take to London, but despite banging on about 'southern softies' all the time, he loved the place. Whenever he went home, he couldn't help feeling Sheffield felt small and while it was nice to visit he always felt more alive when the M1 gave way to Finchley and beyond. He kept busy by doing a bit of consultancy work and mentoring disadvantaged young people. Mostly, though, he loved to get out and walk around the City. He felt uniquely blessed to be in the position to do what he chose every day without having to worry about money. He had plenty to reflect on, and his walking was the best thinking time he could remember. He would then cook for Pearl or take her out for dinner with their many friends or as he preferred, just the two of them.

He never tired of his routine such that it was, and he thanked his lucky stars every single day. He saw something new or interesting every day, he lapped it up, even the sometimes horrific things like the time he came across a body in the canal snaking through Camden. It's fair to say George wasn't squeamish and virtually oversaw the operation to pull the corpse from the water. He then walked on, getting on with his day. It was hard to surprise George Dingle.

Until today that is. He decided he wanted to take a detour along the canal near London Zoo, so he could follow the canal sneaking views of the animals and listen to the strange myriad of sounds that every zoo emitted.

Mac was high up in the canopy struggling to work out his position, he'd lost his radio and binoculars. He also felt dizzy, and a slow wave of nausea washed over him followed by an arctic chill. He was shaking and had never felt more alone. What was happening to him? He was high up a tree, and was that London Zoo he was overlooking? Jesus Christ. He closed his eyes, he felt a very sudden urge to sleep.

The mix of aromas from the zoo reminded George of a tour to Malaysia or Malaya as it was called then when he was part of regular patrols in the jungle. His mates hated the heat and moaned constantly. As a sergeant, he had to lead by example, but apart from the cloying humidity, he liked the jungle, bewitched by the wildlife and awestruck by the people who made life work in the most challenging of conditions. He was startled out of his memoir by a dark shape hurtling in his peripheral vision into the canal with a huge splash. The canal side was busy with mid-afternoon walkers, and there were shrieks of disbelief and everyone crowded in to see what was happening.

George quickly realised the shape was human and jumped straight into the water. He was surprised how cold and deep it was, nearly up to his neck. He grabbed what turned out to be a man in his early thirties with his fishing gear by the look of it, plenty of blokes liked to fish on the canal. He was gasping for air and looked like a trapped animal, looking desperately around at the gathering crowd, he was shaking from the shock.

'Hey, hey calm down, come on, look at me, don't worry about them,' said George urgently while shouting for an ambulance.

'No! No ambulance, I'm ok,' he said spitting rank canal water and clearing green weed off his face.

'Don't be daft, mate, come on, they'll check you over, you'll be fine.'

'No way, I've got to go.'

George looked at the man, wiry frame, closely cropped hair.

'You army?'

'What?' he gasped.

'You know, are you in the army?'

He didn't answer but held his bag closer to him, almost hugging the gear as he started to shake more violently.

'Suit yourself,' said George as he led him to the side as a packed pleasure boat had slowed to take in the scene, the skipper asking George if he could help. George tried to take the bag off the man, but he grabbed it and held it like George was King Herod.

'Alright mate, I'm just trying to help.'

They climbed out of the canal, and George recognised the rattle in the bag straight away but was quickly distracted by the crowd surrounding them.

Given the man seemed ok, no one seemed to know what to do. A group were discussing in plummy tones whether they should donate their picnic blanket, the discussion was becoming animated and heading to a row. George shook his head in despair, and other people started asking him what they could do. George stood up to speak to the crowd who were wondering about an ambulance, calling the police and getting the man some tea. People were looking in all directions, pointing this way and that, some were even filming and tweeting. They could hear a siren in the distance, and when George finally looked down again, the man was gone.

At last, a lead. The incident room was low on incident, high on frustration and tedium. But when Merton took a call from a Yorkshire sounding man called George who thought he might have some useful information for them, there was an immediate buzz. 'I'll come with you, Merton, let's go,' said Jack already halfway out of the door.

Jack warmed to George Dingle immediately. Though expensively attired, it didn't quite sit with him as though he was slightly apologetic about it. The Ralph Lauren shirt didn't quite fit, a little too big, the chinos ever so slightly too short. Not that he was coy or shy, far from it. He bristled confidence and looked completely at home in the dingy room where they normally interviewed suspects. George Dingle looked like he'd prefer to be in a uniform concluded Jack.

Merton and Jack sat before him, and he just looked into Jack's eyes waiting to start. The room was stuffy despite a rattling fan and the strip light buzzed mournfully above them for all the world sounding like it would finally give out. The faint smell of sweat and more insistent disinfectant was very familiar to all three men.

Before Jack could start, George raised both hands. 'I don't know if this is relevant, but something tells me it is.' His voice was loud and proud, unmistakably Yorkshire with that unwavering sense of certainty that dares you to disagree. 'He just fell out of a tree, a bloody tall one too. I couldn't believe my eyes to tell you the truth. I've been all over the world, and I can tell you I've never seen a grown man fall out of a tree before into a canal. Bloody barmy I tell you, Mr…?'

'Love, Jack Love.'

'What rank?'

'Detective Inspector and this is Detective Sergeant Merton?'

George seemed content with the answer. 'Thing is, I've been in the army, and you come to recognise very quickly those who are like you, eh? A nose for those in the job you'd probably say.'

The two detectives nodded. 'Yes, well he was definitely army or ex-army at least. I asked him of course,' said George as if it was the most obvious thing in the world to do.

Jack managed to get a word in as he paused, 'George, just take us through what happened from the start, will you please?'

'Ok right…' Beads of sweat were forming on his forehead, whereas Jack and Merton had long since melted, Jack fantasising about air con.

'I was walking up from Oxford Street after running an errand for the wife,' George tutted and raised his eyes to the sweating ceiling and groaning strip light. 'Go on,' said Jack quietly.

'Well, I headed up through Regents Park loving the shade and peace to be honest with you and decided to head to the canal by the zoo. This weather kills a Yorkshireman.'

'And a Welshman,' smiled Jack.

'And a Croydon boy,' said Merton. The three men shared a brief smile then George continued.

'It was cooler, and I was reminiscing about Malaya, the jungle and everything. The animals always remind me of that time, the smell, the noises, so, you know… foreign I suppose. Anyway, next thing I know, there's a huge splash, and there he is, this startled bloke in the canal struggling to see what was going on. So was I to be truthful,' said George slowly shaking his head, fixing his gaze on the wall behind the detectives.

'Naturally, I jumped in the water to see if he was ok.'

'Naturally,' echoed Jack wondering if he would do the same, rapidly concluding probably not.

'Here's the thing, I helped him out of the water with his gear…' He hesitated.

'What, George? What is it?'

'Well, that's the thing… the gear. I assumed it was fishing gear. It's just he was really protective of it, you know? But it was the rattle that gave it away. It wasn't fishing gear, it was a weapon, a rifle of some sort in my opinion. In the brief touch I managed, it was unmistakable really. I felt the barrel and the sight. In the fuss after, I clean forgot I'm afraid.' His face clouded with irritation.

'What fuss, George?'

'People were crowding round, trying to help, getting in the way, asking questions, shouting, some were laughing, even taking bloody photos, you know? Then I'll be buggered, he disappeared. People were pointing this way and that, banging on about the police and ambulances and that. I stood up trying to take charge, and when I looked down, he had gone, just like that.' George clicked his fingers.

Jack and Merton were nodding in sync both thinking the same thing, they looked at each other, Jack nodded for Merton to ask the big question.

'George, can you describe him for us?'

A look of triumph suddenly beamed on the old soldier's face. 'Oh yes, that I can.'

Mac ran and ran. He whimpered as he ran, tears and sweat breaking into his eyes. He ran barging people out of the way as he went, not caring he was blowing his cover, completely and utterly. He just had to get home, that's all that mattered. The sight of Kentish Town High Street brought a wave of relief, and he pounded up the stairs of his building and collapsed in the cool of his hallway. His heart was beating through his chest as he lay star-shaped on his carpet, fixating on the bulb above him. It was swinging after the opening of the door and Mac watched it swing to and fro.

He woke two hours later soaking wet, a rancid stench of the canal about him mixed with fervent sweat filling the narrow hallway. A pizza menu was stuck to his head, and after pulling that off, he noticed the card for the unit and the bold name of Jane Harkness. He dialled her number and felt relief when Dr Harkness picked up. Emergency appointment with a surprised but composed Harkness duly arranged for the morning, Mac promptly fell asleep again.

Jack was grateful to George, but it was clear when briefing Wallace later that it still didn't amount to much. George's description was adequate, slim and wiry, black closely cropped hair with a light bald patch. He reckoned he was mid-thirties. They would pore through the CCTV footage and appeal for social media photos of course, but Jack still felt they needed more.

Wallace agreed. 'It's progress, Jack, I'm grateful for that at least, but somehow we need more, get Merton on the CCTV as soon as, would you?'

'He already is, he's with Camden Council now, he couldn't wait.'

'Keep me posted.'

'Of course, ma'am.'

Jane was struck by Mac's tone. It seemed desperate. She asked him if he was ok, and he just laughed bitterly and more than a little dismissively. Something about the exchange made her bristle, and she found herself sitting bolt upright in her chair when normally comfort was the priority. Something was going on, and she couldn't wait for the morning. She made a mental note to mention it to Collins and prepared for her next appointment.

12

Jack and Merton were no strangers to the control room at Camden Council, and they nodded to Bob Greening on the way into the blissfully cool room with banks of screens that always reminded Jack of shots of NASA he watched when he was a boy. Bob Greening was 'ex-job' and headed up the Camden Community Safety Partnership. He took early retirement five years ago and, an already large man, gave the appearance of enjoying his less stressful role at the Council as well as his free time. He openly admitted to Jack at the Christmas party that it was the best thing he'd ever done and Jack remarked every time he saw him how well he looked. Retirement scared him to death, so the role was perfect, involved enough to give him focus, relaxed enough to switch off at 5 every night.

Jack liked him a lot and warmly shook his hand as did Merton, a ritual they always observed despite frequent meetings. Bob had become an expert at following the patterns of CCTV and a whiz at operating close ups and producing pin-point photos. They left the buzz of the main room and adjourned to a smaller room rather that Bob grandly called the MCR, the Master Control Room.

Bob affected a studied indifference of a man who did this every day as they took their seats but couldn't hide his intrigue at what they were studying. Jack and Merton sat on the edge of their seats like kids at a Star Wars premiere. It took a frustratingly long time to catch a first glimpse as the canal sections near London Zoo and Regents Park had poor camera coverage. Luckily, the suspect headed in a north easterly direction running past Chalk Farm tube station, battering his way through the slow moving crowds, zombified by the stifling heat.

Jack sighed, 'the way he angles his head, it's like he knows where the cameras are.'

'Come on Jack, be patient,' replied Bob quietly.

Jack sighed again, 'I know, been done by these pictures before, you know that, they're never the panacea to crime everyone thinks they are.'

Despite Bob's insistence on patience, the pictures continued to be of inconsistent quality, a constant bugbear to all concerned. The Civil Liberties lobby often complained but if they could see how haphazard it all was, how many cameras were out of order or just of dismal quality they'd be instantly reassured.

Bob sat forward with his remote control, the indifference long evaporated. 'Hang on lads, this is better, hello matie, how are you doing, nice to see you at last.' The suspect was approaching Kentish Town Road in Camden Town, and it seemed George was spot on in his description. He was indeed wiry and shortish, five foot four or five maybe. He had short black cropped hair with a bald patch.

Jack looked at Merton and felt the slight giddiness of a long-awaited breakthrough. They'd waited a long time for this, and Merton's smile was pure relief. The detectives watched in awe as Bob zoomed in on their man and printed off the many shots they wanted. Bob could not hide his pride of helping in such a big case. He always enjoyed the proper police work element of the job, and this was as good as it gets. They thanked him and observed another time honoured ritual, buying Bob a pint over the Oxford Arms, an offer he had never ever, refused. He collected the photos from the printer, and the three men set off for the pub with purpose despite the steaming heat of the day.

Jack got the drinks in, ice cold bottles of Peroni that lasted a mere gulp or two given the stultifying city heat of the afternoon. Jack ordered three more, a tiny hint of a breeze offering no more relief than a low powered hairdryer tickling his arms. The Oxford didn't stretch to air-conditioning, but all the windows were open as were the doors, letting in the noise of a Camden day and the smell of frying onions and meat. Tourists staggered in gasping like Legionnaires lost in the desert and flopped in seats mopping sweat from their brows. The temperature had hit 39 degrees in parts of the south-east, Gravesend in fact, according to the breaking news ticker on Sky News.

Jack brought the drinks over, and the men sipped at them this time, savouring the refreshing brew without a chorus of shocked belches like the first round. Bob caught up with some Muswell Hill gossip, laughing or nodding gravely as appropriate before they moved onto their afternoon's work in the control room.

'So, what do you think, boys?' asked Bob.

Jack took a sip of his lager and thought for a moment, 'It's good, Bob, no question, but I'm struck by his ordinariness, he's almost too normal looking. Does that make sense?' Jack pulled one of the photos out of the file, 'I mean, I forget what he looks like the moment I put this down, do you know what I mean?' Merton nodded grimly.

'I do Jack but that's not the point is it? The point is we, sorry, you get the photo out and someone will recognise him for sure, bound to.'

'You're right, Bob, of course, you're right, but I get the feeling this isn't the breakthrough we all think it is. For a start, the photos are decent at best, and I'm not convinced he'll be known in any locale.'

Bob shook his head, 'What do you mean? You're not going to give me this hairy old bollocks about lonely old London where everyone is anonymous, and you can hide like a field mouse. What is it about this man? You're being so negative about finding him.'

Jack was instantly reminded of why Bob was so valued in the station and why he was so liked, he suddenly remembered umpteen rallying calls issued from an inspirational Bob Greening with his North London brogue when the chips were down. And yet, and yet…

Jack took another thoughtful sip of his beer as Merton turned to Bob, 'thing is Bob, he's so elusive, we've had a bloody author unable to describe him, others who can barely remember if it was a man or woman. I've never known anything like it. They've all said the same thing, how quickly he moved and how they could barely recall anything about him.'

'Who's this bloody author?'

'Alan Wild.'

'Never heard of him.'

'Can you read?'

'Very funny. He's probably too busy googling himself to even notice the world revolving. You know what those la di da wankers are like up there, not remotely connected to the real world.'

'He was gutted about his dog,' said Merton.

'Nah, just another writing project for his creative writing class in some goddam awful night school class full of tossers pretending they can be the next John Grisham.'

'John Grisham!' Merton and Jack cried simultaneously.

'What's wrong with John Grisham?'

'Used to be a lawyer,' Jack smiled.

'Fair point,' laughed Bob, 'what do they know? Wankers. Mind you, Grisham wasn't CPS was he? What a shower of bastards they are, wouldn't prosecute a mass murderer who did it live on the One Show cos of "insufficient evidence to warrant a realistic prospect of conviction."'

'Might get a knighthood for services to television, though,' said Merton and the three men laughed.

'Thing is Jack, it's more than you've had so far, by a mile by the sounds of it so let it, ride, see what it throws up. Our cameras have given worse and thrown up shots that have given us convictions, stop being so bloody gloomy, it's not like you at all, Happy Jack my arse.'

Jack smiled and nodded. Bob was spot on, he was unusually gloomy about it, maybe it was the punishing heat, but he couldn't shake the feeling they had a long hard road to travel yet.

13

Jane and Major Collins bumped into each other on the river, Collins taking a moment to savour the slight cool relief morning was bringing to Londoners. A breeze threaded along the river from the south-west also helping a touch, and Collins closed his eyes and took a deep breath.

'Penny for them…' said Jane pinching his arm gently.

'Ah, Jane, couldn't sleep either eh?' It was a quarter to eight, and neither of them needed to get to the unit before nine in reality as appointments never kicked off earlier than 10am.

'You were miles away, everything ok?'

Collins seemed thrown a touch by the question. 'Yes, fine thank you.'

Jane hid she felt a bit stung by his defensive reply and actually inwardly reprimanded herself as anything could be going through his mind, given his military experiences. He must have 'moments' every single day. She'd had clients that said their traumatic incident, whatever it may be, was their first thought in the morning and last thought at night. Maybe that's how it was for Collins.

Almost imperceptibly, he shook his head and turned to Jane. 'Coffee?'

Jane looked unnecessarily at her wrist and said, 'great idea, it is way too early anyway.'

'Did your naked wrist tell you that?'

'What?' It was Jane's turn to be defensive though it quickly turned to an embarrassed laugh. Jane had unnecessarily looked at her watch because she had never worn one. She rubbed her naked wrist then hit Collins with her Metro, 'Cheeky! You're getting the coffees in for that.'

'Fine by me.'

They settled companionably on a large brown leather sofa near the window in Waldo's, a coffee shop with killer views of the river, Collins taking a sip of his cappuccino, Jane breaking the end off her croissant.

'I take it you saw the news this morning,' said Collins. Jane blushed, her unintentional avoidance of news still a source of consternation for her despite endless resolutions to 'get with it' as her husband would say. The reality was she was dancing round her bedroom to Bruno Mars this morning, to the hilarity of her boys.

'No, missed it this morning,' she said quickly.

'We have a problem.'

'Oh look, I will start watching it, I always forget, I prefer a bit of music in the morning that's all. Has someone complained?'

Collins, despite the gravity of the predicament, couldn't help laughing.

'Don't be ridiculous,' he said smiling incredulously, 'it's just there have been developments in the dog shooting case. Have you actually looked at your Metro this morning? National and London news had photos from CCTV of a possible suspect.'

'Really? That's interesting, I mean who the hell would want to shoot dogs?' she said as she looked at the front page of the Metro, eyebrows shooting up as she did so.

'Well, it's only a line of enquiry according to DI Love.'

'Who?'

Collins frowned but it lifted as soon as it arrived. 'He's the policeman heading the shot dogs enquiry.'

'Oh right, of course.'

'Anyway,' Collins betrayed he was in the foothills of exasperation, 'the point is the photos looked very much like a certain Capt John MacKinnon.'

Mac had watched the news that morning. From very early, 3am to be precise. He had woken from a particularly grisly dream that involved torture, kidnap and a firefight. He woke screaming as the main kidnapper was about to drive a sword through his belly. He was so wet with sweat it looked like he'd emerged from a pool. He'd also defecated. Swearing profusely he cleaned up, put new sheets on the bed and sat in a blanket in his living room watching the news. He was amazed to see his face third item in after an Afghanistan massacre and a political storm over a cabinet minister's expenses claims.

His mind swam wildly, what were they saying? Shooting dogs? Voices in his head were saying I'm finished and what the hell are they talking about at the same time. One thing was for sure, he was terrified. The policeman, Love was being interviewed saying they want to speak to this man urgently and that people can ring the incident room or contact Crimestoppers anonymously. He also said no one should approach this man.

'Shit,' he muttered over and over and over again.

Jane just stood and gently shook her head.

'I know, I was shocked too, I must admit. These men mean so much to us all, you must know already that you feel each man is our personal responsibility,' said Liam.

'He's due in this morning at 10am, he's my first of the day.'

'I know.'

'What do I do?'

'Well that's just it, Brad Wilkinson from Whitehall met me the other day to tell me Love had contacted him about the possibility the suspect could be services or ex-services given his brilliant shooting ability. Turns out it might just be a very good deduction.'

'Liam, I really feel I'm getting somewhere with him, I'm getting him to talk at least. If he is shooting dogs and I'm certainly not taking that for granted, I don't care what this Love says, then he is obviously really damaged and disturbed and surely doing the right thing by coming to us?'

'I agree, but we have a duty to tell the police, Wilkinson was adamant about this. We always look after our own, and I hate the idea of coppers sniffing around, but we cannot ignore this.'

'I agree but does that mean we have to do something straight away? I mean, I'd really like our session to go ahead as normal this morning.'

'If he turns up.'

Mac was shocked and scared but strangely exhilarated too by his 'appearance' on the news. He knew the papers would be full of it and that his face would be everywhere for a day or two. He deliberately chose to live in London because you could be anonymous, move around unseen and no one bothered you. He veered wildly between the naked fear of getting caught and the challenge of getting to Barnes Bridge unseen. All accompanied by a distant but insistent voice telling him over and over, 'I need help, I need help.'

'He'll turn up, Liam, I'm absolutely convinced of it,' said Jane.

'Ok, I agree, getting spotted won't necessarily faze him, given his training. My hunch is the police will catch up with him pretty quickly, but Jane, I want to see you as soon as the session is concluded, ok?'

For the first time, Jane felt she was being given orders by Major Collins.

'Fine, do you want me to raise it during the session?'

'See how it goes, if you are able to, then do it.' Liam straightened his tie unnecessarily, he was always immaculate. He was concerned but felt very energised too, he couldn't deny it.

The early morning cool had already dissipated as Mac walked to the tube. He knew that looking conspicuous was a bad move, so he strolled almost nonchalantly, no one even glancing in his direction. Part of him expected the 'Butch Cassidy and the Sundance Kid' treatment on opening his building's main door. But no, a homeless man glanced at him then resumed his search for cigarette butts. Mac donned a cricket hat as his one concession to avoiding being too cocky. The joys of good old London Town thought Mac as he strode towards the tube aware his heart was pounding through his chest. He imagined people could see it and phone the police immediately.

Jane was nervous, not a feeling she was overly familiar with. It was rare that her clients had the imminent threat of arrest hanging over them. She had counselled some pretty nasty people or damaged as she preferred to think of them. Drug dealers in prison, rapists and paedophiles, but never someone she was warned would be the subject of arrest on her watch. She flipped on the kettle, looked at the Old Man of Storr print on her wall and imagined Mac running wild up there far from the madding crowd. Did it humble you? Liberate you? What? Jane had never been one for the great outdoors. A stroll along the river was fine, yomping through mountains assuredly wasn't. Too far from a flat white for a start, a thought so silly she couldn't help smiling. It's just how she was really. 'Tough,' she said out loud. She thought how cosseted her life was especially when compared to the horrors her clients had experienced.

Those with their limbs intact – Did they relish the space and freedom far from the noise and bustle of civilian city life? She just didn't know. She would ask Mac.

'Tell you about the Isle of Skye?' said Mac. Often with difficult clients, she'd start the session with a question out of leftfield, she found it disarmed someone with a bit on their mind. Someone like Mac. He laughed, but his eyes weren't smiling. In fact, they darted around as he fingered his hat. He saw the news then thought Jane provoking a sudden wave of heart-breaking pity for Mac.

'Why do you ask?' He smiled again, but he was somewhere else.

'It's just you mentioned it in our first session, and I was wondering about it. I'm not one for countryside myself.'

'Countryside?' he replied sharply, very much back in the room. Jane shrugged and held his gaze.

'I wouldn't call the North West Highlands, "Countryside"'

'Wouldn't you?'

'No,' frowned Mac.

'Mac, indulge me a bit here, I just want to know what the Isle of Skye is like, that's all.' She turned, took a sip of her tea and looked out of the window, the first morning walks emerging beneath her, nurses pushing wheelchairs and chatting away as they headed for the river. When she looked up, he was standing in front of the print. 'There are no people,' he said at last, 'well, not many anyway. You get the tourists holed up in Portree, Sligachan and Broadford, but it's easy to lose yourself.'

'Lose yourself?'

'Yes, get to a place where you don't have to think, or think as much as you like, where you blend in with nature. I've done a lot of training up there, survival, special forces manoeuvres and all that.' Mac waved his arm like he was dismissing some menial administrative tasks he'd done.

'People say it's remote but what does that mean? It reminds me of the desert in a way, the stark beauty but with eagles rather than people wanting to blow you up. I don't like people if I'm honest.'

'Why not?' Mac just stared back at her, all the empathy in the world couldn't compute what was going through Mac's mind. He stared through Jane and was gone again.

'Do you feel you want to hurt people?'

'I have hurt people.'

'In battle?'

'Oh yes, in battle. I've killed people, I've told you that, it's what we do.'

'What about outside the theatre of war?' Jane asked feeling a bit of shame at being so pleased with herself for using military terminology.

'Theatre of war? Jesus Christ,' sighed Mac. Jane blushed and shrugged again.

'What about you? Have you hurt anyone?'

Jane laughed, spread her arms wide, 'Broken a few hearts, obviously. Don't laugh, Capt Mackinnon, I was quite sought after, back in the day, you know.'

'I can imagine...' Jane didn't know or care if he was being sarcastic, it was just good he was genuinely smiling and laughing.

'You sounded pretty distressed when I spoke to you, yesterday.' Mac looked down gravely, brow furrowed like rolls of puppy fat, enough to bring Jane close to tears. 'What's happened, Mac?' He put his head in his hands.

'Honestly? I don't know, I think I'm hurting people, but I don't know for sure.'

'What do you mean, "hurting people?"'

'It's hard to explain, and I'm not even sure myself.'

'Mac, relax and try to tell me what's in your mind, on your mind, what you think you've been doing. Take your time.'

'The police want to talk to me in connection with shooting dogs, you know, that tosser from Mile High and some other dogs. I mean it's nuts, I love animals.'

'So, why you?'

'That's just it, I don't know, part of me thinks it's some mad mistake but then…' Mac stared out over the grounds to the river and the haze beyond, the metropolis grinding on and on, indifferent to whatever the hell this man had or had not done. A barge sounded its horn as if to prompt Mac it was time to continue. 'But then, I find myself on the floor of my flat, and I don't know where I've been. I'm out, and I find myself in bushes or soaking wet or up trees.'

Mac covered his eyes and threw his head back, 'truth is, it could be me, seems so ridiculous, I love dogs but then…' Mac's speech was peppered with contradictions, inner conflict and turmoil laid bare.

'You said you hurt people?' asked Jane.

'I guess by shooting their dogs, I am hurting people, if it's me,' 'Have you ever had a dog, Mac?' Jane asked.

He looked down at his hat, picked at some imaginary dirt. 'Yeah, when I was a kid.'

'Tell me about it.'

'He was a glorious black Labrador, 'Jimmy' we called it, and he was my best friend by a mile, we grew up together for a while really as we got him from a pup.' 'For a while?' reflected Jane.

'When he was three, and I was ten, he got hit by a car, I'd just let him off his lead near the park, and he charged across the road towards the fields. I let him off too soon and bang!' Mac clapped his hands once, startling Jane. 'He never stood a chance.'

This reminiscence didn't bring on any emotion at all. Jane noted that, if anything, he became totally impassive. More than that, he had shut down. She was convinced that at that moment, nothing short of shaking him would bring him round. So she said nothing, sipped her tea, stood up and went to the window.

There was no breeze now, it was sweltering. She wondered how long London could stand this weather. Records were tumbling on a daily basis it seemed to her. Bloody Gravesend had beaten the highest temperature three days running, hitting 40.2 degrees on the third day. The nurses had long abandoned their river walks, and the grounds were empty bar a wiry soldier running with uncanny speed towards the river path and Barnes Bridge. 'Shit.'

Major Liam Collins' ashen-faced countenance quickly gave way to laughter, huge whooping gales of laughter. Jane, so mortified only moments before, quickly gave into the contagion of laughter.

'So, any other clients done a runner and jumped in the river?' They were off again with Jane's stomach beginning to hurt. When they eventually calmed, Collins said he was going to ring Major Bradley Wilkinson in Whitehall and tell him they have their man.

'I don't like you betraying Mac's confidence.'

'But Jane, you know what the rules are, and he knows the police want him.'

'I know, but I think we were getting somewhere, he could be in real trouble if it's him.'

Liam introduced Jane before asking, 'What did he say?'

'He told me he was worried he was hurting people. It's like his mind is fragmented, different parts are thinking different things. He needs help not the police on his tail.'

'But if he is running around with a rifle, and I think we know he is, then we have to stop him, you know we do.' Jane nodded but hated it was true. She catastrophised about what jail might do to Mac. She just knew it wasn't the answer.

Since the photo was released, the press were all over it, it was the only story in town. It was August, the Westminster village was dormant, England was enjoying a steady but unspectacular series against New Zealand and footballers were avoiding the front pages. Papers had withdrawn to their stock issues, the Mail was scaring everyone about immigration, the Express was fixated on the weather and various miracle cures while the Star, Sun and Mirror had the usual tittle-tattle about various celebrities. The initial 'Houndsdead Heath' story had died down, but now there had been a spotting and a photo released, they all seized on it like piranhas. Jack's assigned press officer, Anna, was under siege but calmly dealt with each call in her usual professional manner.

Major Bradley Wilkinson was knee deep in reviews and reports. With the government chasing cheaper and more efficient ways of running the armed forces, it fell to Wilkinson to draft the often bad news that had to be communicated internally to staff. His was a very broad remit that included all manner of bolt-ons such as media relations. It seemed to him that things were just tossed to comms for lack of any better idea how it should be handled.

He sighed and pushed another report to the side of his desk. That was why he had to meet, they literally didn't know what to do with it. Not that he minded really, he liked the variety, and it was good to see Collins and learn a bit about his unit he thought as his phone rang. 'Liam, I was just thinking about you funnily enough, what can I do for you?'

Fully expecting it to be Anna again from Scotland Yard's press office, Jack was pleased it wasn't another media call and was instantly intrigued to hear Major Bradley Wilkinson's voice on the other end of the line. 'Bradley, how are you? Right, give me an hour.' Jack hung up and strode into the incident room. 'Merton, leave that, we've got a lead.'

The imposing facade of the MOD Whitehall HQ gave way to a typically drab civil service interior, all dated and worn greys and beige office furniture and a patchwork collection of chairs and workstations. Wilkinson's office was a simple temporary partition, but at least the door closed firmly, and it had a fan. Even the hairdryer effect of the fan was a relief from the tube journey south on the Northern Line.

Wilkinson outlined what he gleaned from Collins. Jack stopped him and got the name and address so Merton could phone it in. The Major told them Captain John MacKinnon might be able to 'help you with your enquiries' and told the detectives of the counselling sessions and that he fitted the description issued by Jack and his team.

'You should know, we believe Capt Mackinnon to be of a fragile state of mind. Early assessments from the unit indicate severe post-traumatic stress disorder, possible multiple personality disorder and delusional behaviour. We're extremely concerned what being apprehended could do to him. The staff were convinced they could make good progress with Captain MacKinnon.'

'Bradley, I don't need to explain why we need to explore this line of enquiry with great urgency, and if he is our man, we have a duty of care when we apprehend him. I will underline this when I brief the team, you have my word on this. I'll obviously keep you in the loop at every stage.'

They shook hands warmly enough, but Jack could sense Bradley was genuinely concerned, and he understood why. Jack though had a sniper to catch and didn't dwell on his concerns, he couldn't at the moment especially as Merton was taking a call.

'Armed response unit is on its way, sir.'

'Right, good.'

Except it wasn't good. Armed response units weren't known for their duty of care, he knew they had to be involved but treading carefully had to be the first priority in the first instance. 'Shit, get me the boss on the phone,' he barked at Merton as he remembered his pledge to Major Bradley Wilkinson.

14

Mac was stationed in a horse chestnut tree high above his road in Kentish Town. He was 50 yards away from his building and watched wearily as the tell-tale signs of a raid made their inevitable appearance. An urge to survive pumped through him like high-octane fuel and he was more lucid and aware than he had been for weeks. He knew he was in trouble, though he wondered what they actually had on him.

He'd stashed his gun in the top floor's roof terrace, the built-in storage space unused and barely visible should the police ever get that far. The quest to remain undetected gave Mac focus. He pondered his predicament as a grin formed and stretched across his face. The fact is he could avoid detection with minimal effort. But did he want that?

He watched the SO19 officers creeping round like beetles in the dust. Slow, slow, quick, quick, slow. He heard a rapid banging on his door and a series of shouts and finally his door being stoved in. Around 20 officers had burst into his flat and were crawling all over it.

'Can I help you?' Mac stood in the doorway, the familiar sight of his flat disturbed by such unfamiliar beings. His drawers were turfed out all over the floor and cupboards were being taken apart.

'I said, can I help you?' The feverish activity suddenly ceased. The men looked aggrieved someone had the temerity to stop their work. Not a new feeling but Captain

John MacKinnon never expected 20 guns to be trained on him in his Kentish Town flat on a hot afternoon in August.

'Ok, Merton, they've got him, let's get back, sort out an ID parade will you?' With a prime suspect apprehended, Jack could usually sense the end of the case, the taste of the celebratory beers, the paperwork to be taken care of. But not this time. The gnawing uncertainty that had been his faithful companion throughout this case showed no sign of leaving his side. This was enhanced when SO19 told him he just strolled into his flat during the search.

'He asked if there was anything he could do?'

'Yep, as he was bundled into the car.'

'He's either barking mad or the coolest guy on the planet.'

'He's a fucking nutter,' was the SO19 officer's neat summary.

The cool of the cells was almost sensual in the way it wrapped itself around Jack. He took a moment and peered through the small window, the faint aroma of piss and disinfectant battling it out before piss emerged triumphant. He rested his elbows on the door and looked at Captain John MacKinnon, a globe of sweat bursting on his neck and momentarily cooling the middle of his back as it made its unsteady way south.

The captain was sat bolt upright at the table staring straight ahead. Jack blinked and he was gone. Startled he looked left and right, locating him in the right-hand corner two yards from the officer on guard but silent. Looking unblinking towards the opposite wall, a sheen of condensation apparently of great interest. Jack heard a door slam and instantly looked to his left to see if Merton was joining him. He wasn't, a desk sergeant was performing some duty with another suspect. When he looked back, Mac was at the window staring straight into his eyes barely six inches from his face. Jack gasped and stumbled backwards, feeling hot and extremely bothered, the unease spreading through him like jungle fever. When he went back to the window, the captain was seated once again, bolt upright staring at a very uncomfortable guard.

'Are you ok, Jack?' Merton said as he approached with a lawyer looking like she was just stepped out of an ad for some swanky drink in what Jack would swear would be called a 'little black dress.' Jack guessed she could be no more than twenty-five, her black hair, Japanese straight and long with an immaculate fringe. Tabitha Richards introduced herself beating Merton to it, her cold, dry and very firm handshake taking Jack by surprise, as did a cockney accent that would've reminded the Krays of 'their old mum.'

'Yeah, fine thanks, Merton.' He looked at Tabitha, 'good to meet you, Tabitha.'

'Tabby, please,' she spat back. 'now, can we get on please, there's somewhere I'd much rather be and I can't see this taking long.'

'Can't you?' said Jack, instantly admiring the young turk's front, 'your client is suspected of a very serious set of crimes and if it's ok with you, we'd like to explore if he's actually guilty or not so you can get back to the pub or wherever the hell we've pulled you out of.'

'*Client*,' she whispered, shaking her head slowly.

'What?'

'I prefer "punter"', dropping the 't' so spectacularly that all three of them fell into laughing. She was a piece of work this one. Jack found himself biting his ring finger to prevent himself from laughing more loudly. Moments before he had been so disconcerted by the suspect's behaviour and movement and now he was gnawing on his hand.

Tabby snapped back into business mode, 'Good, now we've broken the ice, let's get this innocent man home shall we?' Her attempt to sweep into the room with authority and purpose was stymied by the locked door, and she crashed into it spilling a dog's flob of her coffee down her little black dress.

'Facking 'ell' she yelled. She turned to the bemused detectives with a look that would've frozen molten lava. Jack ignored this and knocked once loudly on the door. The PC quickly opened it, and Jack nodded for him to leave, the relief palpable on his sweating face.

Captain John MacKinnon watched them come in as if they were coming into his living room, he seemed to own the space completely. Jack felt bolts of discomfort course through him again as he watched Tabitha shake MacKinnon's hand and give his arm a reassuring rub, unnecessarily judging by MacKinnon's unmoving face.

MacKinnon intrigued Jack intensely. After Merton did the formalities and started the tape, Tabitha immediately insisted that the proceedings were a farce. Jack, rapt by MacKinnon's presence, simply held his hand up while holding his gaze. The two men looked at each other, reading each other's faces, assessing each other, MacKinnon implacable, Jack realising immediately this wasn't your everyday scumbag.

'I presume you know why you're here?'

'Yes. I came home one morning to find a gang of armed police in my flat, I'm thinking it's not my overdue library books?'

'You thought right, though the books thing is a bit rude, frankly.'

Mac smiled the quickest of smiles before locking back into immovability.

'You were a sniper, is that correct? Special forces?'

'I am a sniper. Discharged now, though.'

'Why?'

'*Medical reasons*, I think you'd call it.'

'Compassionate discharge according to your records.'

'It did say that on the letter, yes.' Mac's voice was flat though his eyes burned with an astonishing intensity.

Though more composed now, Jack was still entranced by this man.

'Didn't feel very compassionate, they wanted me out, another fuck-up basket case to throw on the scrap heap. Another recruit to the silent ghost army roaming the streets. We're everywhere Inspector, the unwanted, fight your wars, lose your friends, your dignity, kill people then ultimately lose your marbles before you lose your life if you're *lucky*. Act a bit strangely, go off the rails a bit then you're out with well-worded letter telling you to kindly fuck off. Back to civvy street and you're despised for being homeless.'

'You're not homeless.'

'Why am I here?'

'Yes, why is my client here, Detective Inspector?' Tabitha said, this time not remotely as in thrall to the proceedings as Jack. As far as I can see you've no weapon, no evidence, just an army rehab unit shitting their pants that one of their clients might be a notorious pooch popper.' Jack knew she had a point. The CPS would need a very good case put together to even consider it, and that meant hard evidence.

'Capt MacKinnon is helping us with our enquiries, you have to let us do our job, *Tabby*.' Tabby grunted and sat back.

'It is the duty of the people counselling you at the unit to inform the authorities if a client discloses information that suggests involvement in a serious crime. They tell me you think you may have 'hurt people' but you weren't sure how and that sometimes you thought it was you shooting dogs, other times not,' Tabitha sighed. 'Also, the unit tells me you've found yourself in various places without knowing how you got there, including rivers, bushes and woodland.'

'Did the unit also tell you my client is delusional?' asked Tabitha, 'And that he is showing signs of post-traumatic stress disorder?' Jack nodded.

'Yes, so isn't this type of behaviour, if not expected exactly, certainly not untypical? What it clearly doesn't show is that he's been hiding up trees taking out the dogs of the chattering classes.'

'Capt MacKinnon, did you drop into the canal near London Zoo recently?'

'I believe I did, it was a rather startling experience, it's all a bit vague if I'm being honest.' Jack couldn't deny the frown was genuine, a look coloured by confusion and fear.

'What did you have with you that day?'

Mac's frown deepened, 'I don't know, I don't remember really, it's all a bit of a blur.'

'How convenient. Do you remember a man helping you?'

'There seemed to be a lot of people around, it freaked me out actually, I don't really like crowds of people, I need to get away.'

'A man helped you get out of the canal that day. He came forward as your behaviour was so odd and he believed you were carrying a rifle.'

'How would he know?' said Tabitha suddenly sitting up.

'He's ex-army himself, but I don't imagine a rifle would be that hard to identify through a long fishing canvas tackle bag.'

'Oh don't you? Someone from Dad's Army rocks up claiming he *thinks* he may have felt a rifle in a fishing bag. This is all rather desperate, it's going to take the CPS, ooh… seconds to stamp *No Further Action* on this.'

As Mac watched this exchange between Jack and Tabitha, sweat formed, beaded then gushed down his face, his expression of a man who was no longer in the room in any measure other than a physical presence.

Released on bail and allowed to go home, Mac went home and headed straight to bed. He woke after a fitful sleep at 6am, his sheets drenched from a sauna of a night, his fan essentially a quiet hairdryer. His digital clock showed it was 24 degrees outside already. He cursed and got out of bed, but he could already feel his mind was clearer now he had jettisoned those pills. He felt better, sharper and immediately went for his rifle.

Jack walked the half mile to Muswell Hill Police Station a little later than usual and skipped Gino's as a result. Never a slow walker, he was perspiring already though that was as much to do with overdosing on Peroni and red wine the night before. Despite the fug and the heat, he was in good spirits. Tabby's prophecy that the CPS wouldn't want a bar of it wasn't quite true, though there wasn't enough to charge MacKinnon. He was released on bail pending further enquiries, and while disappointed, Jack felt they were very much closing in.

He enjoyed reacquainting himself with Annie and having a proper night off more than he would've imagined in the middle of a case. They did also reacquaint themselves with Danny Koumas and Whoosh when they got home, and one thing led spectacularly to another on the front room carpet.

The CPS decision still meant a severe carpeting from Wallace for Jack and the team. Jack came in for particular fire, 'sloppy' and 'lackadaisical' some of the politer brickbats hurled his way. The description of the investigation as 'lacklustre' really stung as the team had worked extremely hard. They had agreed to meet again when calmer.

Yet Jack was fine that morning. His calm manner hid a thick skin, and he knew Wallace had a point. He also knew that this situation was temporary and that Captain Jack MacKinnon was almost certainly their man. They would watch him and would certainly need more evidence. The CPS wasn't keen at all yet something had shifted in Jack, a sense things were rolling his way was beginning to form though the team didn't share his optimism.

'Someone looks happy, blimey, Happy Jack is true isn't it?' said Merton as Jack bounded into the incident room quite unaware he was smiling broadly.

Jack answered with mock mystery that he didn't know what he meant and disappeared into his own office and shut the door. Wallace was soon knocking on the door, and together they went onto the floor for a progress meeting to follow up and move on from yesterday's custody setback. It was a pretty forlorn affair, a sea of miserable and distracted faces. It took Wallace a little while to get their attention.

Mac glided through Highgate Village, for all the world a man on his way fishing, not that anyone noticed. There were a few coffee drinkers catching a bit of early sun outside Costa Coffee and Café Nero, all engrossed in newspapers or their phones. It was 8am now, and the traffic was heavy. No one gave Mac a second glance and he knew it.

Jack thought Stephanie Wallace was going to explode.

'Never mind the Broadway stabbing for a moment, please, please! Can we have some hush, please? Since when have we just packed in on a case because we couldn't crack it or something better came along? Never, that's when. This is not over, we've got officers on the stabbing and all the other new cases so wake up and get out there.'

Merton was having none of this, 'But Ma'am, we have nothing, this bloke moves unseen, witnesses haven't seen anything barring that author, and he couldn't give us a damn thing, not a sausage. Snouts think we're barmy even asking, it's one dead end after another and the CPS is not impressed.'

'Thank you for your positivity, Sgt Merton, it's been noted.'

'You can't deny it, Ma'am, this is a dead set shocker of a case, we're drawing blank after blank, and just cos some past it rock star's mutt is part of it, we have to pile so many bodies into it. I'm far more interested in the mugs that are beating their women up or stabbing people down the road from here.'

This drew a lot of nods and mutters of agreement and a sharp intake of breath from Jack Love.

'Oh, so you all think this is a waste of time, do you? No matter that this has caused a sensation all over the country, no matter some lunatic is running around with a sniper's rifle and has uncanny expertise in its use. We're all okay with the rash of copycat shootings because we're all a bit bored with police work. It's only dogs, eh? Who cares? I fucking well care, do you hear me? I care.'

'Ma'am,' said Jack.

'Oh what Jack? Going to stick up for your shoddy team, are you? Lunatic snipers aren't a priority cos he's only popping dogs?'

'Actually, Ma'am, I was going to say we all need to calm down a bit and that I agree, we cannot ignore this case just because we're firing blanks the whole time. This man is firing live rounds in public places, and it simply cannot be tolerated. Sure, it's hot, it's hard, but that's no excuse for giving up or being distracted by other cases. Yes, we needed more yesterday, and I hold my hands up to that and,' Jack looked at Wallace, 'I know you've worked so hard on this, but we're getting closer. This is our man, it has to be, he's out on bail not free to disappear. So we tail him, watch every move, every blink of his eye, every wipe of his arse, we'll be there, and soon enough, we'll have him. I'm convinced there's something about him that wants to get caught. As he marched out yesterday, do you know what he said to me? 'Try harder', I nearly knocked him out...' Merton snorted. 'Ok smart-arse, I felt like it, but I think 'try harder' means 'I'm here, come and get me if you can.'

The rumble of traffic suddenly died to a whisper as Mac darted down Merton Lane towards Hampstead Heath, early morning birdsong and the throb of jet engine seamlessly taking its place. He hurried on, careful not to let the enemy get sight of him, some generals said the insurgents were a ragged bunch of amateurs, but he saw too many colleagues get shot for that to be totally true. The SAS taught him to always assume your enemy is well trained and deadly, knock any complacency on the head.

He was running now, fleet and silent through the trees and bushes, clocking and logging enemy positions in his head. Visibility was good for attack though obviously he was concerned he'd be spotted, a lone warrior at 11 o'clock causing him to hit the dirt at the double. He gritted his teeth and watched him pass, not 10 feet away. He focussed on the earth in front of his face, a worm and ants sharing his space. He was transfixed on the worm as it made its way through the dust and dirt, twisting one way then the other. He was startled when a blackbird swooped down and took the bacon coloured grub away to feed the chicks Mac could hear nearby crying for food.

Fortunately, he didn't give his position away and refocussed on the mission at hand. He was quickly on his feet and shot through the bushes to the foot of the thickest oak tree he could locate. He scaled the old giant with the speed and dexterity of a squirrel and was soon in the comfort of the canopy, a world that belonged to the birds and insects. Warm therms whispered through the branches. Mac took his bag from his shoulders and removed the rifle. Silently screwing the sight into place, he surveyed the targets patrolling the ponds. There was more activity now, he would need to be quick. The position of the sun meant sight flash reflection might give him away.

Wallace looked at Jack askance but couldn't help a smile of gratitude. A bit less assertively, Merton cleared his throat to speak again, 'Sir, with respect, this is what I mean, it's like a huge wild goose chase. Have you had any joy with the MOD?'

'I haven't Merton, no. That reminds me, I need to follow up with the Major today actually. But look, wild goose chase or not, this is our job, this is what we do, I'll say it again, he's out there, right now for all we know, with a sniper's rifle – actually, we have a sniper operating on our patch, hear that, a sniper taking out targets in our community, hurting the people we serve, keep that in mind when moaning about dead ends and wild goose chases. He might've stopped, he might take out Battersea Dogs Home tomorrow, he still needs to be caught, and the CPS won't get out of the canteen until we have some serious evidence. I strongly suggest we all go through the notes, pore through the witness statements, re-interview all involved and see if anything new sticks out,' the desk sergeant came in, trying to get Jack's attention as well as whispering in Merton's ear. 'Try that bloody author again for a start, his writer's block might've faded now.'

The target moved slowly towards the water, scanning left and right, a warm breeze had blown up from the south clearing the haze a touch that had settled over the city. Mac noted he was in civilian kit making him more dangerous in his eyes, he had to take him out. The breeze was lurching branches and leaves across his line of sight. He started moving towards the tree Mac had climbed, perhaps he was onto him. The adrenaline started pumping through his veins, but a supernatural calm also enveloped him. He could hear air cover approaching but it was too late, he'd been spotted. The target was now within 20 metres of the tree, and a clear sight was seconds away. The breeze cleared as quickly as it arrived and the heat increased its hold again. A crow landed in the branches above Mac and let out its brutal report. Startled, the target looked up, and his last view in this world was a sniper taking aim straight at his head.

He hit the floor, a clean bullet hole through the forehead instantly releasing a narrow but steady stream of blood.

Merton's eyebrows shot up, his surliness gone. 'Sir.'

'What is it, Merton?'

'He's struck again.'

'See what I'm saying…'

'But sir,' Merton was ashen-faced, 'he's taken out a human this time, shot straight through the forehead by the pond closest to the public toilets in Highgate. Died instantly.'

'When?'

The desk sergeant took up the story saying it was in the last 10 minutes.

Mac scrambled down the tree gripped by a lurch of panic. He heard people screaming and quite a crowd had already gathered, two of which were shouting into their mobile phones. An elderly woman noticed Mac jump down from the last branch of the oak, saw his rifle, pointed and screamed. Everyone turned. Two men immediately ran towards him and stopped when they saw the raised rifle. They raised their hands and edged backwards towards the group. Mac looked about him and saw no one was currently where he had entered the Heath. He removed the silencer and aimed a shot above the people tending the body causing them to cower and whimper on the ground. He could hear a siren to the east of the Heath, and he was gone, surging through the trees and foliage once again.

'Shit, Jack, shit,' was all Merton could manage as they tore through East Finchley in the pool Mondeo. They didn't even bother with the blues and twos for the five-minute dash to the Heath. As they hit the Great North Road, Merton screamed for Jack to stop and he obliged with a screech of rubber.

'There, look at that bloke,' a wiry man with what a black fishing rod carrier was sprinting and headed down a gully and was over the fence with cat-like dexterity. They raced to the gully, and both took up the chase leaving the car running on the road, Merton vaulted the fence, and Jack got out to locate the man. He could see a close-cropped head bobbing through the gardens at high speed, Merton was no slouch but looked awkward and slow in comparison in the chase. The man tore through another garden then over another fence into the next gully and back onto the Great North Road. The piercing wheel spin was like a nail being driven through his head, and Jack felt so stupid. Jesus, this man was good, he thought as he reached for his phone. They'd laugh about this one day.

'Suspect heading north down the Great North Road towards Finchley in YT03 RTY… yes I know it's the fucking pool car.'

Merton caught up with him desperately trying to get his breath. He tried to speak but ended just pointing at the road where the car was left running.

'Yes, Merton, he doubled back and drove off in our car, thinks he's fucking James Bond. Wallace is going to love this. Was that a smile? Good.'

Merton pointed towards the village and the Heath beyond.

'Yep, we'd better walk it.' He nodded and tried to keep up with Jack's furious pace.

Jack's mind raced as he tried to absorb the events of the morning. The sniper had switched to killing humans as many feared he would and had shown immense ingenuity in the process, especially in fooling him and Merton like that. He dared to hope they could catch him in their car without any more ado, but this bloke had plenty in his locker and would be a hell of an opponent to track down. Still, this was London, the traffic stinks, you can't get anywhere quickly. That would look after itself, all he knew now was there was a corpse lying on the Heath, the unwitting victim of a psychotic sniper.

Jack looked up as a news chopper flew over them as they dropped down West Highgate Hill. He couldn't believe how quickly news spread these days. Merton had regained his breath but was still sweating profusely.

'Getting past your prime, Merton?' He grunted a reply and desperately tried to cool down. 'This guy's good, very good indeed,' he said at last.

'Yeah, god he was fast, his agility was uncanny, totally chimes with the witness statements.'

He got away. They still hadn't reached the Heath when the call came through. He'd got away, dumped the car and set it on fire in a woodland near Muswell Hill. The fire service was on the scene, and a SOCA team was on their way. Slippery didn't even come close. SOCA would do their best, but Jack didn't fancy their chances of getting anything at all. Fire and water would see to that.

'Shit,' said Jack, 'had some CDs in there too.'

'Oh bollocks, my football boots were in the boot, only had them three weeks,' said Merton shaking his head.

They made their way onto the Heath through the cordon ignoring the beseeching questions of the press. A uniform unnecessarily pointed towards the huddle of the SOCA team and photographer.

'Gee, thanks,' said Merton.

'How would we have coped?' hissed Jack.

The hit was a clean as you could hope to see, literally in the middle of the forehead, the blood ran in a narrow stream running diagonally towards the centre of his left ear when he fell. The man was approximately fifty years of age, expensively clad in a blue Ralph Lauren polo shirt, chinos and timberland deck shoes, no socks and an authentic Rolex on his wrist. He was tall and trim with a full head of light brown hair, a slightly ruddy complexion hinted at a liking for red wine.

'Who is he?' asked Jack.

'Graham Chappell, 51 years of age, resident of 3a, Flask Lane in Hampstead, sir,' replied a uniform, 'his wife, Amanda is on her way.'

'That's all we need, a screaming widow.'

'Sorry, Sir, put the phone down on me shouting she was on her way.'

'Merton, speak to Mrs Chappell, will you?'

Mac couldn't remember leaving the flat, but he was dirty and covered in sweat. He looked for his rifle, and it was in its bag on the living room floor. He got up, unzipped it and examined the rifle, it had been fired. A cold chill ran along his spine as he cried out, 'No, it can't be,' and thumped the sofa repeatedly.

He fell calm and then disappeared into a deep and brutal sleep, scarred by a terrifying nightmare that made him wake with a start that threw him off the sofa. Unable to summon the energy to stand he crawled to the cool and dark light of the hallway and checked the pad next to his phone, knocking it onto the thin light blue carpet. His appointment was the next morning, and he lay his face on the pad and fell asleep again.

15

The incident room was a mess of bodies, shouting and ring tones. Jack surveyed the scene and couldn't help recalling the miserable apathy of earlier. Things were moving quickly - they had CCTV from the Great North Road to check, terrified witnesses to interview and Merton's description to get out in the media. There was a gaggle of reporters outside the station, spilling onto Fortis Green, their satellite trucks relaying live reports to a suddenly news-hungry public. Jack tried to bury the feeling of excitement that bubbled away inside him, knowing even now this wouldn't necessarily be straightforward and that a totally innocent man had been murdered barely an hour ago. He would also have to face those cameras very soon in a hastily arranged press conference in the station to outline the latest developments and ensure the description reached as wide an audience as possible.

He knew that when it came to questions, some tricky ones might emerge, their hitherto lack of progress to date for one, releasing MacKinnon on bail for another. He could say 'no questions' but was always reluctant to do that – it looked shifty, as one of his press officers once told him and Jack totally agreed. He'd cross that bridge later he thought as he made his way to the video suite.

The CCTV images on the Great North Road were going to be key in the investigation that day. He grabbed Merton en route to the suite, made a couple of coffees and fired up the DVD player. Bob Greening was very helpful in copying and biking the DVD to the station but would it be any use?

Jack was hopeful, though. It was a beautiful sunny day, and the road was broad with few obstacles given the height of the camera. It should give a view north as far as the Wrestlers pub before the hill dips significantly. The action had occurred a good distance before that. Bob assured them no maintenance was taking place and that the camera was live.

The cool of the video suite was a welcome relief from the incident room furnace, and Jack slid the DVD into the machine. Wallace knocked unnecessarily on the door and sat down next to Jack immediately taking the same edge of seat position as the other two detectives. As is the norm in this footage, there was no sound, but there was colour, to Jack's relief. The technology was such that zooming in was an option and in good quality too. Jack's one major fear was that the route taken by the sniper meant there was a good chance all they'd see was the duck pond and the back of his head.

Merton fast forwarded the tape til the time code showed a minute or so before the incident. Wallace said to check for other people on the road who could be witnesses, and suddenly there was their man sprinting across the road and down the gully. Their Mondeo quickly came into shot, stopped with a cloud of burnt rubber and swung round to race up to the entrance of the gully. Jack said stop there, but Wallace intervened. 'No Jack, let it run through, we'll go through it minutely afterwards, ok? By the way…'

'Ma'am?'

'That car looks familiar.' Merton and Jack shared a quick look before Merton pressed play again and let the scene play out.

Jack winced as he watched themselves give chase with the car left idling on the kerbside. God, he was quick, in less than a minute he appeared again bolting out of the next gully down, turning left away from the camera and making like a tracer bullet for their car. They watched as he sped off. Unlike Jack and Merton, he put on the blues and twos, traffic would pull over to let him through. Clever, very clever indeed.

They ran it again in slow motion, zooming in when the man first shot across the road. His head was slightly angled away from the camera, but they managed a reasonable view of his profile. When he reappeared, he was looking north, but they got a quick view of the other side of his face but nothing that meant they could look into his eyes. They watched the back of his head sail towards their Mondeo and that was it, other than Merton re-appearing exhausted. Despite the lack of a face-on view, they knew it was their man. Wallace asked Merton to zoom in at himself.

'Christmas Party will be fun this year, don't you think Sgt Merton?'

Sometimes Jane liked nothing more than returning to a house that was almost supernaturally still. She stood statue still in the hallway, the cool of the house so welcome after the furnace heat of the tube. She fought the urge to shower and drink tea and absorbed the silence. Little streams of sweat meandered down her neck and back as she listened to her own breathing. Ray had taken the boys to the cinema, and she smiled as the hints of bacon sandwiches lingered in the air. They'd also had a bit of a tidy, bringing a wave of gratitude washing over her.

The house felt like a living entity, breathing and moving. She was aware of floor boards gently creaking, her phone vibrating and muffled echoes of traffic on Balham High Road. She closed her eyes and breathed in deeply and let out a long sigh, heavy with contentment. Jane stifled a scream as on opening her eyes she saw Capt John MacKinnon sitting on her stairs.

Remembering she could feel her phone vibrating constantly as she entered the house, Jane's heart began to beat that bit quicker. Despite increasing alarm, she simply asked, 'Tea or coffee?' Mac, disarmed, took a moment before answering tea. Putting the kettle on gave her a moment to compose herself. She decided it was unusual but nothing she couldn't handle. She also couldn't deny she was thrilled by his presence, a dancing mass of turmoil that had chosen her to make him feel better.

Major Liam Collins put the phone down to DI Jack Love and cursed. His first thought was to call Jane and cursed again as he failed to get through. He called the staff at the unit to let them know a manhunt was under way for one of their clients and to call him immediately if Mac turned up or contacted them in any way. That done, he tried Jane again. She wasn't great with technology, but she usually got back to him quite promptly.

He grew uneasy the longer the radio silence continued. He checked his contact list for a landline number and realised hers wasn't there. As calmly as he could, he rang the office who supplied Jane Harkness' landline number.

Mac startled Jane again by moving into the kitchen unheard and was directly opposite her by the sink as she turned from flicking the kettle on.

'I never get used to that, Captain.'

'What?' Mac's face clouded, cleared, clouded, cleared…

'Why did you do a runner from me?' Despite laughing with Liam Collins, Mac doing a bunk out of a session rankled. She couldn't deny it, it hurt. Without her hearing a thing too, she was in mid-sentence when she noticed for god's sake.

'It was time to go.'

'Was it? What does that mean, Mac?'

'It means it was time to go.' Mac stared straight at her, through her even, causing a chill to brush her spine. 'That annoys you, doesn't it?'

Just as a blush formed on her face, he was suddenly alert, he looked out of the kitchen window, but he was listening rather than looking.

'What is it, Mac?' He didn't answer, and again the rhythms of the house reclaimed the kitchen, every creak on the stairs, every tick of a clock and every fleck of landing dust rang in Jane's ears. She screamed when the phone rang.

'What's wrong, Jane?' The pair looked at each other as the beseeching tone rang out. 'I should get that, excuse me.'

She cleared her throat, and the tone died as it clicked to the answering machine. Major Collins' calm but insistent voice suddenly filled the kitchen.

'Hello Jane, please call me as soon as possible, thanks.'

Collins kept it simple not to alarm anyone in the family who may pick up the message. He cursed as he remembered being told she had the house to herself this evening. The feeling something wasn't right was growing. He knew they had a connection, a bond, even. MacKinnon was on the run, had killed someone, was mentally unstable and volatile.

'That's odd, wonder what he wants, I'd better…'

'He can wait, aren't you wondering why I'm here?'

'Of course, but believe it or not, you're not the first client to break into my house.'

'You left a window open.'

'You know what I mean, Mac.'

'I killed someone.' Feeling ridiculous even as she formed the words, she said, 'That was your job.' Mac sighed and looked at the brown tiled kitchen floor. He quickly looked up again, alert again, cat-like instincts warning of imminent danger. A car door shut outside causing Jane to look down the hallway. When she looked back, Mac was already scaling the fence at the bottom of her narrow garden. 'Bollocks,' she muttered as she went to the front door opening it as a policeman was about to ring the bell. Mac's visit was already feeling dream-like.

Merton knocked on Jane's door. 'Good evening, Jane Harkness?'

'Yes?' The detectives introduced themselves and walked in as Jane stood aside. 'How can I help you?' she asked doing her best to grab some reality and snap back into the moment. Jack looked briefly at Merton. 'Are you ok, Ms Harkness?'

'Yes, fine thank you.'

'We're here to warn you that a Captain John MacKinnon might try to visit you.' She tried and failed to suppress a smile. Jack returned the smile but asked, 'Is that an amusing prospect, Ms Harkness?'

'Oh Jane, please. And yes, your assertion, no, deduction would be better, is absolutely spot-on DI Jack Love, in fact, he's just jumped over my fence.'

Jack tilted his head, Merton nodded and was off, mobile already to his ear.

'What did he want?'

'We were just getting to that when he seemed to sense you coming. Let's just say he's very perceptive and intuitive, our Captain Mac.'

'He's also extremely dangerous. We believe he shot a man dead today.' Jane gasped as she digested this news, her hand flying to her mouth. She fought back tears, partly for the victim but she couldn't deny it was mainly concern for Mac.

'Jane, you need to tell us anything that might help us catch him, for his and everyone's safety. Jane? I know this must be difficult.'

She looked at Jack, eyes two glistening puddles. 'I really thought I was getting somewhere but...'

'But...?'

'We had a connection, I felt there was trust there.'

Jack bristled despite himself, remembering being dumped by a girl in college who banged on about another student she had a 'connection' with. He'd hated the phrase ever since. He smiled inwardly at his idiocy or thought he had.

'Something funny,?'

'No, not at all,' Jack felt a blush billow on his cheeks for probably for the first time in 30 years.

'No, go on, I'm curious, have you got something against counsellors?'

'Far from it, I know from my wife's school what a great job they do.' This wasn't defensive bull to patronise Jane either. While Annie Love was a de facto social worker on a daily basis, the school's two overworked counsellors were in the front line dealing with raped teenage girls, self-harmers, bullied wallflowers and victims of abuse to name but a few, every day.

Jane tilted her head slightly trying to work out if Jack was lying and seemed to conclude he wasn't. 'Ok,' she said eventually, 'as I was saying, I felt I was getting somewhere, but it was clear very early on how troubled he was. He had trouble remembering things, short term memory especially. He would form a vague memory… he would say he thought he'd hurt someone but couldn't remember how or even if it was him. He found it terrifying. Not nearly as terrifying as his nightmares. He would wake up under his bed or cowering in the corner of his living room or lying on his hall carpet drenched in sweat, his sheets often soiled when he went back to bed.' Jane shook her head gently as she recounted the last part of her account.

'Why hasn't he been referred to mental health services?'

'He has been, it's incredibly slow, and actually, the military link and our approaches here offer a faster route to getting care and attention.'

'But surely him being a threat to himself and others would make him a straightforward candidate for being sectioned?'

'It would, but this behaviour is just coming to light. When he first came to us his symptoms were in the range that we felt we could deal with and like I say, he had a quicker route to being seen. His poor GP resorted to various combinations of anti-depressants and they clearly didn't work.'

'Poor GP?'

'She tries her best, but it's fair to say her surgery is very overrun like a lot of inner-city practices. She was relieved when he got in touch with us on his own volition.'

Jack nodded and thought again about the first interview in Muswell Hill Police Station, his cool demeanour and other-worldliness. 'We interviewed him last week, he was very cool, totally in control it appeared to me, something quite mesmerising about him.'

'Yes, there was always a dream-like air to proceedings and his movement.'

'His movement?'

'Yes, he would suddenly appear in a different position in the room, where you least expected normally.'

'I noticed that too, and we've been unable to get a witness to nail a really decent description of him. It's like they instantly forget him when he leaves. Even an author couldn't manage it.'

'An author?'

'Yes, he shot an author's dog on Hampstead Heath. You surely knew that, right?'

It was Jane's turn to blush. 'Yes, of course. Funny thing is, I'd take really extensive notes after a session, and when I'd read them back later, it was like I didn't believe them. Hand on heart, he's the strangest and most interesting client I've ever had. The best way to describe him is that you remember a feeling, an impression of him if you like and you dearly want to see him again but details are hard to recall. My notes have been imperative in this case.'

'Do you mind if I read them?'

'I do actually.'

'It's a bit late to play the patient confidentiality card I'm afraid, Jane,' said Jack softly, 'I can make it official if you like.'

'No, it's ok, feels very intrusive that's all, it's easy to forget a man was murdered today. He has that effect on me I'm afraid.' Jack understood but found it anything but easy to forget the body he had looked at just hours ago, flat out in the dust, life seized from him in the cruellest way, the look of shock still evident on his face. He was trained to piece together a victim's last moments and re-membered each and every dead person he had encoun-tered.

Jane excused herself and went upstairs, her footsteps heavy on the wooden stairs, the heat and situation bringing deep sighs and gasps as she went. Jack moved into the liv-ing room and admired the many photographs of what looked like the perfect family. His education and training once again taught him to question everything, but he was confident this was a happy home. Sometimes you could just *tell*.

She returned to the living room and handed over her notes, a plain A4 pad, to Jack. Seeing the look on her face, he said, 'Don't worry Jane, I'll look after them.'

'It's not that, I'm sure you will. It just feels like a total betrayal. I've only done this once before, a drug addict who had killed a dealer. I felt like I was getting somewhere there too. She was very damaged and lived a hideous life really. I was called to give evidence, even then I thought I could help, but in the end, I did no good at all. She got life, of course.'

Jack nodded, 'Are you still in touch?' Jane just shook her head slowly. 'No, she killed herself a week into her sentence.'

'You really care for these people, don't you?'

'*These people* as you call them are invariably deeply troubled, and sometimes a perfect storm of circumstances conspires to make people do awful things. Sandra was raped repeatedly as a young girl by her father and went through the care system before ending up on the game, on the streets, just about surviving. She didn't stand a chance.'

Jack wasn't unsympathetic, and he knew he was considered soft and a bit of a bleeding heart in the station. In the canteen, suspects and criminals were often subjected to what Jack called the MMP test, Mug, Maggot or Psycho. He knew it was nearly always more complicated than that.

'Everyone has a story, Jack. Capt Mackinnon has seen and experienced things we can only have nightmares about. He's very damaged, and I can't see this ending well.'

Jack nodded, 'Yes, but it certainly didn't end well for the man lying on the Heath with a bullet in his head. We need to catch him fast, and I repeat, for his good as much as anything else.'

'I know, the one thing I must warn you about is that when Mac feels cornered, he disappears, he's bloody brilliant at it.'

Jack couldn't resist a smile. 'Yes, we know that already, Jane, believe me.'

'Keep me posted, Jack and call me if you need me.'

Capt John MacKinnon was running, and clarity was forming in his mind. It was as if the adrenaline and perpetual motion of running were acting as a window into his predicament. He was remembering things, and he knew now he'd killed a man, some dogs and was wanted by the police. He smiled as it dawned on him he was being pursued, he was back on active service. Suddenly a map of what he could and couldn't do was spread out before him.

Jack called Merton, who breathlessly reported nothing much at all. Uniform were crawling all over Balham, but they had nothing. Mac's mastery of evasion was getting tedious. It was late afternoon, and Jack decided to beat the rush hour hell, and get back up north and read Jane's notes in the shade of his garden. His shirt drenched in sweat, he could almost taste the first sip of ice cold lager from his fridge but knew that was a terrible idea.

Knowing Annie would be there only quickened his stride as he disappeared into Balham tube station. The smell of sweat agitated his taste buds further as he picked up a discarded paper in the carriage. A cursory glance at the cricket report didn't detain him long, though at the Oval they had had their first ever 'heat stops play' incident, much to the amusement of London-based Australians. Australian-based Australians too, no doubt especially as it was a Kiwi batsman whose collapse prompted the stoppage.

Jack marvelled at the weather and remembered the dire summer of 2012. The wettest summer *since records began* and bang on cue for the London Olympics. This reverie drew a smirk from Jack as he recalled with a wince the fascist grip the dreaded London Organising Committee of the Olympic Games, LOCOG, had on anything from traffic control to closing down Olympic kebab houses in the East End. The elements deliciously proved they could never be controlled despite the overwhelming success of the games.

He put the paper aside and opened Jane's notes. Her handwriting was big, not especially tidy but mercifully easy to read. Deciphering other peoples' writing was not his favourite pastime, but Jane's openness translated well into her note taking. He smiled at the little asides – '*how does he do that?*' and '*what a fascinating client.*'

She outlined in detail the loss of a female companion in Afghanistan, a member of the media from what Jack could tell from Jane's description. 'Unusual closeness' had developed, and out on patrol, he watched her get blown up, literally witnessing her head being blown off her torso. Words like 'unimaginable' and 'incomprehensible' peppered her notes, and it wasn't hard to see why she was so captivated by this man. This was a window on human experience so removed from western civilian life as to render you almost a voyeur or an observer of some grisly human experiment.

Jane's description of the attachment as unusual explained her initial frustration in the notes – '*he just won't let me in!* 'She also describes how his eyes appeared to burn into her as he described his battlefield experiences as if he was saying you could never ever understand what I've been through. Jack knew he was right. All someone like Jane could do was try to understand, to empathise. Counsellors were big on empathy. She would have heard many terrible stories, lives ripped apart by drugs, child abuse and domestic violence and all the other woes humans seem intent on inflicting on themselves. She might have suffered terrible cruelties in her own life, you never knew. *Everyone has a story, Jack.*

Jane was further up the conveyor belt of human trauma and misery from Jack really. The police and the criminal justice in general were stationed right at the end of the line witnessing the consequences when troubled humans had slipped through teachers, youth workers, social workers, counsellors and the health service into the lap of the police. Then they were punished, and many would simply not make the return journey back to respectability, whatever that was.

He had seen far too many dead people, poor souls who haunted the outskirts of his consciousness like lost refugees, unloved, unwanted but never quite forgotten. He had even taken someone's life too and while he never felt a moment's guilt - it was him or Jack - he still looked down at his shocked face most days, the blood matting his hair as he gasped his last moments.

The sudden burst of brilliant sunlight cutting through the carriage as the train emerged out of the tunnel at East Finchley startled Jack who had planned to get off at Highgate, the stop before. Seeing the next train south was a full five minutes away he decided to walk, pulling out his phone as he clicked his oyster card at the exit. The wall of heat engulfed him as he emerged from the shade of the station, instantly regretting the decision to walk.

Mac had to stop running, of course. He wasn't Forrest Gump, and despite endless desert combat operations, he had to conserve energy in this heat especially given the journey ahead. He had reached the road bordering Hampstead Heath to the north, close to the Spaniards pub. He darted into the trees with only the clothes he sweated in and his fishing bag. The woods were cooler, but the heat was still oppressive and humid, a storm a near certainty in the coming hours.

He lay on the ground staring up through the canopy to the sky. The sunlight was sliced as if a child had drawn it. He felt calm yet could see his heart beating through his black t-shirt. Parakeets let out their shrill and rapid cries as a crow took watch 30 feet above him. Blackbirds foraged around him, and a pair of magpies noisily fought over scraps of food before flying to the top of the trees and out to another part of the Heath. Mac felt safe here and knew he could hide out in these conditions. Food would be plentiful and wouldn't be a problem.

He closed his eyes and allowed the wood to engulf him. He heard creatures around him, felt a bird land on his leg and fly off again. The lo-fi whine of jets holding their pattern high above him soothed him.

'You failed me, Mac. Why didn't you stop them?' He was looking at Charlie Grey.

'You left me behind, Mac, you fucking left me behind with those bastards. You get home alright, did you, Mac?' His face was a hideous mix of terror and fury with blood openly flowing from wounds and gashes all over his body, barely covered with ripped fatigues. He faded as quickly as he appeared and it went black. He couldn't move, he couldn't even slide his eyes from side to side. He became aware of wailing, an insistent primaeval scream of 'What could I do? What could I do?' over and over.

Mac was wailing in the wood. He woke immersed in sweat and metres away from his rifle covered in soil and twigs. When the terror finally subsided, he knew he had to see Jane Harkness again. He grabbed his gun and headed south again.

'Jesus, look at the state of you,' laughed Annie as she joined Jack in the garden. He looked like he'd just emerged from the sea with not quite the élan of Daniel Craig. 'Is that just from walking from the tube?'

Annie, on the other hand, looked adorable; Jack's heart lurching as he spotted her approaching with Earnie. Most importantly, she looked totally relaxed, her end of term torpor dispatched for another year. Unruffled in a vest, denim shorts and cream converse, Jack started to lose interest in Captain John MacKinnon for a moment. He watched her sashay into the house for drinks and a bowl of water for a hot and bothered black Labrador. Earnie, never a fan of heat, enjoyed a bit of attention from Jack but was far more interested in the bowl of water when Annie came back to the shaded table. His nose also bristled at the grilled meat sending aromas into the garden from a neighbour's barbeque.

'Hate to say it, but I want autumn now, how British is that?' said Annie taking a large sip of her bottle of Peroni, letting out a satisfied sigh in the process. Jack nodded. Autumn was his favourite time of year. It had always been a busy time in his life, the beginning of college, the football season, his police career and some relationships, including Annie. He also loved London in the autumn, fewer tourists and the parks looked fantastic, it felt like you'd got the city back after the summer invasion. It was cool and easier to get around. Annie was right, it'd be particularly welcome this year. 'The *lovely Helen Willetts* said there was no let-up in sight, this heat could continue well into September.'

The heat, Annie and the *lovely Helen Willetts,* a BBC weather forecaster Jack found particularly attractive, were making him dizzy. As if sensing this, Annie asked, 'So what the hell are you doing at home when there's a renegade sniper on the loose? It's nice to see you and all that…'

'We've got the whole Met chasing him, and Merton is keeping me up to date on the search, not that we're having any joy.'

'No, Sky News is saying how embarrassing it is for you.'

'Oh, are they? Balls to Sky News. Anyway, I've got a sheath of case notes from his counsellor I want to go through, see if I can get any clue over what he might do, any new angles at all really. The more I know about him, the better our chances of catching him I reckon. Even Wallace agreed with that.'

Annie nodded, 'Just don't tell her your chosen location for such a vital task.'

Jack saluted, 'Yes ma'am, I said I needed some peace and quiet, that's all she needs to know.' Annie nodded and ran her hand slowly along his thigh.

'That's not helping.'

'Sorry.'

Mac could hear sirens screaming out along the west of the Heath. He shinned up a tree as close to the fields of Parliament Hill as he could. The higher he climbed, the safer he felt. Being pursued as often as he had been in the army, he had quickly learnt that assuming an elevated position was crucial to survival. The dense foliage of summer trees was perfect. The taking out of targets was different; you

194

had to be sure you didn't give your position away, getting the balance between optimum shooting and the ability to get out unnoticed was central to survival. He knew too many brave men who paid the ultimate price for concentrating too much on taking out a suspect. Brave but stupid.

People rarely looked high up into trees and today was no exception. Not that many people were out today. There were plenty of uniformed police officers walking in pairs around the Heath however, none of whom even considered the world above them. They seemed content to talk to each other and take constant swigs out of their water bottles. They assumed, not unreasonably, that their presence was enough. He knew that regular soldiers on guard often adopted the same approach. This was fine by Mac, it would help him move about with impunity.

He would have to change his route south, though, even he couldn't just stroll across the Heath to the relative safety of Camden's streets. He dropped down to ground level as a pair of patrolling officers passed, moaning about 'this pissing heat.' He headed through the woods towards the eastern side of the Heath and Merton Lane.

Jack quickly became compelled by Jane's notes, passing the pages to Annie as he read. Jane's words echoed in his head, and he understood why she was so concerned about him. He was completely damaged, paranoid and delusional, so when you read it in black and white, you wondered how he could react in any other way. As fascinating as the notes were, however, he questioned how useful this exercise was. A sixth form psychology student could tell you he was likely to be a danger to others. The fact he had already killed someone would've alerted students much younger than that. He sighed and rubbed his sweaty brow.

'What's wrong?' asked Annie.

'All I'm getting from this is that he's dangerous. I'm genuinely sympathetic to how he got in that condition, but you always end up with he's loose and dangerous. The system has let him down, you know? He was referred for psychological treatment, but he didn't show, and it was never followed up. I'm not getting anything fresh on how we catch him, and that's my job. This would definitely be an excellent case study on post-traumatic stress disorder or whatever for an academic, but I don't have that luxury or the bloody time.'

Annie nodded, 'It's completely fascinating, no doubt about that. It's like he's created the conditions where he's being hunted again. He's experienced so much horror, so much tension, it's almost as if it's the fuel he needs to run on. He's gone from hand-to-hand combat with the Taliban to *Cash in the Attic*. The rest of us lead lives where real tension – you know, the risk of dying - has been removed as well as the need for food and a roof over our heads, all these things are taken for granted. I'm not saying that's good or bad, just a fact of our civilised existence.'

'I see that, the shock of safety, the lack of tension. But how does that help us catch him?'

'I'm not sure,' she paused, taking a sip of her beer. 'I could probably take a stab at how not to do it.'

'Go on.'

'How you're doing it now.

'What do you mean?'

'Well, you're pursuing him, you're giving him what he wants. He doesn't know he wants that, but he does.'

'So if we don't chase him, he'll cease being a danger to dogs and humans and we can all crack on with our lives?'

'Maybe. Either way, I'm struck by Jane Harkness remarking on how he said he would do anything possible to survive. Being delusional, he thinks he's in a war-like situation, and that's why he felt he had to shoot that poor man. If, as she also says, he's ditched all medication, it's highly likely these delusions will get worse.'

Jack felt a huge pang of love for his wife, he loved how she engaged in his cases, how interested she was and the enjoyment she got from mining her psychology degree. But he was still troubled.

'I agree with you totally, the only problem is we have to chase him, we can't stop that, on a couple of levels. Most obviously, he's a murder suspect, but we've both also read that he's engineered circumstances to become a hunted man. We call off the search, which we can't do, and won't he just engineer the same again cos that's what he feeds off?'

Mac reached the toilets at the bottom of Merton Lane and relieved himself, aware two men in a cubicle engaged in activities and unlikely to hinder his progress, and left the building. Two uniforms were stationed at the bottom of the hill stopping anyone attempting to access the Heath. He looped around the toilet building into the bushes that fenced off the adjoining North London Bowls Club. The thick shrubbery presented no problem to the captain as he reached the club. He looked over the fence at a scene so peaceful and at odds with his state of mind he was momentarily disarmed. He stood mesmerised as he watched the game between Finchley and Muswell Hill unfold.

'There's a gate over there.' Startled by the first spoken contact with someone since he left Jane's house in Balham, Mac turned to look at the source of this contact. An elderly man with a ruddy complexion, black glasses and a white cap perched on his silver hair looked at him through twinkling, if slightly, rheumy eyes.

'Right, thanks,' said Mac, his eyes darting all over the new surroundings, plotting escape routes and any clear and present threat to his person.

'I know, it's a big game, but it's free to watch, and you can just walk in. What's with the histrionics?' The man's North London accent was soft, and his tone was kind, if teasing, decades of a being a clubbable sort around various, football, cricket and now bowls clubs in the Highgate area.

'Histrionics?'

'Yeah, piling over our fence as if you're being chased by wild dogs. Mind you, we get all sorts coming through here, druggies, poofs, bored kids looking for a laugh and a bit of trouble, you know? Poofs mainly, though, bloody nuisance. Each to their own and all that but why do they have to have a bit of a slap and tickle on our grass of an evening?'

Mac couldn't help but smile. 'You might get a couple more through in a minute.'

'How come?'

'There was a couple getting very well acquainted in the toilet just over the back there.'

The old man laughed. 'Better tell Burt then, he'll pre-pare a nice welcome for them. Enjoy the game, son.' But when he turned to look at this strange man who had popped over the fence, he had gone. 'Strange,' he mut-tered to himself and wondered if that odd little exchange had actually happened, concluded it probably had, shook his head and returned to the keenly fought local derby.

Mac squirrelled along the fence through some more bushes and shinned up the wall of a huge house with a superb vista over central and west London. He perched on the wall and paused a moment. Despite living in Kentish Town, he rarely strayed this far north; in fact, when he stole the copper's car that was among the only times he'd been to Highgate apart from his target practice on Hamp-stead Heath. He knew it was 'posh', but it was clear it of-fered critical hiding spots that he really needed now. This ridiculous pile he had happened upon for example was being renovated and so large, he reckoned he could live for the rest of his days here unhindered if he wanted to.

He looked along the wall and saw a small security por-takabin stationed outside the main gate. There was a cam-era or two, but none of this presented a problem. The southern and eastern parts of the house were covered in scaffold, and the extensive gardens provided plenty of cover. There was also a summer house, numerous sheds and a bandstand as well as all the tree cover you could wish for. He looked south onto the rambling grounds of Highgate Cemetery charting its various paths, nooks and crannies. Less luxurious but more dense and impenetrable than here especially on the western side, it could definitely be an option too.

He pondered these options and was surprised he hadn't thought of this before. He also remembered reading an article about Bishop's Avenue and was convinced that was close to here. Thought to be one of the most expensive streets in the UK, the article also pointed out that many of the houses were empty for much of the year or were being prepared for demolition as 'foreign oligarchs' designed and built 'ghastly' new properties. Whatever angles the architecture debate threw up, it meant only opportunities for Mac.

He always felt the grime and transient nature of inner-city areas like Kentish Town were perfect for anonymous living and they were. But when you were on the run, it only took one sighting and you were in trouble, he saw that now. He jumped down into the gardens and liked even more what he saw. What looked like a summer house was on closer inspection a large swimming pool with jacuzzi and steam rooms. Despite the major works, it was all ready to use, and he wondered if that was a sop for the workers and security staff. Again, it was perfect.

He decided to head south happy that he had somewhere to sleep tonight, away from the madding crowd, the thought of sleeping south not entering his troubled mind. Decision made, Mac easily evaded security and began what he knew as 'hedge hopping', making his way to the A1 by running through rear gardens. As a very athletic young boy, he was exhilarated by other people's gardens. Growing up in a flat he was always envious of friends' houses. He thought it was fantastic that families had a place to play, hang washing up or store things. It felt like another world and having mastered climbing trees, he would climb them in large gardens and watch in awe as people went about their domestic business. It was another world, and this expedition felt like another universe.

The gardens of Highgate were immense as he headed up towards Pond Square with beautiful landscaped terraces and swimming pools in what seemed like every other house. Where it was obvious no one was home, he'd quietly submerge himself in a pool, the shaded ones providing merciful moments of cool and calm. He dried in minutes in the oven of the early evening heat and moved on.

Dogs were few and far between, and those he encountered were quickly calmed by the captain. Most of the gardens had plentiful cover, but one where everything had been cut back revealed an elderly couple enjoying a gin and tonic perched under a dark green sun shade. Mac simply walked across the bottom of the sparse space waving like it was the most natural thing in the world. The old lady waved, and the couple carried on talking.

The gardens became smaller around Pond Square, and Mac could smell the restaurants and bars of Highgate Village, an enticing mix of sweet garlic and frying potatoes filled the air. He could hear the clink of glasses and the chatter of people enjoying a bite to eat and a cooling glass of beer or wine. It reminded him he was ferociously hungry and utterly alone.

Seb Marshall enjoyed the sweeps of the Heath in the news chopper at first. He loved the hazy view of the city and the close-up vistas of an area he enjoyed walking with his wife, Penny. As a senior Sky News reporter, it made a change from pieces to camera on College Green or some other building of national significance like the Old Bailey. This was also such a unique story that any reporter would want a piece of it. He still marvelled at being able to report live from an aircraft over London, the hard-bitten cynicism of so many in his profession failing to pollute this assignment.

He knew his editors were beginning to tire of the frequent flights over the Heath and stopped them as the case grew cold. It was obviously very expensive, and the breathless pieces to camera were beginning to grate. The Independent had commented that it was the news equivalent of bombing sand. However, with a man shot dead they were airborne again. The choppers were given permission to fly slots from Kenwood House on the northern boundary of the Heath. Seb would ask the pilot to fly directly south to Parliament Hill and sweep around the southern boundary and up to the ponds where the majority of dogs were shot and where the first human was murdered.

Given the loud protests from Hampstead residents, he also liked to hover over their village, particularly Buchanan's house as it had relevance to the story but more because he couldn't stand the man. Some of the early live pieces were punctuated by Buchanan running onto his lawn and giving him all manner of obscene gestures including an inevitable and prolonged moon, all instant and massive YouTube sensations now.

His usual pilot was a squat Australian called Les who had the irritating habit of laughing wearily for a second whenever Seb asked him anything from a route to whether if he fancied a beer after a flight. The longer they did these things, the more annoying it became. Today, Les had disarmed Seb by suggesting a change of route, a sweep over the northern woods before heading over the borders of Highgate Village. Despite himself, he couldn't help giving a little knowing laugh before replying 'why not?'

It was early evening, but the Heath was largely deserted. While dogs were being shot, some people still ventured out. Now it was humans, the atmosphere had deteriorated further. Even the tea rooms at Kenwood House were empty save for some plucky elderly ladies who he made a mental note to *vox pop* on their return. Wonderfully British, they were totally determined not to change their lives. They reminded Seb of the 'Spirit of the Blitz' but also the 'not scared' movement that formed in the aftermath of the 7/7 attacks on London that he had covered so extensively. A website appeared with pictures of Londoners out and about with 'not scared' on placards, postcards and t-shirts.

His camera woman, Beth Evans, ran out from the ladies' and jumped aboard. His stomach lurched as the helicopter tilted into the air. The horizon shifted and the deep haze engulfing London became visible with the tops of the Gherkin, the Shard and further to the east, Canary Wharf peeking out of the steam. Les evened out the aircraft at 300ft and headed for Highgate. Headphones on, Seb could hear the gallery clearly back at Isleworth telling him they were going live in 30 seconds. On camera, Beth was following the boundary of the Heath before they flew along a wide arc taking them east towards Merton Lane.

He was cued down from 10 and Seb began broadcasting live to the world. '*As police continue their search for prime suspect Capt John MacKinnon, we are live above the place where today a man was so cruelly shot to death as he took a walk in the beautiful summer sunshine on London's Hampstead Heath. Somewhere in this picturesque and wealthy pocket of North London lurks a man who began shooting dogs and is now killing innocent people, as many people suspected and feared he would …*'

As Seb continued his piece, Beth noticed movement in the gardens below. She took her eye away from the viewfinder. Sure enough, a wiry male with a long narrow bag was scaling the wall of a large detached property. '*… this elusive man has evaded police and can disappear at will.*' Beth felt a chill zip up her spine. She knew this was a gamble, to interrupt a live piece, especially on the key 7 o'clock bulletin. Seb was reading from his script but was taking in the scene below him intermittently, and she knew she had to get him in shot for a shot to camera as he ended his report. The best bet was to alert Les and Seb would obviously notice. She leant over and poked Les in the back, he looked round to see Beth urgently making circular motions with her right index finger.

Seb was straight on it. *'I'm just getting information from the pilot and Beth on camera that they have spotted something of interest below. Stay with us as we circle round and take another look and I check what has alerted the crew.'* The anchor filled as 'breaking news' graphics appeared on the bottom of millions of TV screens. Beth had put her camera in a fixed position and told Seb and Les what she had seen.

'Fucking hell,' Seb shouted, grateful it was off mic and relayed the news to the gallery. He heard a similar refrain in his earphones followed by instructions to get lower and 'find the bastard at all costs'. Les was already reducing altitude and following the same course far more slowly. Beth's head darted back and forth from her viewfinder convinced he would be long out of sight.

'There! There he is,' she shrieked. Seb was immediately live, *'We've had a sighting of a man closely resembling the description of Capt John MacKinnon climbing walls in Highgate Village, and there he is.'* Les brought the helicopter to a hover, and sure enough, the man had climbed to the top of a large ivy-clad wall and was sat on the top as if it was the most natural thing in the world.

Jack could hear his phone trilling in the bathroom through the merciful jet of cold water hitting his shoulders and the back of his neck. He let it go to message as the wonderful chill attacked the heat of his long day and the two lagers that had gone straight to his dehydrated head. It went again, and with a groan, he peered through the curtain to see who it was and spied Merton's name flashing on the screen. He stepped out and seeing Annie skipping past the bathroom in her underwear tried to concentrate on the task at hand.

'Jesus, Jack, where have you been?'

'Just showering before heading back to the incident room, Jane's notes were really interesting…'

'Never mind that, just put Sky News on.' The line went dead. The TV he had resisted having in their bedroom for so long came to life, and he tuned to Sky News. His eyes could not believe what he was seeing, Capt John MacKinnon, larger than life on top of a wall live on Sky News in a very leafy North London suburb Jack instantly recognised as Highgate Village. Jack sat dripping on the edge of the bed mesmerised as the Sky News chopper circled around 100 feet above the most wanted man in Britain. The chopper circled, but the camera never left his face.

He stared blankly into the camera, arms hanging limply by his sides. Jack was convinced he saw the 'four seasons' racing across his face like TV interference. Jack could hear sirens racing towards the village and started to get up and get going when he watched the captain slowly reach down into his long narrow bag, all the while never taking his eyes off what was now becoming an unmissable target. Jack yelled 'No' and watched as the expert sniper lined up the easiest shot of his life.

Beth realised first what was happening and shouted for Les to get out of there. In the excitement of 'getting the story' and actually finding this man, Seb had clean forgotten how dangerous he was. It was the last thing he was to forget. *This man, who police believe has brought chaos to a steaming British summer, is looking up at this very aircraft with his capture a mere formality now we have located him.'*

Mac stared at the enemy aircraft and cursed how careless he had been. He had observed aircraft all through this mission, but they were at an altitude unlikely to worry him at all. This chopper had come out of nowhere and surprised him. They looped round ready for the kill and Mac couldn't deny he froze. The climb in the heat was punishing, and there was no cover either side of the wall, not for at least 50 yards.

But they sat hovering above him, an officer speaking furiously into a microphone and a camera trained on him. Whatever they were doing he calculated he may have a chance of getting a round off. Not taking his eyes off the enemy he reached for his rifle.

'Oh my goodness, I do believe he is now taking aim at us in the Sky chopper, and it is clear we have to leave this scene as soon as possible.'

The last thing the viewers saw were large specks of red material cover the lens of the camera and Mac lower his rifle before the broadcast was cut. The news anchor in the studio screamed, a noise so unbridled it could only be of a creature watching another member of her species die in front of her at the most unexpected moment. Sky News went off air for the first time in its history for reasons other than technical fault and did not appear again until 8 o'clock, a full 50 minutes.

The bullet had hit Seb Marshall in the right cheek of his face and splattered grey matter all over Les, Beth and the interior of the helicopter. It exited through the back of his head and went through the ceiling such was its velocity. Beth had filmed in war zones before settling for less dangerous assignments in London and despite intense shock thought first of making sure Les was ok. It was preposterous to her that they were under fire over North London and had lost a man. She looked at Les's blood-spattered face and was relieved he was concentrating on getting them out of danger. He quickly gained altitude and speed and looped quickly back to Kenwood House radioing for police and ambulance as he flew.

Beth, assured they were now safe, went to Seb already knowing he was dead. His face was horribly gashed on one side, and his eyes were locked in terrified surprise. She did not know Seb that well, but he was always charming to her when they worked together. She looked away, holding his hand and fixing her gaze on the giant red sun setting in the west criss-crossed by vapour trails.

Jack sprinted the short distance to Muswell Hill Police station where Wallace was waiting for him parked outside. He jumped in, and they sped off down Fortis Green towards East Finchley screeching round the junction at the High Street. Crowds of Friday night revellers gathered outside the pubs and looked on anxiously as they flew past as the busy Friday evening traffic made as much room as it could for the speedy procession of police cars.

'Jesus, they're brave,' cursed Wallace pointing to the sky as another news chopper made its way to the scene.

'Who gave them permission? Madness, our own helicopter must be there too, surely?'

'It was scrambled and is all over the area praying for anything like as good a sighting as Sky managed, for all the good that did, must be media crews from all over the world heading there.'

'Christ, this has to end tonight.'

Danger averted, for now, Mac quickly sought cover. He reckoned there was still an hour or two of daylight to negotiate before the relative safety of darkness. The air was still but far from quiet, the throb of helicopter blades and the urgent sirens saw to that. The cover was patchy, and he decided the next garden looked far more promising with its ancient trees and almost orchard like selection of smaller fruit trees providing brilliant cover from aircraft.

He had no time to linger on the wall so threw himself over and landed awkwardly but safely in a hydrangea bush. Perfect, tidy but lacking in any signs of human life, he'd be ok here until darkness set in. He could hear doors being knocked along the road and hoped he was right about the house being unoccupied or at least deserted for the evening. He sat against the thick trunk of a horse chestnut tree and tried to calm his breathing. He listened to the sirens come and go and the loud banging of door knockers by the police. He closed his eyes as a door was knocked urgently. He opened them again to check there was no way to walk around the back, assured there wasn't he closed his eyes again as the police approached the next house.

Jane looked at her phone and saw sixteen missed calls and umpteen text messages beseeching her to put the news on. Each of the missed calls was from Major Liam Collins. She'd been walking through Balham, picking up bits and pieces for dinner, and as usual, her phone was low on battery and set to silent, the bugbear of virtually all her many friends. She mumbled a quick 'whoops' to herself, sighed and listened to the first and only message he had left.

'Hi Jane, god, trust you to be on radio silence now of all times, if you get this soon, put the bloody news on. I'm on my way.' She ended the answer-phone call as she turned into her road and immediately saw the tall imposing figure of Liam Collins leaning against his car outside her house.

'Bloody hell, what's going on, Liam?'

'We need to go inside, it's John MacKinnon, he's killed again…'

Jane gasped and dropped her shopping, the bottle of red wine she was looking forward to loudly clanking but not breaking, fruit and veg spilling out of her tote bag. Liam quickly bent down and gathered the shopping back into the bag. 'We might need a drop of that in a minute, he did it live on Sky News' he said, pointing to the wine as Jane unlocked the front door and they entered the cool of her hallway.

Jane quickly ran to the TV in the kitchen and flicked it on. Sky was still off air, but the pictures were being played on a loop on the other news channels. BBC interspersed the footage with live shots from their own chartered helicopter cutting the film as Mac raised his rifle. The reports also featured shots of distressed Sky staff coming in and out of their Isleworth HQ as well as a growing pile of flowers at the gates. The breaking news graphic remained fixed on the screen 'Sky News senior reporter shot dead live on programme.'

'Oh my god, Liam, oh my god.' She repeated this in an urgent whisper and threw her head into her hands. When they repeated the film of Mac once more Jane just stared at his lost face looking up into the camera it was as if he was looking right into her eyes.

'How does the clip end Liam? I want to see it.' Liam shook his head.

'Liam, I want to see what happened, I'm 45 years of age for Christ's sake, show me what happened. Now.' Liam looked around the kitchen and into the living room. He walked into the living room and fired up the PC stationed in a large space behind the brown leather sofa with an acoustic guitar leaning against the desk. While the computer booted up, he imagined Jane swinging round on the chair to watch something her boys were telling her about on the TV with a big warm grin on her face, genuinely interested to see what it was about. He looked at her ashen face and hoped a similar happy gathering was just around the corner for her.

The shooting was already all over social media in its entirety, racking up hundreds of thousands of hits in less than an hour. 'Are you sure you want to see this?'

Jane's shaking hand went to press play itself but was intercepted gently by Liam, he didn't let go. His left hand pressed play. Liam had already viewed the footage many times seeing it through Jane's eyes gave him fresh insight to the horror that had befallen Britain that day. Liam's own battle experience had inoculated him to a certain degree especially in terms of the defence mechanisms he employed, but listening to Jane's gasps and feeling her shake to the point she might levitate brought on a wave of feeling he almost couldn't control.

He concentrated on Jane and watched grimly as Captain John MacKinnon again raised his rifle and sent a wash of blood over Sky News that would be forever etched in the minds of those who saw it, the men, women and children sat down gripped by a developing story in North London. 'Ok Liam, enough,' was all Jane could manage as she buried her head in Liam's shoulder as the screams of the Sky News anchor echoed around the coving of her living room. Liam hit stop, and birdsong filled the airless evening again.

16

Wallace had clearly forgotten nothing of her advanced driving test. Despite himself, Jack was impressed and felt she was enjoying her rare stint away from her desk. She flung the old Mondeo into East Finchley High Street and south towards Highgate Village. She cut across the A1 with a screech and hurtled through the fork that divided into two the road to town and the village.

As if reading his mind, she simply said, 'Flying Squad.' Jack nodded and watched as crowds of Friday drinkers gathered to shout and wave them on past the Victoria, Old Bull and Wrestlers pubs before hitting more organised crowds at Highgate. Wallace brought the car to a halt a couple of feet before a startled Merton and two uniformed officers demanding an update.

'Ma'am, we've got teams going house to house, the chopper has been scrambled and given the fading light, their infrared and searchlight will come into play, we're bound to get him, now.' Jack sighed, and Wallace just raised her eyebrows.

Jack leaned across, shouting above the howl of sirens 'I admire your optimism, Merton, I really do but listen, don't pussyfoot around on the door to doors. People might be out or away, once you're in the back garden of any house, get over the walls with teams of four or five and comb as many back gardens as you can. They might complain but bollocks, we'll deal with that afterwards; besides, no one will care if we bag MacKinnon tonight.'

'Ok Jack,' said Merton and got straight on the radio barking the orders out to the teams sweeping the Merton Lane houses.

Wallace pulled over to give full and clear access to the cavalcade of response vehicles careering back and forth. She sighed deeply, 'Jesus, he's making mugs of us again isn't he?'

'I can't help feeling he is, ma'am, yeah.' A moment passed, the two senior officers lost in contemplation before Jack spoke again, 'I wonder to what end?'

'What do you mean?'

'Well, you think about it, in a battle scenario, he had a clear aim and a purpose for doing what he was doing. What can he hope to gain? For all his expert avoidance of those pursuing him, what can he possibly think is the point?'

'So you think he'll just give up?'

'No, I really don't. We are closing in though, I'm sure of that. Without a clear purpose other than his own survival, I feel he'll make mistakes. Whether that makes him more dangerous or not, I don't know.'

'Jack, second guessing this man hasn't got us very far at all before has it?'

Mac had chosen well. His garden had a selection of very old and tall trees that made him invisible from above and enough places to deposit himself off the ground to avoid detection from below if his hunch about search teams not looking up proved right. In the still dead air with darkness increasing by the minute, the sound of the search throbbed in his head, the helicopter blades, the sirens, the radios, the shouts… in Mac's head the sounds were blurred and indistinct like he was under water. He shook his head, desperate to stay alert while blades of torch light arced across the garden next door. Urgent mutterings and the sound of shed doors being opened and closed. Officers hissing 'clear' and 'no, nothing'.

His eyes adjusted to the increasing murk, Mac watched the search team, noting they were armed and preparing to enter his garden. He could hear laughter, piss takes and commanding officer chastisement when it got too much. There were six men scaling the six-foot wall coated with thick ivy and landing with heavy thuds. The fifth man slipped on his arse with a flurry of expletives to an explosion of laughter from his comrades and calls of 'twat', 'idiot' and 'muppet.'

The merriment quickly gave way to an urgent shout of 'sarge!' and the men rushing to a corner of a garden where torches had picked out the unmistakable glisten of a pair of eyes. The urgency quickly died away as they realised they had cornered a startled fox, frozen in the thick unforgiving confluence of six torch beams. Mac was mesmerised by the stillness of the creature he knew to be a female, healthy and fully matured. She tilted her head slightly as another wave of expletives exploded from the men as they turned to the rest of the densely vegetated garden.

Now the men were directly below him, but the torchlight rarely went over shoulder height. So Mac relaxed in the layer of darkness sandwiched between the sporadic overhead searchlight and half dozen scatter-gun torches below. Like a short, sharp shower, they were soon gone.

He looked to where the fox was, and despite the return of peace and darkness to the garden, he could just make out the two tiny dots of her eyes. She paced warily out to a patch of lawn and looked up at Mac. He put his finger to his lips, and she held his gaze for a second or two before retreating back to the safety of her corner of this secret garden.

Wallace thumped the thick plastic of the steering wheel, the thrill of being in the chase and not chained to her desk wearing thin. She fired up the Mondeo and raced around the cordoned off streets as if randomly driving up and down the deserted streets would throw them a break. Jack just shrugged as she barked, 'got any better ideas?' at him. After failing to spot a sleeping policeman on the east side of the Heath, they nearly took off with the suspension making a fearful bang.

'Shit, sorry Jack, pass me the radio will you? Merton? Wallace.'

'Ma'am.'

'Any update for us?'

'Negative, ma'am.'

'Well, god help us, Merton, we're ducking out of the wild goose chase for a while, and you're in charge, call us the minute anything changes.'

'Of course, ma'am.'

'Right, your DI is buying me a coffee.'

'You'll be lucky, over and out.'

'Cheeky bugger,' said Jack as they screeched off in the direction of a roadside coffee shack on the northern fringes of the Heath.

Jack did actually have an idea. It involved Jane Harkness, Major Liam Collins and Major Bradley Wilkinson. It wasn't much of an idea.

'That's not much of an idea,' said Wallace, taking a large sip of her milky white coffee.

'I know, but I just feel his only redemption, his last mission, if you like, is to get somewhere safe. With his home no longer an option he needs what he regards as his base.' Wallace nodded, 'Go on, Jack.'

'I know second guessing MacKinnon has been impossible so far, he's made total mugs of us, we've already said as much. But given his issues and reading Jane's notes they were getting somewhere, he was responding. Now he's a hunted animal looking for some sort of position where he can contemplate survival.' Wallace was slowly nodded her head. Jack paused, and they both looked at the TV rigged up behind the counter showing the fabulous gardens of Highgate from the air, library shots showing swimming pools, lush, dense greenery, elaborate summer houses and terraces.

'I'm calling Major Collins, he's going to try and see Jane. What that means I just don't know, but he will go there. We'll piss about playing keystone cops up here, but that's where's he's going.' He pointed at the TV. 'He's there in one of those bloody gardens, and we won't catch him, he's too damn good for that.'

He picked up his phone. 'Major Collins, DI Jack Love here. Look, I need to meet you and Jane Harkness as soon as possible. You're with her now? Excellent, we're on our way. Yes, I know the address, thanks,' Jack hung up and finished his coffee, energy beginning to course through him, banishing the heat-induced torpor and reek of failure.

Mac jumped down from the trees as its upper branches began to sway and in the midst of all the others doing the same the noise was deafening after the dead heat of another hot day. Infused with a new sense of vigour, he had to get on his way, darkness was his friend as he headed south once more. The fox had come onto the lawn again and was looking up at the trees as the wind whipped at them. Leaves were falling, and she tried to catch one in her mouth. She looked at Mac, stood stock still, absorbing the change in the air. She looked north and took a run and jumped over the heavily creosoted fence that separated the house from the woods. Mac looked south and scaled the wall, scanned his way for danger and silently jumped onto a path that would take him to the A1.

It was approaching 10pm when Jack hit the A1, and the traffic was light. Radio 5Live had cleared their schedules to draft their most well-known anchors in to follow the story live. Jack snorted at the talking heads, opining various theories including MacKinnon disappearing altogether and living wild indefinitely 'outside the law and hapless efforts of the police.' He found himself speeding up when one expert, a criminologist argued that it would 'end tonight.'

'I agree, it ends tonight,' he said to himself, putting his siren on as he approached the thicker traffic developing at Archway.

Mac evaded the knots of uniform at Highgate with ease and blended in with the Friday evening crowds. He looked for all the world like a normal member of the public walking through Archway towards the tube, and no one batted an eyelid. He hurried across the A1 when an unmarked Ford Mondeo with its urgent siren demanding he got out of the way. He stood on the inside lane watching the silver car bullet past. He raised his hand slowly as it passed and thought he recognised the driver.

Jack raced under Archway and towards the junction by the hospital, intent on getting to Balham as quickly as possible. People often wandered into the road in London nonchalantly making it to the other side when in reality they've nearly been knocked down. Jack had done it himself and convinced himself his timing was perfect despite the beeps and the shouts. Seeing it as a driver was very different indeed, but this joker standing in the inside lane was ridiculous, a Friday night drunk asking to be hit. He was thankful the man was standing still, he even raised a hand to wave like the revellers had done when he and Wallace were heading to Highgate Village. But this was different.

'Shit.' Jack brought the car to a howling stop just short of the interchange, the acrid smell of burning rubber filling the car. He looked in his rear-view mirror and the man, now unmistakably Capt John MacKinnon, was leaning on the pavement side of the barrier staring at Jack, a mere 50 yards away, his face impassive. He knew before he moved to open the door that he would be gone and Mac hadn't let him down. There was no sign of him.

Jack ignored the horns and abuse and walked slowly along the road deliberately looking in the direction where he guessed Mac would have gone. He surmised that he would be watching the road planning his next move. So Jack walked even slower, staring into the trees and houses lining the A1. He reached the railings, the wind disturbing his hair but energising him. With the aid of a lamppost, he hauled himself on top of the narrow railings, a path and elevated litter strewn grass area separating the houses from the road. He held his position and looked straight at trees he picked out in a back garden between two semi-detached houses.

At the top of his voice, he shouted, 'This ends tonight,' remaining on the railings a moment or so before jumping down and returning to his abandoned car, engine still running with the experts still hopelessly second guessing Jack's quarry on Radio 5 Live.

Mac was 100 yards away running like the hunted animal he was. He was aware of shouting, horns blaring and the roar of car engines. A particularly vivid shout pierced the air, but he couldn't quite make out the exact words. He navigated the lower gardens and fences in Archway with ease and continued heading south crossing roads and walking through crowds unseen. Just another anonymous Londoner.

Jane poured the wine, vowing it would need to be the one given they had no idea what lay ahead that night. Liam noted they were hearty glasses just the same, full bodied Rioja too. He sighed, took a sip and thought what would be would be. The wine was delicious, and he felt a little giddy. He wasn't a big drinker these days, finding alcohol didn't help him at all. He loved the taste, liked the buzz a small amount gave you and left it at that. Compared to his hard drinking active combat days he found this far preferable. No crippling hangovers, no chunks of time unaccounted for, no brawling... yes, it was much better these days.

'Liam?' said Jane, 'Penny for them?'

'Ah nothing really, just thinking about the 'demon drink,' that's all. The amounts we used to put away as young blokes was frightening.' Liam shook his head slowly in wonderment at his younger self. 'Then the army came along, and it was premier league drinking all the way, part of the culture, you had to join in, not that I needed persuading in those days.'

Jane nodded, 'I've never really been a big drinker.'

'Too busy talking I'd imagine.'

Jane threw a faux wounded look at Liam before smiling knowing that Liam had several lunches with her when his meal would be finished and food would be dangling off her raised fork with the rest of her meal untouched and cold, such was her urge to talk.

'Anyway,' she continued, 'I'm what society would see as a light or moderate drinker, always have been. Boring, I guess you might say.'

'What's so exciting about drinkers? It's odd how society can be so beholden to drink, and I say that as someone who likes the stuff. Non-drinkers always have to explain themselves, it's almost like they're viewed with suspicion. I even knew a girl who once said she couldn't trust a man who didn't drink. Imagine that? In Barrow, lasses were getting thumped all the time by drunken men. What are you smiling at?'

'I love the way your accent drifts back in every now and again like a lazy tide, it's lovely.'

'Are you flirting with me?'

'No, don't be silly, Liam, she laughed. 'Well, might be...' They both laughed. They were sat on Jane's three seater leather sofa, and Jane noticed that Liam had his feet up on a footstool. She felt glad he could relax and that they could sit so companionably together. She took a sip of her wine; forgetting momentarily that Mac was heading towards them.

'I've seen the destruction booze can cause in my work. It breaks my heart.'

'Is it the booze or how the individual uses it that is the problem?'

'Damn, you're good. You haven't forgotten your training have you?' Liam just saluted wearily.

Central London was even easier to navigate for Mac, having deliberately chosen the crowded areas and he resisted the urge to move too quickly. He mooched along at times, looking in shop windows and even laughed along with a passing stag do heading for Covent Garden. He was less impressed when they thought it would be hilarious to 'kidnap' him and take him to the next pub. There were thirty blokes, and they winched him up on their shoulders thinking he was skinny and light. He asked one of the lads to 'hold his fishing rod' who didn't bat an eyelid. 'Course I will, mate, enjoy the ride,' he cheerfully slurred. Hoisted aloft, Mac took in the faintly lit stars and the rhythmic blinking lights and dull drone of jets preparing their approach to Heathrow. He laughed loudly, the stag party unaware their prey was also being pursued with more serious vigour so close by.

They made him have a jagerbomb, and with a wave and a big cheer, he was on his way again, heading over Waterloo Bridge, the strong north wind driving him relentlessly south to Balham.

'What I mean, Major Liam Collins, is that I've seen people and whole families get destroyed by what alcohol can do,' said Jane, warming to her theme. 'It's the grip it has on people that is so fascinating to me. What is this urge to take themselves somewhere else, to change their state of mind?'

'Yes, is it a bad experience?' Liam was sitting up now. 'Or indeed experiences? It's tempting to take a Daily Mail view and imagine 'getting off your tits' is a relatively new phenomenon, but it's been with us for centuries, of course. Drugs, alcohol, nicotine, you name it, we use it to change our state of mind and have done forever.'

Jack was racing through Whitehall towards Westminster Bridge in silence now the radio debate had run out of steam. Big Ben's floating, glowing white face was showing it was close to 11 as he swung onto the bridge, the traffic mercifully light. Merton called and said they'd lifted the cordon and moved away from the Highgate area, aside from SOCO and some uniformed officers. They knew Captain MacKinnon had long gone and Jack confirmed he'd had a brief encounter with him in Archway. Wallace had relayed Jack's theory upstairs and in the absence any other ideas, armed officers were also heading to Balham.

Mac's seamless progress gave him the courage to jump on a bus and try to get to Jane before she went to bed. He was like a homing pigeon or an automaton, heading somewhere with no idea what it would bring. His mind, so focussed on survival, was now collapsing. He felt dizzy and nauseous on the bus, the bus sticky after the refreshing cool change that had hit London that night. A couple, stinking of alcohol and emerging from a row, moved away from him thinking he was in a worse state than they were and therefore dangerous.

He closed his eyes and was back in the desert, a passenger in a Land Rover en route to a mission, the adrenaline starting to course through his veins. He opened his eyes and saw he was on Balham High Street. A young lad in his twenties and tooled up with the latest smartphone sat in the seat opposite Mac. He had over-ear headphones on and was gripped by something on his phone. He started looking back and forth at Mac and the screen, urgent tinny whispers escaping from his cans.

Mac was aware he was being observed and snapped back into attention. Mac got up and leaned over the now cowering young man, his studied cool long evaporated. Mac looked at his smartphone screen and watched himself raising his rifle slowly before aerial shots of Hampstead Heath played behind the breaking news graphics and ticker.

'You're not going to say a word, are you?' The man just looked stunned. Mac flicked the headphones off his head with the back of his hand causing the man to squeal. Mac shook his head slowly. 'You're not going to say a word are you?' He put his finger to his lips and gently placed the headphones back on his head. He was very close now and cursed that he had placed himself in danger on a brightly lit bus. He got off the bus, quickly checked it was clear and took out his rifle.

Greg Cooper was heading south after enjoying a third date with a woman he had met in work. She was smart, funny and, Greg thought, very pretty indeed. They had enjoyed a somewhat passionate farewell outside the 100 club on Oxford St before deciding to call it a night, Martha grabbing the last tube to Walthamstow while he took a bus south to Streatham. He was catching up with the news on his iPhone after multiple texts alerting him to 'unbelievable' and 'amazing' footage on all the news channels. As an IT worker, it was assumed he would have been all over it that evening, so details were sparse, but his reception was poor in the gig, and for once he wasn't exactly that focussed on his phone.

Saying goodnight outside the club, he was aware of the insistent buzzing in his pocket. 'Someone's popular,' breathed Martha in his ear.

'Undeniable' he whispered before kissing her again, the delicious mix of fresh lager and a hint of garlic reeling him in as well as the intoxicating feeling of someone new. They looked at each other, desire and resignation doing battle in their eyes. They hugged one more time at the top of the stairs of Oxford Circus tube and made their separate ways home.

He floated down Regent Street not bothering to stop the smile forming on his freshly kissed lips enjoying the slow burn of this fledgeling relationship. Now just 40 minutes later, a man he had watched on his news app pointing a rifle at the camera was doing the same at him as he tried to call the police. He froze, and the last thing he heard was the breaking of the bus window as the single bullet headed for his brain and then there was nothing.

Mac heard shouts from two men emerging from a kebab shop and ran for cover, heading down a side street he hurtled over a fence and into a side alley, sirens throbbing in his head. He had to get to Jane's as soon as possible. He was very close but sat on his haunches as doubts and confusion furred his mind. What would happen there? What would she do? How long could he stay there? The one thought that kept chugging along in the background like a subtle bass line was safety. Jane was safety to Mac.

Jane and Liam sat in comfortable silence pondering their conversation about the 'demon drink', as they called it. The chat meant they had momentarily put Mac to the back of their minds, but with the wine remaining largely untouched the friends and colleagues were aware they needed to keep their wits about them if their assertion that he was coming to Jane was to be proved correct. She felt a burst of tiredness in the conversational lull and noticed Liam's eyelids were beginning to droop.

'Coffee?' Liam looked at her, smiled and nodded slowly before stretching his arms wide and releasing a long deep yawn. 'I'll put the kettle on.'

Jane went to the kitchen, filled the kettle, flicked it on and got the cafetiere and coffee out of the cupboard. The kitchen window was open, and though it looked out on to the sheltered garden, a fierce breeze blew through causing goose bumps to form on her arms. She shut the window and stared out into the pitch black of night, a lit window or two puncturing the darkness. She shivered and rubbed her arms as the kettle got into its stride. As it reached the boil, she thought she heard a crash in the garden, but all she could see was a wall of black and thought of the vicious wind that had whipped in from the north.

Mac arrived in the garden with an unfortunate bang as he knocked over a large piece of heavy wood onto the concrete path. He didn't know what to do. He watched transfixed as Jane pottered in the kitchen, making coffee, unaware of his arrival. His single-mindedness in getting to her meant he assumed she would be on her own. Jane reaching for two cups showed how wrong he was. He moved along the garden and peered through the window and saw Major Liam Collins sat on the large dark brown leather sofa looking at the ceiling. It took him a moment to recognise him in his civilian clothes, but it was him alright. What was he doing there? He definitely wasn't expecting the Major. He took out his rifle, loaded it and walked up to the floor to ceiling glass doors. He pressed his face against the window.

Liam listened to Jane rattling round her kitchen making the coffee. Any little lull even now would prompt memories of battlefield horrors. They were always there, ghosts behind the curtains. Such was his own experience of therapy was that he no longer feared these ghosts returning, instead, accepting them. The ferocity sometimes took him by surprise, and it really was darkest before dawn whenever he woke in the early hours. The sights, the sounds and the smells were as vivid as the days these events happened, more so in a sense after you had processed horrors that had occurred so quickly at the time.

Friends appeared before him now to a backdrop of screams and the sound of gunfire. Burning flesh and the smell of blood filled his nostrils as screaming jet engines and exploding shells thumped in his eardrums. His best friend appeared, bloody with a look of indescribable desolation on his face. Tears began to tumble down his face.

Mac looked intently at this man covering his face and wondered what private grief he was witnessing. No matter, he was an obstacle in getting to Jane. He took three steps back from the window, raised his rifle and watched as Major Liam Collins put his hands down and looked squarely at him, a look of recognition, bafflement turning to abhorrence spread across his face. Mac pulled the trigger, shattering the huge glass door and putting a small hole in the major's forehead. A veteran of the Balkans and the first Gulf War, a man who had witnessed so much death and destruction and had dedicated his life to helping others, had been shot dead on a sofa in a comfortable south London suburb.

Lights came on, and dogs barked in the tightly packed terraced houses backing onto Jane's house. Mac could hear sirens in the distance, not an unusual sound in London but then the air filled with a piercing scream, Jane had walked into a room that once would have represented the hub of joyous family life but in a second had changed forever.

She fell to her knees in front of the stricken major and cried out in anguish. With no thought for own safety, she tried to revive Liam, the neatness of the wound fooling part of her that he may still be alive. The wind roared through the shattered window, but she felt nothing in the urgent need to help Liam. His eyes gazed forward blankly as the little trickle of blood made its way down his forehead to the bridge of his nose. She brought his head forward and screamed again as the exit wound was far less neat and grey matter spattered her brown sofa.

'He's dead,' a voice said to her.

'I know,' she replied, her voice a strangulated whisper, 'I know.'

'I'm sorry, he was in the way.'

Jane quickly turned to face Mac, 'What? What did you say?'

Mac's face was grimly determined, but his eyes darted around the room struggling to focus. Jane kept closing her eyes as if this grisly scene might magically disappear. Every time she opened them, Mac was in a different position in the room.

'Please keep still, Mac, please.' She started to shiver and then cry uncontrollably. Mac raced upstairs, found a blanket and raced back to Jane. She was hugging Liam's legs, juddering with huge sobs. He wrapped the blanket around her shoulders and stood back, pondering his next move as the urgent sirens came closer and closer.

Jack took two calls as he pulled over on Balham High Street to double check Jane Harkness' address. The first call was from Merton telling him a 23 year old male had been shot dead on a bus on the High Street twenty minutes ago. He called back virtually straight away to say gunshots had been heard in the vicinity of the Harkness household and to proceed with caution.

'The thought had occurred to me, Merton.'

'You are unarmed, Jack, and MacKinnon has obviously totally lost it. Please wait for SO19 to get there.'

'Can't I'm afraid, Harkness must be in severe danger, I need to get there now, Merton. Tell Wallace, will you? Make sure SO19 liaise with me on arrival, no bloody Rambo acts tonight. Get the street sealed off and no chopper. Whatever you do, call the chopper off.'

Relieved he was so close, he sprinted to the houses adjacent to Jane's. A few people were out on their doorsteps wondering what was going on. He flashed his badge and told them to get indoors and to stay away from their windows knowing damn well that last nugget would be completely ignored. He couldn't worry about that. Jane's next door neighbour was also out on her doorstep, about to knock on her door from what Jack could see. He caught her in time, an elegant woman in her sixties, smartly dressed after an evening out.

'Madam, please do not knock that door.' He flashed his warrant card again, 'what have you seen or heard here tonight? And can you tell me inside your house please?'

'It's Grace and yes, come in, please.'

They hurried in, Jack quietly closing the door.

'I haven't been in long after going to a show, and it was all very quiet. Then I heard a huge smashing of glass out the back then a scream like I had never heard before. It really chilled me to my bones. I don't know the family that well but they seem very nice, especially the lady, Jane.'

Jack nodded and thanked Grace. 'Grace, can you show me to the back of your house please?'

Without replying, she walked through the modern and expensively assembled kitchen. Jack quickly told her to stop and put the lights out. 'Grace, please wait in your front room, thank you.' Without fuss, Grace nodded and quickly made her way to the front of the house.

Jack could see the bright lights of Jane's kitchen extension burning brightly but as yet could not see any movement. He unlocked the back door of Grace's kitchen and slipped into the small garden space, concrete dotted with large tasteful flower pots and a table of chairs. He crept on his hands and knees to the low red brick garden wall. He peeked over the wall into the kitchen and saw that a cafetiere of coffee had been prepared and was still steaming on a tray with two mugs. He looked as far as he could beyond the extension and saw the thousands of tiny bits of glass from the door windows.

'We need to go upstairs, Jane. I need to get you away from this, come on.' Jane, numb with shock, simply stood up, and Mac helped her slowly through the living room to the hall and stairs.

Jack climbed over the wall and crept along the side of the kitchen extension all the while getting a better view into the house. He heard a voice and stood stock still. Through the kitchen door, he saw Captain John MacKinnon carefully leading Jane Harkness through the hallway to the stairs. She had a cream blanket wrapped around her shoulders and appeared to be crying. MacKinnon's rifle was over his other shoulder as he led her upstairs. Jack was puzzled, why the smash, gunshots and commotion? What had happened here? Emboldened by Mac heading upstairs, he quickly went round the extension, and the answer took his breath away.

Major Liam Collins stared at Jack through the smashed window. He got on his phone for a whispered appeal for an ambulance, however futile, and a status update on his armed support.

Jane's violent trembling was subsiding, like she was entering the earth's atmosphere again. She recognised her bedroom and called Ray's name. The silence that greeted her plaintive calling surprised her. She felt anger too that he wasn't there. Where the hell was he? The main light was on, harsh and unkind like an interrogator's lamp. She never put that on, preferring the softer shades of her bedside light. She noticed the blanket around her shoulders and again felt a chill, but the terrible automatic shivers did not return. She licked her lips and recognised the taste of wine. She felt so tired and being sat on the bed she just wanted to lie back and close her eyes.

Instead, she started to get up and go to the bay window at the front of her house. She gasped as someone said 'no' quietly but firmly behind her. She turned slowly to face the stranger in her room. When she saw Mac, the previous hour flashed past her, and she struggled to stay on her feet.

'Sit down Jane. Please,' he said simply. She did what he said, the full horror returning to her like a kick in the throat. She fought the urge to dissolve into tears and concentrated on Mac. His face was full of the squalls of thoughts she was so familiar with from their therapy sessions. He at once radiated concern, confusion, doubt and remorse but most of all an almost savage air of sadness.

'Why Mac? Why?' Jane asked. 'Liam, of all people, Mac. He understood you, he knew what you were going through. He only ever wanted to help you, he devoted his life to helping people like you and you shoot him dead.'

'He was in the way.'

'In the way of what?' snapped Jane. 'In the way of what, Mac?'

'My only mission was to get to safety. Only you can help me, nothing and no one can get in the way.' His expression immediately seemed to question the words he'd just said.

'Brilliant, so what now, Mac? You going to shoot me too?' He looked alarmed at this prospect like it was the most ludicrous notion in the world. Surprised too by Jane's anger, he simply said, 'no.'

'So what then, Mac? Tell me, because the police will be here very soon, they will be armed. You've got to give yourself up.' Mac shook his head slowly.

'I've never been captured, and that won't change tonight.' Mac's words immediately haunted Jane, the sudden realisation that she was in very real danger in her own home, the place you should always feel safest. She thought of Ray and the kids, her elderly parents.

'I can run rings round these jokers.'

'They will catch you, Mac. And why run anyway, what are you going to achieve? What sort of life are you going to have?'

'Jane, how will I ever be free of this? I can't be locked up, and it's not going to happen. That's why I'm here, you know what I should do. After all I've told you, you think I should hand myself in?'

'Yes I do, they can help you. Might seem desperate now, but there will be help.'

'From you?' Jane couldn't answer this question immediately, she didn't honestly know the answer, but Mac's agitation ignited.

'So I get sent to some nutjob hospital with the Yorkshire Ripper for the rest of my life? Without you? How can you desert me now?'

SO19 informed Jack by text that they were outside and standing by, awaiting a status report on the situation inside the house. Relieved he had put the phone on silent and that SO19 were mindful enough to contact him that way, he asked their CO to join him at the rear of Grace's house. He inched his way into the kitchen and to the hallway. He listened intently and could hear Mac's voice, agitated and confused. He heard Jane pleading with him and his heart thumped through his chest. Satisfied it was just the two of them up there, he carefully retraced his steps back to Grace's kitchen where the incongruous sight of a burly man in full black combat gear greeted him. He offered an iron-fisted handshake and raised his visor to introduce himself as Commander Mike Harrington. Jack introduced himself and quickly appraised Harrington of the situation.

'Is she a hostage?' he asked.

Jack replied, 'No, I don't believe so, but as you know, he is extremely volatile. He has killed twice already tonight, we have to conclude Jane Harkness is in very real danger up there.'

'Ok, I've been briefed on the nature of the suspect, do we try and negotiate with him? We have trained people in the squad, not sure we've had such a wild card before though.'

Jack had also had siege and hostage negotiation training and was willing to try anything. Judging by Mac's actions this last day he doubted if it would work. He had taken out the Sky reporter, a man on the bus and Major Liam Collins, all seemingly en route to Jane and with his mental condition rapidly deteriorating. That made him an extremely dangerous individual indeed. He remembered Major Bradley Wilkinson telling him to tread carefully and that they were making progress with Captain MacKinnon. He'd love Wilkinson's take on this now.

Nevertheless, he wanted no more deaths tonight, and something about Wilkinson's words and Jane's protective feelings about Mac reinforced that view.

'Of course, I won't desert you, Mac, that just isn't going to happen. Whatever else happens tonight, I will be there, I'm not giving up on you.' Jane knew she was in survival mode now and would say anything to walk out of this alive and into the arms of Ray and the boys.

'Do you really mean that, Jane?'

She did. Despite Liam lying dead on her sofa downstairs and the other innocent people who died at Mac's hands, he still had a hold on her. The feeling was forming in her that somehow this was a man who was failed by the system, a man who was completely and utterly lost and had abdicated all responsibility for his actions. This was the logical yet grisly conclusion to a situation that had had its touch paper lit years ago and now, due to a rapidly worsening mental state, had cost lives.

He had seen things very few people could begin to imagine. One of those few was Liam, and he had paid the price for caring about these troubled men. She couldn't go the same way as Liam, and she also had to help Mac or at least convince him that she could help him.

Mac went to the window and looked out onto the street. He could see men taking up positions behind trees and cars all along the road. He could see the road was cordoned off and that neighbours were taking a peek at proceedings from behind their curtains. His head started to thump, and he felt nauseous and dizzy. He looked out again with the enemy closing in, and he knew he was in serious danger of capture. Previous grave situations played in his head like TV repeats, how he escaped, how he killed his way out of seemingly doomed scenarios. Cunning mixed with sheer brutality, living on his wits, high on adrenaline, losing comrades as he went... was that his fault? It probably was in some predicaments, some men just couldn't keep up or react like he did, the sheer freedom of running, the feeling of invincibility. It was a blessing and a curse how his survival instinct kicked in to such an extreme extent.

There was always relief when he made it back to base of course, but it was quickly followed by what muppets on TV would call 'survival guilt', a load of bollocks in an era when every condition needed a label to give it legitimacy. On too many occasions he lost people he liked and respected and that hurt so much. It wasn't guilt, it was bloody grief. Sometimes, an action of a comrade helped him survive but the comrade didn't make it, but there was no guilt about that, just grief. His head felt it was going to explode. It was all too much, he didn't really know where he was. He had nowhere to escape to, and that realisation exhausted him.

'Mac, talk to me, you're shaking, why are you clutching your head?' asked Jane. He turned around and looked at her but said nothing. She watched his face and the storms he couldn't hide. She got up and joined him at the window.

'We're surrounded,' he said.

'Surrounded? I can't see anything.'

'Come here,' said Mac, clarity quickly returning, a soldier assessing the enemy and a strategy for surviving or winning a battle. 'See that glint of light just over the blue saloon by that tree?' Jane nodded in the direction Mac was pointing.

'That's a rifle, look two cars down on the left, rifle, two more cars – rifle.'

Sure enough, once her eyes adjusted, she could see the firearms trained on her house. Worse, she could now see the men in black combat uniform, some watching through binoculars. The wind had dropped again, but the air remained cool, and the street was Sunday morning calm. She looked down to the High Road and saw her road had been cordoned off.

'Mac, we can end this now, and I can help you.'

Sergeant Stuart Brock was surveying the house through field glasses. He watched as MacKinnon talked to Harkness clear as day in the bay window. They could take him out immediately, but they were under strict orders to wait for orders from Commander Harrington. He was transfixed by the comfort the two people appeared in each other's company. They were briefed that this was a hostage situation, but Harrington warned them this was no normal hostage scenario, whatever that was. He reached for his radio to update Harrington.

The stillness was broken by Harrington's radio piercing the night with an update from the street. He broke off his conversation with Jack to reply, his Home Counties baritone filling every inch of Grace's kitchen. Jane turned to Mac but he was gone, and she heard fleet-footed steps on her wooden stairs. He appeared in Jack's eye line, and before he could speak, a bullet tore through the Harrington's left cheek and into his brain, his face retaining the calm demeanour as he slumped on Grace's kitchen island his head smearing the work surface with a swipe of blood before he hit her tiled floor.

Grace had walked into the kitchen at the moment the bullet had hit Harrington and started screaming wildly. Jack looked to where Mac was, but he'd gone, so he dived on Grace to take cover and tried in vain to calm her. She was shaking as if a fit had overcome her and Jack did his best, holding her tight and thinking this might be it for them. All he would need to do was walk calmly into the kitchen and shoot them both. A thousand thoughts flickered through his head, images of his parents and then Annie as a massive crash came from the hallway.

Brock, alerted by Grace's screaming, frantically waved his men towards the front door and, leading the way, Brock smashed his way through, the men all shouting in time-honoured fashion, all adrenaline after so much watching and waiting. The sight of the stricken Harrington staring up at the kitchen ceiling in a growing puddle of blood stopped them in their tracks.

'Jesus Christ,' hissed Brock at the head of six stunned SO19 officers. His radio was ablaze with urgent requests for information as Grace kept screaming as the clatter of a helicopter overhead added to the sense of chaos.

'Mac, what happened? What did you do?' cried Jane, tears streaming down her face. 'Why is Grace screaming?' Mac slammed the bedroom door and scanned the ceiling before his shoulders slumped, and he looked at Jane utterly tortured and terrified. He didn't speak, he just stared at Jane, his eyes also full of tears. The noise of the chopper was so loud they couldn't hear each other anyway, so they just looked at each other.

Brock allowed his training to kick back in and turned to Jack.

'Is the woman, Harkness... is she still up there? Have you heard any other shots? Do you think she's alive?'

'I heard her speaking until the noise of the helicopter drowned everything out,' said Jack as loudly as he could.

Brock nodded and pulled one of the men away from looking at Harrington's body to take Grace into her front room and try to calm her down or at least stop the screaming. 'What do we do, sir?'

'We can't charge up there, sergeant, I'm as sure as I can be that he wouldn't harm Harkness.' Jack noticed the look of disappointment on the young sergeant's face, the need for vengeance bubbling just beneath the professional surface. Jack held firm. 'Somehow I need to make contact, have you got a loud hailer?' Brock nodded and disappeared into the front room. Jack looked up and saw that the five SO19 officers were staring straight at him, eyes nearly demented with rage. Every police officer feels a colleague's death on the job like members of the public feel the death of a close relative, but it was clear the tight-knit unit was consumed with the need for vengeance. They looked at Jack with a potent mix of fury and longing, none of them older than about twenty-five.

Jane looked at Mac, amazed her spell in army counselling had led her to this moment, standing in her bedroom surrounded by armed police with a fugitive who had killed a colleague in her living room. The one thing she didn't feel now was fear and that thought occurred to her. She wondered if that would bite her on the arse down the line but quickly resolved to worry about that later.

Mac looked again at the ceiling then went to the door and opened it slightly. He watched for some time and listened as best he could as the chopper hovered and its searchlight laced the room. He could see the tops of helmets and raised voices but not in anger he thought, more to make themselves heard. He closed the door again and surveyed the room. His training taught him to assess every dangerous situation and think what can be used in his immediate vicinity to aid escape. Jane's bedroom provided slim pickings on first viewing. If the enemy charged, he was at least elevated and he had Jane. He was hopelessly outnumbered, and no doubt surrounded from all sides and above.

The noise of the chopper grew quieter as it moved away from the target site. Mac wondered why and soon he got his answer.

'Captain MacKinnon? Captain John MacKinnon, can you hear me? This is DI Jack Love from the Metropolitan Police. Please confirm if Jane Harkness is alive and well up there please?' said Jack through the SO19 megaphone. Mac looked at Jane and put his finger to his lips. Jack had climbed the stairs and was lying on the mini landing just as the stairs turned to reach the top of the house. Brock had given him a pistol, helmet and flak jacket. It was quieter, but the megaphone was definitely required. He had no idea if Harkness was alive and establishing her situation was his first priority. He asked again.

'Captain MacKinnon, please confirm if Jane Harkness is alive. If you do not answer, I will have no option to send a SWAT team in to the room.' As Jack started pondering his next move, he heard Jane Harkness' voice.

'Yes, I am here and unharmed.' Mac didn't look perturbed and just shrugged when Jane looked at him palms outstretched.

'That's good, I'm glad to hear that. Now, Captain MacKinnon, this is a very serious and dangerous situation but one we can end in total safety now. Just lay down your rifle and walk out very slowly with your hands up and I guarantee your safety. We are here to help you.'

Jack looked down at the accompanying officers joining him on the stairs and saw their response to that statement. He knew of Mac's service record, the incredible operations he'd been involved in, the friends and comrades he'd lost. He thought of the raid on the Taliban communications outpost, just 10 of them disrupting a desert encampment. Surely they didn't expect to come out of that alive? Half of them didn't, of course, including his close friend who met an unimaginably brutal ending. What a pathetic way to end his freedom this would be, after all the missions he taken part in. He shook his head slowly.

Jane was relieved she was no longer alone in the house and found Love's voice a comfort as the feeling things were about to unravel uncontrollably grew inside her. She didn't fear for herself, but looking at Mac, she knew he wasn't about to walk into the DI's handcuffs. All manner of storms were breaking over his face, he rubbed his right hand through his tightly cut hair as he frantically thought. He looked at Jane, a slight grin forming on his lips. He beckoned her to come close which she did without hesitating.

'Is there a skylight in your attic?' He immediately shushed her beginnings of a protest and asked again. She simply nodded. They were face to face now, Mac giving off an earthy mix of stale perspiration and dirt.

He whispered in her ear, 'Do not argue or try to stop me. I am going to get your bedside chair, place it under the loft entrance and pull myself up through it. Once I am in your loft, you will wait 20 seconds before saying to Love that I am releasing you and that you will walk out slowly and into his custody.'

'You won't make it,' she whispered furiously back. 'It's suicide.'

He simply looked at her, his faced flushed with sadness and confusion before he looked down and muttered, 'I can't stay here, you know that Jane don't you? It's time to go.'

'We can help you, you can't keep running Mac, presuming you get out of here alive.'

'What, you and Love? The unit? Liam?'

She thought of Liam lying dead downstairs and stopped herself wondering what would happen to Mac now. She looked up at him and gave the briefest of nods. In the blink of an eye he had got the chair, loosened the loft cover, and with his rifle over his shoulder he deftly pulled himself up. He knelt and looked down into the bedroom at Jane Directly below, tears running down her face. He held her gaze, giving the briefest of smiles before flicking both hands twice reminding her to speak to Love in 20 seconds. He placed the cover back on the loft opening.

Albert Johnson left his Highgate cottage around 10pm that night and walked down to the Prince of Wales in the village, grateful the awful cloying heat had at last lifted and that a bracing breeze was now rattling through North London. He could not sleep with all the sirens, helicopters and flashing blue lights tearing up the place, in fact, he'd never known a night like it. Since Prince had been shot dead, he had slept so much with the heat adding to his malaise, reminding him of the heat of Malaya during the war and the brutality of his Japanese POW camp.

The nightmares that were his regular night-time companions for years after the war had made an unwelcome return and life felt very uncomfortable indeed. He just couldn't settle, he missed his Prince so much. That night in his armchair, the temperature dropping by the minute, he picked up his favourite framed photo of his wife. 'Bugger this for a game of soldiers love, I'm going for a pint.'

Aidan Buchanan was very drunk, not a new feeling he'd admit. But he was also bored. He looked around the table in the pub and saw a lot of mouths moving but couldn't really make out a word, there was a lot of uproarious laughing and people taking the piss, and his shoulder was getting slapped a lot. He turned to the bloke sat next to him and asked who he was. The man looked surprised but not offended so answered Buchanan.

'Barney? Who the fuck is Barney? I don't know anyone called Barney.' The table went quiet as Aidan got up, took a last sip of his lager looked around the table once more, shook his head and walked out. He thundered back through the door.

'And what kind of fucking name is *Barney*?'

Back on the street, the cool breeze surprised him and gave him some energy the booze and heat had robbed him of. His phone buzzed with text messages. 'Just fuck off,' he muttered to himself as he checked the messages. Then he saw one from Ellen, his housekeeper. 'Hate to interrupt your evening but if you're near a TV put it on.' 'On my way home, put the grill and kettle on, will ya?' he answered.

Danny Koumas was also out, dinner in Nobu with his manager, Paul and in truth, he was bored now the wonderful food had gone. Their business had been concluded, and both men were thinking of home. They both checked their phones and looked at each other at the same time.

'Are you reading what I'm reading?' asked Koumas.

'I am indeed, siege in Balham? The dog killer, holed up with a woman, news channels all over it.'

'Night cap in Shepherds Market?'

'Lead on, MacDuff.'

Annie was enjoying the peace and a damn good read. The Da Vinci Code was her guilty pleasure, and once again she was totally gripped. Her phone had started buzzing an hour ago and god it annoyed her. She put it upstairs out of the way so she could concentrate. Earnie joined her on the sofa, his wet nose resting on her bare feet. The cool change sweeping through London had Annie popping upstairs for a cardigan and some socks. She checked her phone while she was upstairs in case Jack had texted her. It was doubtful when he was so embroiled in a case, and he wasn't the most prolific of texters anyway.

Magda among others had texted her things like 'dramatic isn't it?' and 'are you watching this? Hope Jack is ok.' She raced downstairs and put the BBC news channel on.

Albert enjoyed the walk to the pub, the cool air such a blessed relief after the tortuous heat. He felt lighter and really fancied a nice pint of London Pride, his tipple for over 60 years. It was nearly midnight when he walked in, but no one looked round and said hello, every punter was gripped by Sky News. He got the attention of the young girl from New Zealand whose name always escaped him.

Something daft like Brian, but how could it be? Anyway, she poured him a perfect pint, and he joined the throng mesmerised by events south of the river.

The regulars filled him in without taking their eyes off the screen, but Albert was also reading the moving news ticker and the other graphics that filled the modern rolling news programmes. His heart sank as he was taken back to the horrible moment Prince was shot. He was amazed at the events that followed and avidly took in every detail. That avid interest was only heightened by the fact the 'Houndsdead Heath' killer was ex-army and had seen serious action in the Gulf, the Balkans and Sierra Leone.

Albert read every detail in the papers and wondered what state you had to be in to do such things. There was even sympathy in some of the tabloids for MacKinnon, tapping into the rapidly growing 'Help for Heroes' movement. That changed the moment humans started to die at his hands. Yet Albert was as captivated by Mac's plight as he was horrified by his actions. He had been an ordinary grunt in the army, an infantryman who made it as far as corporal but had never worried about rank, staying alive was his only concern along with the welfare of his mates in the regiment. They all felt like that.

He wondered what horrors MacKinnon had witnessed. The papers had long since stopped calling him a war hero, but the fact he was SAS still got plenty of attention, especially on the rolling news channels as so-called experts endlessly speculated on how he was surviving and how long he could hold out for. He heard about the exploits of the same regiments in the war, the sheer bravery of these men took his breath away. People assumed he was brave during the war, but all Albert remembered was utter terror in battle. The Japanese were fearsome, and they went toe-to-toe with them in the jungle in sapping heat.

He saw men shoot themselves rather than get captured and he didn't blame them after looking into enemy eyes at the closest of quarters. The day he was captured he was convinced he was going to die. Cornered, out of ammo and outnumbered, Albert and about 20 men charged with only their bayonets and engaged the enemy in hand-to-hand combat. He still has no idea how long it went on for but did know he killed at least 5 Japanese soldiers and in trying to escape with the six remaining comrades, he was eventually captured.

They stood with their hands up, covered in sweat and blood and waited to die. The officer in charge was shouting in Japanese, and his eyes never left them.

'Christ, is that him?' someone shouted in the bar, yanking Albert out of his reverie. And there he was, Captain John MacKinnon, emerging from a skylight in the house in an unremarkable south London street being watched by millions of gripped viewers around the world. Shouts and gasps filled the bar as the skylight opened and Mac climbed out surveying the scene comfortable as a mountain goat on the apex of the roof. Seeing the road block to his right with its flashing blue lights and TV crews he turned and moved towards the network of streets that branched out from the High Road.

Sky News was quickest on the draw. They had several cameramen in the vicinity, and one enterprising journalist gained access to the roof of a pub that had an unhindered and elevated view of the road. Jenny Rowland, normally an entertainment correspondent and bagging the best vantage points on the red carpet had spotted it and took Jim Baines up with her. Despite grumbling about the lateness of the hour, all he could say when he saw the shot was 'beautiful'.

Jim was taking time out after long spells in the Gulf and Helmand Province and had an excellent eye, quickly spotting the skylight opening. Jenny called it into the gallery, who couldn't believe their luck. 'We're the only ones with this shot,' she said as she ended the call.

They were indeed. The BBC and ITV only had ground level shots of the road and were oblivious to the movement on the roof. When they became aware, it was too late, and Sky refused all frantic offers to get the feed. Jenny had also paid the pub enough to stop any other crews getting the same access.

Despite armed police saturating the front and rear of the property they didn't have an elevated view and the helicopter had moved to allow Jack to negotiate. It took a quick-thinking member of the public watching Sky News shouting out of a window that their man was on the roof to alert them. As one, they all looked up. An officer got on the radio to Brock and Jack as well as aerial support.

The Sky anchor was speaking quietly from the studio as if not to disturb the scene. '*And in incredible exclusive live pictures of who we believe to be Capt John MacKinnon, prime suspect in the killings of dogs and at least three murders, we are watching him walking on the roof of Marius Road in Balham, South London in a daring attempt to escape armed police.*'

Jack ran out into the street and could see MacKinnon nimbly walking, almost running, along the roof from chimney to chimney. He barked into the radio, 'I want him alive' but just as he issued this order, Mac re-arranged his rifle, and this was interpreted by a hungry SO19 as a threat to life and limb, and they opened fire.

'*Oh my goodness,*' said the Sky anchor, '*the police are opening fire on the suspect as he runs along the rooftops of south London to an impossible freedom.*'

Captain John MacKinnon had never felt more free, the ping and whoosh of bullets strafing his precarious path. Thirty houses he reckoned until he could perhaps get into another street and some back gardens for cover. The chopper banked and turned slowly towards him, side door open and opening fire. Plan B flashed into his mind. They'll be no one in the gardens just below.

In the Sky gallery, the director, Sue Mannion knew she had a call to make. The anchor, her close friend, Debbie Reynolds, was hesitating but holding it together as she expected to have the footage cut at any moment. But Sue held her nerve, the gallery was looking to her to give the order to cut. Senior producers were yelling in her ear piece, 'Sue, are you sure about this? Are you fucking sure?' 'She was shouting "hold, hold"'

'Sue, they'll have your arse in a sling.'

'They can have it.' As Mac got further away, it was getting less clear what was happening. Not that difficult, but perhaps enough to argue a case for holding Jim Baines' shot.

In The Grape in Mayfair, Danny Koumas turned to his manager, Paul, 'Fuck me, Paul, they're going to show this bloke get killed live on TV.'

'Surely they'll have to cut it now.' Was the reply, while hoping with all his heart they would carry on showing this incredible spectacle.

Aidan Buchanan stood in his dark living room yelling, 'Come on, shoot the bastard, fuck me I would've blown his head off by now.'

Richard Simmonds was patrolling his lonely beat in Soho, his head hurting as he had run out of cider over an hour ago. He passed The Three Greyhounds pub on Greek Street and wondered why so many people were crowding around the TV. It was dark, and everyone was distracted by the television, so he crept in, no one noticing or caring about the rank smell he gave off. He knew Mac was in trouble, it's all anybody seemed to talk about. He worried about his comrade and there he was on Sky News, a still photo of him in the corner of the screen and long shots of a man hurtling along the roof of a strip of terraced houses somewhere in London. They had the sound pumping through the speakers.

'The *helicopter has turned towards the suspect, surely he will surrender now, or he will be shot dead.*' As if he was listening to the commentary he turned around, and Jim Baines did his best to get in as close as he could. 'He's *stopped, and he's looking down into the garden below him, maybe he will surrender now. He's turned again and looking into the street and…Oh no.*' Sky News cut the feed as two bullets hit him, one in the head blowing out a vivid cloud of red and one in the chest ripping a hole in his sodden black t-shirt. He tumbled down the roof and onto the telephone wires where for a grotesque moment he swung before falling again to the street below.

Postscript

The press conference was long and gruelling. Jack joined Wallace and the Head of the Met, Sir Colin Birkstock with the questions as wild as they were varied. The tabloids were fixated on the details of the chase and 'the kill' and the broadsheets and broadcasters more focussed on Captain Mackintosh's mental state and whether he could and should've been 'taken alive.' Jack fervently wanted to capture him and watching the coverage back, that passion shone through.

The police came in for severe criticism across the board as Jack knew they would. The IPCC had opened an inquiry as was mandatory in these cases and Jack wasn't relishing it one bit, but for now, he craved time with Annie. There would be no knees-up in the Clissold this time, and he just wanted to go home. Before he could do that, he had further meetings with Wallace and Sir Colin to negotiate and the day stretched interminably ahead.

Jane Harkness was spirited away by Ray and the boys to the Suffolk coast eschewing all the many interview requests for now. She sat in the car as the boys gently bickered with Ray refereeing when required. He rubbed her leg on occasion, snatching a sideways look that radiated love and concern. She smiled momentarily and closed her eyes – the processing well under way but feeling safe with Ray and the children enveloping her. The hum of the engine and motion of the car lulled into her sleep, and it took her right back to three nights ago and standing face to face with Mac.

Not so much a nightmare as a thudding sadness that she couldn't help him. The fleeting smile before he lifted himself out of the loft crushed her as the memory shot through her dreams, and it invariably jolted her awake. She knew Ray's horror was diced with fascination over what had unfolded that night, and he had bought all the papers and watched all the news items on TV. For Jane, it was a private experience with the media storm feeling like another story far removed from her. As such, she didn't read a word or watch a minute of the news and knew Suffolk would prove a perfect escape. As Ray often joked, 'Tonight, we're going to party like it's 1953,' and that sense of a preserved version of old England couldn't have been more suitable as they walked, talked, swam in the sea and just stopped.

The media noise was intense, but gradually the shrill headlines, the finger pointing and bandwagon interviews ebbed away, and more thoughtful analyses took their place. The plight of veterans and the prevalence of mental illness was high on the agenda with interviews conducted across the broadsheets and current affairs programmes with soldiers who had suffered PTSD and service personnel that had known Captain Mackintosh as well as experts in the field.

The cool change in the weather on the night of Mac's death didn't last, and the heatwave returned like it had never been away the very next morning. The dramatic end to the case had seen people returning to parks and open spaces despite the heat and a sense of normality reasserting itself.

The leave Jack had booked with Annie was delayed a day or two, but they had decided to stay in London anyway. Not one to dwell on a case, Jack had still devoured every inch of newsprint about Mac discussing at length with Annie what had happened and furore that followed.

They attended the victims' funerals and reclaimed the Heath, making a point of taking Earnie early in the morning and long into the evening.

The day of Sky reporter, Sebastian Marshall's funeral was the hottest of the summer with central London temperature gauges hitting the 36 degrees mark without a hint of breeze to alleviate the early afternoon furnace of heat. The congregation sweltered in the small Chiswick church with the bank of photographers and well-wishers locked outside faring little better. The service was carried live across all the news channels with the great and the good in attendance.

Jack and Annie were glad to push through the crowds and head back to North London after the service. It was the last of the four funerals, and suddenly Jack felt the full force of his exhaustion hit him. They quickly changed into shorts and headed to the Heath with Earnie, glugging on ice cold bottles of water as the temperature showed no sign of abating despite being after 6 in the evening.

They entered the Heath from Merton Lane with Earnie taking off immediately on being unleashed and jumping straight into the first pond causing a commotion among the ducks feeding in the early evening sunshine. Jack was heartened to see so many people out and about enjoying the spectacle of the Heath bathed in red sunlight as knots of evening cloud drifted by. Despite the heat, they held hands tightly and made for a bench with a bit of shade to watch Earnie terrorise numerous species of birds in the pond.

As welcome as the shade and water were, the couple started making eager plans to hit a beer garden and soon, the thought of a cold crisp lager almost unbearably alluring as was the prospect of a good meal, sharpened by the many barbeques firing up around them. As they finalised a well-worn plan of the Lion and Sun's beer garden then pizza, an elderly man silently joined them, the couple barely noticing until he quietly spoke to them.

'That fine black lab yours eh, Inspector?'

'Yes.' Jack turned to their new guest on the bench, Jack instantly recognised as Albert Johns, his dog Prince, Mac's first victim. 'That's our Earnie.'

'He's a fine dog for sure.'

'Not sure the ducks would agree.'

'My Prince was the same. Never let them have any peace, not that he ever caught one. He wouldn't have known what to do if he had.'

Jack just nodded, and Annie smiled sadly.

'Did you ever work out why he did it?' The old man asked.

'No, all we really know is that he was very badly disturbed, delusional and in the end, in no sort of control of what he was doing. There are all sorts of theories, of course.

'Yes, I've read a few of the stories.' Albert nodded.

'What do you think as a soldier yourself?'

'Bus driver you mean, I never felt like I was a soldier, I'll tell you that much. But you can't unsee the terrible things you're witness to, that's for sure. Even now, I have flashbacks of cruelty you couldn't guess men were capable of.'

'How did you and your mates cope?'

'Hard to say. People always said I was calm, unflappable even. I've never been one to wallow about anything, but those flashbacks are buggers and can catch you at any time. But some blokes in the regiment went off their rockers and Mackintosh did, as you more politely put it. We saw things…' Albert hesitated and then simply stopped talking.

Jack nodded, looked down and noticed that Annie was holding Albert's hand, the three of them watching as Earnie bounded towards them through the picnics and the barbeques and the people enjoying a hot evening on the Heath.

Printed in Great Britain
by Amazon

21758694R00137

For Catherine